THE
VILLA

ALSO BY RACHEL HAWKINS

Reckless Girls

The Wife Upstairs

The Ex Hex

Hex Hall

Demonglass

Spell Bound

School Spirits

Rebel Belle

Miss Mayhem

Lady Renegades

Journey's End

Ruby and Olivia

Prince Charming

Her Royal Highness

THE
VILLA

RACHEL
HAWKINS

HEADLINE

First published in the United States in 2023 by St Martin's Press
an imprint of St Martin's Publishing Group

First published in the UK in 2023 by
HEADLINE PUBLISHING GROUP

Cataloguing in Publication Data is available from the British Library

Paperback ISBN 978 1 0354 0957 0

Offset in 10.08/15.03 pt Sabon LT Std by Jouve (UK), Milton Keynes

Printed and bound in Great Britain by Clays Ltd, Elcograf S.p.A.

MIX
Paper | Supporting
responsible forestry
FSC® C104740
www.fsc.org

Headline's policy is to use papers that are natural, renewable and recyclable
products and made from wood grown in well-managed forests and other
controlled sources. The logging and manufacturing processes are expected
to conform to the environmental regulations of the country of origin.

HEADLINE PUBLISHING GROUP
An Hachette UK Company
Carmelite House
50 Victoria Embankment
London EC4Y 0DZ

www.headline.co.uk
www.hachette.co.uk

For Mary and Claire

Houses remember.

That was what Mr. O'Hare had said to Victoria the first day she and her family came to Somerton, the day that began the end of everything.

At the time, she'd liked the sound of that. Somerton was an old house, after all, and the idea of its papered walls and mullioned windows holding the secrets and dreams of all who had walked its halls appealed to her. She hadn't thought that perhaps houses hold on to the bad with the good, just as people do.

But why would she ever have thought that there might be bad memories in such a place? That summer, the last good season of her life, was such a glorious one, full of blue skies and lemon-yellow sun, and there was no sign of all the horror to come. There were only warm, lazy days, the soft hum of bees in tall flowers, the silky feel of grass against her calves as she walked through the fields surrounding the house.

She had forgotten, as we all do, that beautiful things can contain their own darkness.

—*Lilith Rising*, Mari Godwick, 1976

With its publication in 1976, *Lilith Rising* blew open the doors of the Boys Club occupied by such horror authors as William Peter Blatty, Jay Anson, and Thomas Tryon, a feat made even more impressive by the youth of its author. Blatty was forty-three when *The Exorcist* was published, Anson fifty-six when *The Amityville Horror* was unleashed. Tryon had already had an established Hollywood career as both an actor and writer before *The Other* put him on the map as one of America's preeminent writers of horror.

But the author of *Lilith Rising* was a girl just barely over the drinking age, a petite English redhead named Mari Godwick.

Of course, by the time *Lilith Rising* was published, her name was already famous. Infamous, even. But even if it hadn't been for the events of the summer of 1974 (sometimes luridly referred to as "The Villa Rosato Horror"), *Lilith Rising* would've caused a sensation. Horror had, after all, been mostly the territory of men, until Mari Godwick and her creation—some say avatar—Victoria Stuart stormed onto the scene.

Even divorced from its real-life history of violence, the book shocks. Victoria is no victim, no screaming girl covered in blood. She brings about the destruction of those she loves with no regret, single-minded in her focus in the way teenage girls certainly are in real life, but had not been permitted to be in the realms of horror fiction.

Mari Godwick was asked time and time again if she was Victoria, and her answer, given with an enigmatic smile, was always the same.

"We all are."

—*The Lady and the Monster: Women in Horror, 1932–1990*, Dr. Elisabeth Radnor, University of Georgia Press, 2001

CHAPTER ONE

Somewhere around the time she started calling herself "Chess," I realized I might actually hate my best friend.

It was the third name she'd given herself in the nearly twenty years I'd known her. When we'd met in fourth grade, she was just Jessica. Well, "Jessica C.," since there was also "Jessica M.," and "Jessica R.," and then one girl who just got to be Jessica, like she'd claimed the name first, and everyone else just had to fucking deal with it. So I guess it wasn't a surprise that by the time we were sophomores, Jessica C. had turned herself into "JC," which eventually morphed into "Jaycee."

That lasted until halfway through college. Sometime between her third and fourth change of major, she became simply, "Jay," holding on to that moniker until ten years ago, right after we both turned twenty-five and she'd finally broken up with that asshole, Lyle. That's when Chess was born.

Chess Chandler.

I can't deny that it sounds good, and it definitely looks good printed in giant font on the book I'm currently holding in my lap as I wait for Chess to meet me for lunch.

She's late, because she's always late, even though I'd purposely shown up fifteen minutes after I'd told her to meet me, hoping to avoid this very situation. But of course, just as I sat down, I'd gotten a text from her. *Leaving now!*

So I was on my second iced tea, and my third piece of bread at this little café in Asheville, the kind of place I'd thought Jessica—*Chess*—would like, waiting for the real Chess while the picture of her splashed across her book cover beamed back at me.

She's sitting on the floor in the photo, wearing a white shirt and jeans, her feet bare, her toenails painted a bright melon, pose casual and smile bright under the title *You Got This!*

That's her thing: the self-help beat. She sort of fell into it when a friend of ours from college, Stefanie, started a website, some kind of women and wellness thing that I can't even remember the name of. Chess started out doing a little advice feature for the site, and one of her answers, encouraging a woman to break up with her shitty boyfriend and leave her shitty job, went viral.

I understood why. The response was classic Chess: breezy and funny, but also getting to the heart of the matter in a way that was blunt without being cruel. *You know what you have to do here—I mean, you wrote to me, you're obviously smart (except where it comes to guys. And jobs. But we can fix that).*

I'd been getting pep talks like this from her for years, after all. Still, I thought the biggest it would get was a BuzzFeed article called "Twenty-seven Reasons We Want to Make This Advice Columnist Our Bestie!!"

But somehow, it just kept growing. Suddenly, her Instagram had thousands, then *hundreds* of thousands of follow-ers. She stopped writing for Stefanie's site and took a job at Salon, then the Cut, and then there was a book deal. *Things My Mama Never Taught Me* hit every bestseller list there is, and before I knew it, Chess was famous.

And honestly, she deserved to be. She was *good* at this stuff. I've read all her books and watched all her videos, in-cluding her big TED Talk that has something like twenty million views on YouTube. I've also spent a lot of time won-dering how someone you once played Barbies with can now be talking to Oprah—at *Oprah's damn house*, no less—telling women how to get their lives on the "Powered Path."

I tear off another hunk of bread.

My life is most definitely not on the Powered Path these days, and if I'm honest, that might be part of the reason I don't like Chess that much anymore.

Well, that and the fact that she's now—I check my phone—*thirty* minutes late.

Just when I'm starting to think I should go ahead and order, the door of the café opens, and she breezes in, tall and very blond, a whirlwind in shades of white, one hand already lifted in greeting as she shoves her giant sunglasses on top of her head, a pearl-gray leather bag slung over one shoul-der. She's always like this, perpetually in motion, her body seeming to move in ten directions at once, but every gesture somehow graceful, fluid.

Heads turn when she enters, but I can't tell if that's be-cause people recognize her or if it's just her—that energy, that glow.

I stand up too fast to hug her, my thighs hitting the edge of the table, ice rattling in the water glasses, and then I'm enveloped in a cloud of Jo Malone perfume.

"Emmmm," Chess says, hugging me tight.

And even though I was thoroughly irritated with her just a few seconds ago, I instantly feel that familiar warmth in my chest. She's the only person who ever calls me "Em." I've been Emily to everyone my entire life except her, and hearing it drawled in that low-country accent she's never lost brings back all the good memories—the years of slumber parties, driving in her car with the windows down, scream-singing with the radio, sitting on her couch at her beach house on Kiawah Island, giggling over glasses of white wine. A million things that immediately outweigh her perpetual lateness and make me feel guilty for ever thinking anything bad about her.

As she pulls back, Chess studies me, putting one cool palm against my cheek. "You look better," she says, and I manage a smile, patting her hand before returning to my seat.

"I feel better," I tell her as I sit down. "Mostly."

I brace myself for more questions, and given how sick I've gotten of talking about my health over the past year, I'm already formulating a way to brush her off, but then Chess spots her book on the table, and gives a pealing laugh.

"Oh my god, did you bring that for me to sign?"

Her green eyes are bright as she sinks into her chair, slinging her bag over the back. "I would've sent you one, you know."

It's stupid to feel embarrassed around someone who has held your hair back while you puke, on multiple occasions, but my face goes a little hot as I wave at the book.

"It's my mom's," I tell her. "I made the mistake of telling her I was seeing you today, and the next thing I know, this is in my mailbox with a Post-it."

Get Jessica to sign this, please! She can make it out to me. (Deborah.)

Chess snorts now as she picks up the book. "Classic Deb," she says, and then once again, she performs one of those magic acts of hers—pulling a pen out of that enormous bag, signing the book, signaling to the waiter, ordering a glass of wine, all as she scrawls her signature across the title page.

Sometimes I feel tired just watching her.

Handing the book to me, Chess leans back in her chair and pushes her hair away from her face.

She looks different these days, thinner and blonder, but I can still see the girl I met the first day of fourth grade at Johnson Elementary, just outside of Asheville. The girl with a splash of freckles across her nose, big eyes and wide cheek-bones, who'd leaned forward and conspiratorially whispered, "I'm glad I'm sitting next to you."

It's funny how such a little thing can form a lifelong bond.

"So, how's your writing going?" she asks as the waiter brings her wine. I'm sticking with iced tea, still on a handful of medications that I don't want to mix with alcohol, and take a sip before answering her.

"It's okay," I finally say. "Been a little slow getting back into it after . . . everything."

Everything.

It's the only word that can sum up what a complete and utter shit show this past year has been for me, but it still comes nowhere close to touching it.

Career stalling out? Check.

Health suddenly terrible for no reason that any doctor can figure out? Check.

Husband deciding to leave after seven years of seemingly happy marriage?

Fucking *check*.

It's been over six months since Matt left, and I keep

waiting for all of it to hurt less, for it to be less messy, less . . .
I don't know. Clichéd. Humiliating. My mom actually asked
me the other day if I was thinking about moving back in
with them, and given the state of my finances—between a
late book and an increasingly expensive divorce—I'd actually started considering it. Chess watches me now, her brows
drawn together, and then she pulls her leg up, her heel on the
edge of her chair, her arms wrapped around her knee, a position I've literally never seen anyone contort themselves into
in a restaurant. I guess once you've pulled the same move on
Oprah's couch, you can do what you want.

I wave a hand. "Seriously, it's fine," I tell her. "The latest
book is, like, epically late, but it's book ten in the series, and
book nine's sales weren't exactly setting the publishing world
on fire, so I don't think anyone's all that concerned." No one
except for me, but that's a different story.

Chess shrugs, the silver bangles on her wrist rattling.
"People have no taste, then. *A Deadly Dig* was my favorite so
far. That bit at the end on the beach where you're, like, 'Oh
shit, the wife and the best friend did it *together*!'" She leans
forward, beaming as she grabs my hand across the table. "So
damn smart!"

Flopping back into her chair, she keeps smiling at me.
"You were always so damn smart."

Feeling almost absurdly pleased, I pick at another piece of
bread. "You read *A Deadly Dig*?"

You write for long enough, you stop expecting anyone in
your life to actually keep up with what you're producing. My
mom only got through book five of the Petal Bloom Mysteries, *A Murderous Mishap*.

Matt, my ex, never read any of them other than the first

one. It had really never occurred to me that Chess would even keep track of the titles, much less read them.

But that's the magic of Chess. Just when you're kind of over her shit, she does or says something genuinely kind, genuinely lovely, something that makes you feel like the sun is shining right on you.

"Of course, I did," she says, picking the last piece of bread out of the basket. "You read mine, right?"

I have, more than once, but not for fun or because I genuinely enjoyed them. I think of lying in my bed, exhausted and nauseous, so sick and tired of being sick and tired, reading *Your Best Self* and then *You Got This!*, shame pricking hot under my skin because I was looking for shit to dislike, looking for sentences to roll my eyes at. What kind of person hate-reads their best friend's books?

"Obviously!" I tell her now, a little too bright, but she must not notice because she just smiles at me again.

"Good. I never would've written them without you."

I blink at her. It's the first time she's ever said anything like that, and I have no idea what she means. By the time Chess launched herself as this weird combination of Taylor Swift, Glennon Doyle, and a girl boss Jesus, we weren't talking all that much. I was wrapped up in my own writing, and Matt, while she was taking over the world.

"Oh yeah, I was very vital to your process, hanging out here in North Carolina," I joke, but she shakes her head.

"No, you were! You were the one who actually got me to commit to writing, you know? You always took it so seriously with your little notebooks, blocking out those . . . what did you call it? You had a little timer for it."

It's called the Pomodoro technique, and I actually still use it, even though it's not exactly doing me much good these days. I wave her off.

"I was just a nerd," I tell her, and she reaches across the table to swat at my arm.

"That's my best friend you're talking about, bitch."

The rest of the lunch passes by quickly, so much so that I'm actually surprised when the check comes. Chess swipes it up before I even have a chance to pretend I was going to pay, and then we're outside on the sidewalk, the late May afternoon warm and rainy.

"I've missed you, Em," she tells me, giving me another hug, and I smile against her collarbone, shrugging when I pull back.

"I'm always here," I tell her. I don't mean for it to come out quite as sad sack as it does, but it's the truth. Chess is the one who is always on the go, but I'm still here in Asheville, the same town where I grew up. We only managed this lunch because Chess had a signing at the local bookstore this weekend.

"Well, good," she tells me now, flashing me a wink. "That way I always know where to find you."

CHAPTER TWO

I don't expect to hear from Chess again for a while.

That's always been her style. Okay, to be fair, it's always
been *our* style. We were in each other's pockets every day
for such a long time, all the way through our years together
at UNC, but after college, that changed. It happens, right?
Lives go in different directions, you make new friends, new
connections. Chess had moved to Charleston with Stefanie,
both of them working at some fancy restaurant while Stefanie worked on getting the website off the ground, and I'd
come back to Asheville with a B.A. in English, and not much
else. Chess had invited me to move to Charleston with her,
had even insisted she could get me a job at the same restaurant, but I missed home, and my parents thought it would be
smart for me to save some money by moving back in with
them. Dad was still holding on to his dream that I'd go to
law school, but I hadn't been ready to commit to another

expensive degree, and had ended up substitute teaching and occasionally answering phones at Dad's accounting firm.

I'd be lying if I said I hadn't been a little bit jealous, watching Chess's life unfold through social media. I mean, sure, she was just waitressing then, but she was living somewhere new, meeting new people, and I felt like maybe I'd somehow fallen back in time, still sleeping in my childhood bedroom under a poster of Justin Timberlake.

It had all worked out for the best, obviously. If Chess hadn't been living with Stefanie, she wouldn't have started writing for Stefanie's site, and if I hadn't been so depressed staying at home and contemplating law school, I never would've randomly picked up a cozy mystery I saw at the library, drawn in by its colorful cover and silly title, wouldn't have read dozens more just like it and then, finally, started writing my own. Petal Bloom owes her whole existence—and I owe my whole career—to the fact that my life had diverged from Chess's.

Even if we are ships in the night most of the time, she is still my oldest and best friend. Which these days means we text when we can, call hardly ever, and see each other once a year if we're lucky.

So, I'm surprised when I get a notification from her the day after our lunch.

I have a crazy thought.

With Chess, that can mean pretty much anything. She might be thinking of marrying a stranger or it could just mean she's thinking about reintroducing carbs to her diet. Hard to say.

I leave it on read, telling myself that it's only because I'm supposed to be working right now. My phone technically shouldn't even be in my office—that's usually a strict rule of mine. It stays in the kitchen, sitting on the counter until I'm through with my work for the day.

But I've been slacking lately, spending more time looking at my phone or dicking around on Twitter than I do actually writing. That must be why my intrepid heroine, Petal Bloom, is still stuck in chapter five of *A Gruesome Garden*, caught by her private investigator not-quite-a-boyfriend, Dex Shanahan, as she hangs out of the window of the murder scene.

I read the last sentence I wrote again.

Of course it was Dex.

The readers will like this, Dex showing up again. I'd kept him way in the background in the last book, and had the angry emails to prove just how popular a choice that had been. I should be excited about writing him again, about getting Petal and Dex back together.

Instead, I kept thinking that maybe Petal should turn out to be the murderer in this book. Maybe *she's* the one who couldn't deal with Mrs. Harrison, queen of the garden club, found dead with a pair of hedge trimmers in her back?

That was a detail I was pretty sure my editor was going to make me cut—you can get away with some violence in a cozy mystery, but for the most part readers want their victims very cleanly dead. No blood, no mess, certainly no horror or pain. A quiet, picturesque death by poison, and not one of the ones that made you vomit or, god forbid, shit yourself. Just enough for you to give a dramatic croak at the Christmas party or the cider pressing or the spring wedding, whatever festive occasion required an untimely death for my plucky heroine to solve.

In the previous book, Mrs. Harrison had been a real bitch to Petal. Maybe this was her revenge, and Petal's pluckiness was actually just a deep well of rage against the town of Blossom Bay and the Mrs. Harrisons of the world. Maybe Dex, who always thought he knew better than Petal, had finally reached the end of his rope.

I let myself type it out for thirty minutes. Thirty glorious minutes, and over a thousand words of Petal Bloom hauling herself through that window and doing away with the frustratingly noncommittal Mr. Shanahan before revealing her big plan to wreak vengeance all over Blossom Bay.

It is fun.

It is bloody.

It is the most I'd written in three months.

And when I'm finished, I sit back, read it over, and then, sensibly, delete every single word.

No one reads my books for chaos and bloodshed. They want small-town atmospherics and familiar plot beats. They want Petal Bloom to save the day while Dex looks on indulgently.

And that's what I'll give them.

But I spend another thirty minutes trying to start a new chapter, one where Petal lets Dex pull her up through the window, and of course there's a moment when they almost kiss, but oh no! What's that? A sound from outside! They must go investigate!

At the end of that thirty minutes, I have 282 words, all of which I hate.

I never should have made Dex so much like Matt. In the early days of our relationship, it had felt . . . inspired. Cute, at the very least. Taking this guy I was crazy for and crafting a fictional version of him, who adored the fictional version of me that I'd created. Dex is definitely better looking than Matt—how many times have readers written to me, wondering why a man like Dex didn't exist in the real world?—but there are many other similarities. He has Matt's love of Talisker whisky. He has a battered brown leather jacket he cares for more than a human baby. He doesn't have a dog, but he wants to pet every single one he sees.

All of those things *are* Matt, and when I was first writing Dex, it made me so happy, spending time with this version of him even as I fell in love with the real one.

But Dex hadn't left Petal when she got sick. Hadn't cheated on her with some unknown woman, hadn't deleted every picture of her from his social media.

Dex was still out there, being the Good Guy, the one our heroine could depend on. Meanwhile, my own Good Guy was actually an asshole who had bought a condo in Myrtle Beach and was, according to Instagram, suddenly getting very into craft beer.

Also, Dex would never have tried to take Petal's hardearned money.

That was one detail I hadn't mentioned when Chess had asked how things were—that my ex-husband has decided to go for the jugular.

It started with the divorce negotiations. Matt claimed he was entitled to a bigger cut of the Petal Bloom book royalties than I'd been prepared to give. The books have sold well, and I've made a decent living, but I wasn't rolling around in money. I drove a car that was six years old, still shopped at the cheaper grocery store, and honestly, Matt's paycheck had been floating us once I got sick and started missing deadlines.

I'd thought maybe that's why he was going for a bigger share—the health care costs he'd covered while I was on his fancy insurance. But when he and his lawyer doubled down, I quickly understood that it was more than that.

It wasn't about money, it seemed. It was about *ownership*. Because I'd talked out my plots with Matt, because he'd made some suggestions when I was stuck and because, stupidly, I'd once said in an interview with *Mystery and Suspense* that "the Petal Bloom books wouldn't exist without my husband, Matt," he now argued that he was entitled to a lot more than a couple of dedications and a mention in the acknowledgments. He wanted a cut of my earnings—not only of what I'd already made, but anything else I *might* make in the future from Petal. Apparently, I only had a career because of him.

I probably shouldn't have been so surprised he felt this way, though. I'd written the first few Petal Bloom books before we'd gotten married, so they were under my maiden name, Emily McCrae. I'd planned on keeping that name for professional use even as I took Matt's last name, Sheridan, personally, but apparently it hadn't even occurred to Matt that I wouldn't use Sheridan on my books. It had bothered him enough that I'd relented, insisting on the change even though my publisher had been less than thrilled about it.

So yeah, I probably should have seen this coming, but I'd thought it was just a ridiculous money grab, that any judge would laugh it out of court.

So far, no one is laughing.

Just last week, I had to turn over the past five years of contracts, check stubs, and royalty statements to his attorneys, and at night, I lie awake wondering what it will feel like if he actually wins.

If every time I sit down to write, for the rest of my life, I'll be putting money in the pocket of a man who left me the second that things got hard.

I'm so busy feeling sorry for myself that I realize I've missed two texts from Chess.

HELLO!!

SERIOUSLY EM I HAVE A—PLAN—

That makes me smile in spite of myself.

Chess was always big on plans, only about a third of which actually came to fruition, and that's me being generous. There was the costume party she wanted to make our entire dorm participate in (she dropped it after she couldn't find a costume she liked). The scavenger hunt senior year (she forgot to actually make a list of things to find). A trip to Cabo for my bachelorette party (straight up never happened).

And of course, there was always the Book.

That's how we used to talk about it, the Book that we were going to write together, the searing exposé of girlhood and sex and academia that was going to make us both literary darlings. That plan had almost gotten off the ground. I think we got about ten thousand words in before Chess lost interest. There had been a new guy, someone she'd met at some random bar, and with him had come an entirely new set of friends to hang out with and impress. I had gotten used to it by then, how when Chess dated someone new, she seemed to become an entirely new person. I'd just assumed she'd get tired of him and his crowd like she always did, and then we'd get back to the book.

The guy had eventually—inevitably—gone away, but she never mentioned working on the book again.

I sigh, getting up from my desk. Outside, it's already getting dark, and I realize I've wasted another day, working and yet somehow getting nowhere. Across the street, the Millers have already turned on their porch light, and I can hear the sound of kids laughing, bicycle tires bumping from street to sidewalk and back again.

Matt and I bought this house six years ago, firmly ensconced in Family Territory, because we thought we'd be one of them soon enough. We were planning on having kids soon, living that suburban dream, but then I'd gotten busy with the books, and just as that had slowed down, I'd gotten sick, and now here I was, the one single lady stuck in a two-story, four-bedroom house that didn't feel like mine at all.

I take my phone into the kitchen, opening the fridge and seeing if I have anything that isn't completely depressing to heat up for dinner. There's a pot of soup from the other night, so I grab that, sitting it on the stove before studying the few bottles of wine left in my wine rack, the reds that Matt didn't bother taking.

I think about all those orange bottles still in my medicine cabinet.

Antibiotics. Those were the first things the doctor prescribed when I started getting sick, just over two years ago. I was nauseous all the time, prickly sweat beading my upper lip and the small of my back.

Matt had been sure I was pregnant, but the tests were always negative, and when I'd finally gone in to see my gynecologist, she suggested I might actually have gotten a really bad case of food poisoning, something my body couldn't fight off on its own. I left with a prescription for these big horse pills that made my arms and feet break out in an itchy rash, but didn't do a thing to curtail the nausea. If anything, it seemed to get worse, accompanied by a fuzzy feeling in my head, an inability to focus on anything.

That had led to CT scans, to ENTs, to a different kind of antibiotic and then, finally, when no one could find anything wrong with me, a prescription for intense motion sickness pills.

Those had at least kept me from throwing up, but the brain fog only worsened. My thoughts felt scattered and slow, and by afternoon, my eyes were drooping with drowsiness.

And then, a few weeks after Matt moved out, I woke up one morning and realized that I felt more like myself again. It's still hard for me to trust this run of good health—even though some of the pills have technically expired, I've been reluctant to throw them away, afraid that I'll need them again. But it's been months since I've been nauseous, my brain foggy, thoughts thick, months since I've spent the day curled in a ball in front of the toilet.

Months since I've trusted myself to have a glass of wine.

Maybe that one naturopathic doctor friend of Matt's was right—it was just stress, my body trying to make me slow down, or at least give it more attention. Or maybe I was just allergic to Matt, and now that he's gone, my body is slowly healing. The thought simultaneously makes me want to laugh and sob.

Regardless, I'm tired of tiptoeing through my life. "Fuck it," I mutter, and I open a bottle of Cabernet Sauvignon.

Glass of wine in hand, I settle on the couch and rather than text Chess back, I call her.

"Okay, this is a direct violation of the Bestie Code," she says when she picks up, and I smile.

"What, calling instead of texting back?"

"Yes. I'll have you know I've broken up with men for less."

"Well, since you can't break up with me," I tell her, settling deeper into the couch, "I decided to risk it. Besides, I know you. Whatever plan you've cooked up, it'll sound better if you just say it rather than text it."

"Right, because in a text, you'll have time to poke holes in it and tell me just how crazy it is," she counters, but I can hear the smile in her voice.

"Exactly," I reply. "I'm saving you from yourself."

She heaves a dramatic sigh. "God, I hate having someone who knows me this well. But I'm actually glad you called because you're right. You need to hear it. Are you ready to hear it?"

"Ready and waiting."

"What if," she starts, drawing the words out, "you. Me. Italy."

"Italy," I repeat, and I can practically hear her roll her eyes.

"Don't say it like it's a death sentence, Em. Italy! Italy!"

"I'm familiar with the concept," I tell her, taking another sip of wine. "I just don't know exactly what you mean. You want us to go to Italy? When?"

"Next week."

I almost laugh. How . . . completely, typically Chess.

And she must hear that in my silence, because she goes on. "I've already got a place. This amazing villa outside of Orvieto called Villa Aestas. You will absolutely *die* when you see it, Em. And I was planning on writing the whole time I was there, but *you* could write, too. I mean, you're healthy again, and I haven't seen you in forever, and when we had lunch the other day, I was like, 'Why am I not moving heaven and earth to spend more time with one Miss Emily Sheridan?'"

She's drunk, I think. Not *too* drunk, but definitely a few cocktails in. Chess always gets chatty and grandiose when she drinks.

"Admit that this is the most genius plan you've ever heard in your whole life," she finishes, and now I do laugh.

"It's pretty fucking genius, yes."

But something is holding me back from saying yes.

For one, it's a little embarrassing to freeload so openly off of Chess's newfound wealth. Am I *that* friend, the one she'll tell people about later?

Oh, poor Emily, you know, we've been friends forever, and she was going through a divorce, so I wanted to do something to cheer her up.

Thinking about that makes my stomach lurch, but then I think about Italy. Sitting in the sun, soaking up new surroundings, new people, a new language. Plus, pasta.

"It's six weeks, Em," Chess goes on. "Almost the whole summer. Or the good parts of summer, let's be real. There's a pool, there's a gorgeous cathedral nearby. . . ."

It isn't really the perks that suddenly make my heart speed up. It's the time. Six weeks. Six entire weeks out of this house, out of this life. Six weeks to try to get my career back on track and reignite my sense of purpose.

And, let's be honest: six weeks of glamorous photos to post on Instagram and Facebook, where Matt still follows me.

"Okay, I'm in," I tell her, closing my eyes as I say it, and on the other end of the line, Chess cheers.

"Yes! I knew you would be. I'm gonna send you all the information about the house, and then I'll book your ticket."

"I can get my ticket," I say, and I can, although it's definitely going to push one of my credit cards to its max. But if Chess is renting us an entire house for six weeks, I don't want her to also buy my plane ticket. I have some pride, after all.

And Chess, thank god, doesn't fight me on it. Maybe she knows better.

"Perfect. I'm leaving in two days, so don't make me wait too long by myself, okay?"

I don't point out that she could've invited me earlier. Instead, I promise her that I'll find a flight soon, and when I hang up the phone, my face is almost aching from how much I'm smiling.

A summer in Italy with Chess.

A chance for a hard reset, something I desperately need. Something I *want*.

Something I deserve.

Fwd: Reservation for Villa Aestas June 6–July 29

To: EmilyLSheridan@PetalBloomBooks.net
From: Chess@ChessChandler.com

Here you go! You won't need to print out the parking pass they attached, I'll deal with all that. But LOOK AT THIS HOUSE, EM!! You can google it and get even more pictures, it's completely insane.

To: Chess@ChessChandler.com
From: Amanda@BespokeTravel.com

Buongiorno, Chess! Your stay at the luxurious Villa Aestas is all set! Thank you again for trusting me to set up the PERFECT summer vacation for you. I think you're absolutely going to be delighted with Villa Aestas and the entire Orvieto area. Here's a bit from the website:

Nestled in the hills around Orvieto in Umbria, Villa Aestas is an oasis of calm and serenity, full of historical charm while still catering to the sophisticated twenty-first-century traveler. While many of the home's original furnishings from the 1800s have been preserved, the kitchen is fully modern, and the property's three bathrooms have recently been remodeled. Only a fifteen-minute drive from the city center, Villa Aestas provides privacy and convenience, and for an added fee, a daily maid and chef service is available. Enjoy your stay in one of Umbria's hidden gems!

To: Chess@ChessChandler.com
From: EmilyLSheridan@PetalBloomBooks.net

Chess, you neglected to mention that this is a Murder House.

To: EmilyLSheridan@PetalBloomBooks.net
From: Chess@ChessChandler.com

Does one murder a Murder House make? Besides, it was a
bunch of rock star types in the seventies—honestly if murder
hadn't happened, it would be more of a surprise.

To: Chess@ChessChandler.com
From: EmilyLSheridan@PetalBloomBooks.net

I do think one murder makes a Murder House, as a matter of
fact! There's a podcast about it! If some guy in an ironic graphic
tee and stupid hat has spent ten hours narrating the terrible thing
that happened in the house, it is a verified Murder House!

(But you're right, this house is also gorgeous and I'm excited,
and I promise to only mention the murder five times AT MOST.)

To: EmilyLSheridan@PetalBloomBooks.net
From: Chess@ChessChandler.com

There's my girl.

I see you in my dreams, he says to me as we lay together/Girl, you haunt me every night.

But he haunts my days, every waking moment/when he's with her, there in the light.

And I wish I could hate her/wish I could hate him/ wish I could set myself free.

But we three are tied together/a golden chain unbroken/and I think it's strangling me.

"Golden Chain," Lara Larchmont,
from the album *Aestas* (1977)

It's raining again.

But then it's always raining, the rainiest summer Mari can remember, and as she sits at the kitchen window of her more-than-slightly shabby flat, she leans her forehead against the glass, watching the water run down the wavy glass, the people on the street rushing by in a mass of black umbrellas.

The smog mixes with the rain, the sky more of a noxious yellow than gray, and she suddenly longs to be anywhere but London. Back to Scotland, maybe, where she'd spent a year when she was thirteen, living with friends of her father. The air had been clear there, cold and crisp, and she thinks air like that might be the only thing that can clear her head, that can sweep away the pain of this disastrous year.

In the other room, she hears Pierce laugh, and she knows she needs to get up from this hiding spot, to go talk to the various people gathered in their living room, and play the part of Pierce's loving girlfriend. It's what she's been doing for the past year, after all, ever since they moved to this flat.

It's too quiet here, he'd said, and had proceeded to fill the place with noise at every opportunity.

Mari understood that he thrived with an audience and didn't blame him for it, but she'd wanted to write today—he *knew* she'd wanted to write today—which is why she's holed up

at the kitchen table they've squeezed into this tiny corner of
their tiny kitchen, a notebook open and only two words written across the top of the page.

Houses remember.

She has no idea where she's going with that thought, but it
had popped into her brain this morning, and she'd written it
down, sure it was the beginning of . . . something. Something
big, some story just sitting coiled inside of her, ready to spring
out fully formed.

Mari used to have these moments more often. When she
was a kid, scribbling in her journal on her bed, the words
had poured out of her, fragments of stories that never managed to materialize into anything as formal as a book, but
still. Everything she read, she wanted to write. When she got
into her stepmother's collection of Victoria Holts, she wrote
Gothic melodramas. When her father's history books caught
her eye, suddenly her journal was full of Napoleonic battles
and tragedy on the high seas. Mari felt she could write anything, everything, and she had. She had reams and reams of
paper stuffed in her tiny bedroom, peeping out of drawers,
crumpled between books on her shelves, stacked up on her
desk in messy piles.

She'd thought the words would always be that easy, that
free.

That's what life with Pierce was supposed to be about, after all. Both of them pursuing their art: Pierce through his
music, Mari through her writing.

A lovely idea. An idyllic one.

The only issue was that it didn't bloody work.

It was hard for two people to be artists when the rugs
needed hoovering, and food needed to be purchased, dishes
washed. And somehow, those things kept falling on her.

She might have had a perfect line in her head this morning, but when she'd gotten up, she'd discovered they were out of milk, out of bread, and, most important, out of wine, and Pierce was already strumming his guitar on the sofa, so she'd been the one to go to the shops.

And then of course there had been the rain, of course her shopping bag had broken, sending her items tumbling to the wet pavement, of course the milk bottle had shattered at her feet, so another run to the shop, another four p she didn't really want to part with.

And by the time she'd returned home, there had been people in the flat, a record playing loudly, blue smoke drifting up from cigarettes and joints, and that slightly sour-sweet odor of too many bodies in too small a space on too warm a day.

It was a sight—and a scent—she was used to. Her childhood home had been like this, too, friends of her father's always stopping by, taking up all the space in their semidetached in Camden. And there had been so little space to begin with, or so it had always seemed to Mari. When it had just been her and her father, it hadn't been so bad, but then her father had met Jane Larchmont, a single woman with a daughter Mari's age. Jane had heard there was a handsome widower living just down the street, and once she realized that said widower was also the semi-famous writer William Godwick, she had set her cap even more firmly. Soon she'd been at the door every day with tea, with cake, with a book she thought William might like, and before Mari had known it, Jane was living in her house, and her daughter, Lara, was sharing Mari's room.

One of the reasons Mari had left was to escape that cramped, claustrophobic feeling, but apparently it was going to follow her forever.

From the living room, she hears the thunk of heavy glass

hitting the rug, a high, shrill laugh, and she sighs, knowing that was an ashtray tipped over, knowing she'll be hoovering up ash out of that rug tonight.

She'd just bought the bloody thing, too. She'd liked its bright green pattern, hoped it would make the flat a little less gray.

She turns back to her journal as there's an abrupt shriek from the record player, the song cutting off to be replaced with Pierce's guitar and his soft, deep voice.

Houses remember.

It was a good line, but where was it leading? What kind of story followed that?

And did she even believe it, that houses had memories? Did the little house near St. Pancras hold on to Mari's past? Did it see her mother leaving for the hospital one August morning, never to return? Did it see Mari's father coming in the door, face ravaged with grief, the tiny, screaming bundle that was Mari herself in his arms?

Did it see her slipping out the front door in the middle of the night, just three years ago, her heart pounding, her smile giddy, as Pierce took her hand and led her away?

It's a romantic sentiment, she thinks to herself, tapping her pen on the paper. *But it could also be a sinister one, if the memories are bad. What if the house holds the bad memories inside with the good? What does that mean for whoever lives there?*

Her pen scratches across the paper, but before she even finishes the sentence—*Mr. Wells says that to her the first day*—the music shifts from the living room, and Pierce launches into another song, this one even louder and more raucous, eliciting cheers from his friends. Mari's next thought skitters right out of her head, like something sliding down a drain.

She puts her pen down.

Pierce is sitting on the arm of the sofa in the living room

when she walks in, his head bent over his guitar, his bare foot tapping out the rhythm as he plays, and he's smiling. This is the smile that first made her fall in love, when she walked into the cramped but cozy front room of their house on that quiet street in Camden, to see her father holding forth with a group of university students. It wasn't an unusual sight. Mari's father had been a noted intellectual and writer in the forties, and while a good deal of his glamour had faded—and his literary production had all but stopped—his open-door policy and his love of a good debate meant that there were always some shaggy-haired young men sitting on the sofas: artists, or poets, or musicians.

Pierce was among them that September afternoon, and Mari had felt like she'd been struck by lightning. Only sixteen, she'd never felt anything like that before, hadn't even known that feeling existed.

Pierce had come back to the house the next day, and then the day after that, and by the time she kissed him in her back garden on an autumn night, the smell of wood smoke and the damp wool of his jumper all around her, she was completely gone.

She'd known that he was married, but it hadn't made any difference. She was never not going to belong to Pierce, and he was never not going to belong to her.

Mari had known that as well as she'd known anything.

She moves into the room, scooting in close so she can watch Pierce play. There aren't quite as many people in the flat as she'd thought, just two of Pierce's old university friends, a couple of girls she recognizes from the pub down the road, and a third woman she's never seen before, one with long dark hair who shoots Mari a look she's gotten very used to.

But she ignores it, just like she ignores the girl in the flat across the way who always seems to be coming down the stairs just as Pierce is going up. It's the price of being with him, and it's not really even his fault. He can't help the way people look at him, can't help that he's the sort of person people are naturally drawn to.

It's what will one day make him a star.

That, and his natural talent. Mari's been listening to him play for years now, in bars and clubs and smaller music festivals. Pierce Sheldon is a name people are starting to know, and if he's not quite there *yet*, it's coming. She can feel it, this whole new life waiting right around the bend for them. If they could just get that big break . . .

They'd been close last year. Pierce had been the opening act for this American acid-folk band that was touring England, the Faire. They'd had a couple of top-twenty hits, and the shows were the biggest Pierce had ever played. It was a whirlwind of crowded vans and tiny rooms over pubs and late nights, but Pierce was the happiest she'd ever seen him, and every time he stepped onstage, it seemed like there were more people there just to hear him.

She still remembers standing in a field on a cool September evening, her baby in her arms, asleep despite the noise, swaying as people in the crowd sang along with Pierce's lyrics. Lyrics he'd written for her, songs that had seemed so personal and private now on the lips of strangers.

It had felt like magic. A spell Pierce had conjured up spreading through the crowd, and even after all the awfulness that had followed, the memory of that night—it still gets to her.

He still gets to her.

And now, when he looks over at her and winks, she still feels that little thrill rush through her.

He's mine.

No matter what, he was hers. And she was his.

The door to the flat opens, and Pierce lifts his eyes.

Mari doesn't have to turn around to see who it is. She can tell from the way Pierce's face seems to light up.

Lara.

Her stepsister lives with them, crashing on the very sofa Pierce is sitting on, and when Mari does turn to look at her, Lara is grinning, her dark eyes wide as she waves for Mari to follow her into the kitchen.

Mari untangles herself as Pierce keeps playing, stepping over his friend Hobbes, ignoring the way the man's hand briefly touches her ankle, his touch hot and slightly oily on her bare skin.

Pierce has told her she ought to sleep with Hobbes.

"He's fuckin' mad about you, Mari, and you know you're free to do what you like."

She does, and she is, but what she doesn't like is Hobbes, or the voice in her head that sometimes wonders if Pierce occasionally tosses her at his friends so that he doesn't feel guilty about his own indiscretions. But then that feels unfair. Pierce has always emphasized the importance of freedom, how just because they choose to be together, that doesn't mean he owns her or has any say in what—or who—she chooses to do. It's been that way since the very beginning.

Lara is waiting for her at the counter, a lit cigarette in one hand, practically bouncing on the balls of her feet. Her dark hair is damp from the rain, curling over her shoulders, and her mascara is smudged, but she's still pretty in that way Mari thinks of as uniquely Lara. Maybe her nose is a bit too narrow, maybe her chin is a little too sharp, but she's always just so damn excited about everything, and that gives her face a glow even in the dingy kitchen.

Pierce's song finishes, and now a record is playing again, somehow even louder this time. It's George Harrison, Mari's favorite Beatle, but she's still casting glances at her journal, wishing for a little quiet again. But now that Lara's here, she knows there's no chance of that happening. This has the makings of one of Pierce's all-night parties, the kind that end with strangers sleeping on her floor, in her bathtub.

She already feels tired thinking about it, and wonders how exactly someone gets to be *this* tired at nineteen fucking years old.

And now there's Lara to deal with.

"Okay, obviously something has you all jazzed up," Mari says, reaching around her stepsister to pull a lukewarm beer out of the sink. The ice Pierce had put in earlier has already mostly melted, and the bottle drips water onto the floor as Mari opens it.

"Let's go to Italy," Lara says without preamble.

Mari pauses. "What?"

"Italy," Lara repeats, blowing out a stream of smoke as she props a hip on the counter, her free arm folded around her waist. Mari realizes Lara is wearing her top, the blue one with the flowers that she just bought a week ago. There's already a tiny stain there on Lara's right breast, and Mari bites back a familiar irritation.

"We did Italy, remember?" she nearly shouts. Has the music somehow gotten even louder? "It wasn't that great of a time."

When Mari had run away with Pierce three years ago, Lara had begged to be included, and even though the idea of taking her stepsister with them had ruined Mari's vision of a romantic escape, Pierce hadn't been able to tell Lara no.

And Mari couldn't tell Pierce no.

So, off the three of them had gone, leaving Mari's father's

house in the middle of the night, a note hastily scrawled left behind on the kitchen table. Italy had been their second stop after France, and it's still something of a blur.

Cramped rooms, cramped cars, the smell of her own sweat, the heat that had felt invigorating at first and then slowly grew more oppressive, making her nauseous nearly all the time. Of course, she hadn't known yet about the baby—about Billy— and later, all her discomfort would make more sense, but at the time, she'd been certain it was some kind of cosmic punishment. Out of money, slinking back to England with nothing to show for their grand adventure except sunburns and a newfound antipathy for one another.

And now Lara wants to go back there?

Lara rolls her dark eyes, standing up straight as she flicks ash into a nearly empty wineglass.

"That's because we were skint and on our own," she says. "This time, it'll be different."

The cigarette sizzles as Lara drops it into the glass, and she reaches out, taking Mari's hands. "At a villa, Mare. With"— she drops her voice, leaning so close that her forehead touches Mari's—"*Noel Gordon.*"

Mari rears back at that, eyes going wide. "Wait, as in—"

"No, the Noel Gordon who works at the chip shop," Lara says, laughing before she swats at Mari's midsection. "Of course, 'as in.' As in *Glasgow* Noel Gordon. *When She Goes* Noel Gordon."

When She Goes is Mari's favorite album, one she actually had to buy a second copy of when fucking Hobbes scratched the first a few months back. She even had pictures of him up on her wall, when he was in his first group, the Rovers, back before he'd gone solo.

But now, Noel Gordon is *famous*. Properly famous, a rock star, an idol that Pierce respects and envies all at once.

"How do you even know him?" she asks Lara, and Lara giggles, turning in a little half circle as she flutters her eyelashes.

"Fate," she says, popping the "t" sound in a way that makes Mari grit her teeth. "I was standing outside this pub in Soho, with Bonnie. You know Bonnie, right?"

Mari doesn't, but she nods anyway because if she doesn't, Lara will get distracted and launch into a half-hour soliloquy about her new best mate, Bonnie. Lara makes and loses friends with such speed that Mari rarely bothers to learn their names.

"Anyway, we were chatting and smoking, and then all of a sudden I hear this . . . *voice* ask, 'Either of you lovely creatures happen to have a light?' And I look up and it's *him*. Bloody Noel Gordon, and he is *so* handsome, Mari. The pictures don't even capture it, hand to god. And then we started talking, and he invited me to this party, and now he wants us to go to Italy with him."

"Okay, but after one party, why would he—" Mari starts to say, but then she looks at Lara's pink cheeks, the way her tongue is poking her cheek, and she understands.

"Of course," she says, and she hates that she's a little impressed. "You're shagging him."

"You can't tell anyone," Lara says immediately, but Mari knows she's only saying it because she thinks it's the thing to say when you're having sex with a very famous married man. Knowing Lara, Mari is sure her stepsister would love nothing more than to march through Piccadilly with a sandwich board announcing the fact.

And what a coup for her stepsister. Mari may have her own musician—Pierce's reputation is growing steadily in the bars and nightclubs of London, after all—but Noel Gordon is in a whole other stratosphere.

That's probably why Lara slept with him in the first place.

Ever since Jane married Mari's dad, when both girls were twelve, they've been locked in this unspoken competition. If Mari got good marks in school, Lara's needed to be better. If Mari bought a new 45, Lara would have two the next day.

Mari hadn't even been all that surprised that Lara had tagged along when they'd left England, and that she had stayed with them when they'd returned. Lara claimed it was because there was nowhere else for her to go, but Jane would've convinced Mari's dad to take her back, Mari is sure of it. It was Mari who'd run off with the married man, Mari who had committed the unforgivable sin. Lara was just being a good sister.

It's been on the tip of her tongue for months now to suggest this to Lara, but something keeps holding her back. Strange as it seems, given how often Lara irks her, Mari still wants someone else with her on this adventure, someone familiar. A person she can talk to who isn't Pierce.

"Gotta say, Lara," Mari says drily as she puts her beer on the counter, "if we spend a summer with him in Italy, I feel people will probably suss out what's going on between you."

Lara snorts, waving one hand. "People will think he invited us because he heard about Pierce's music. Or maybe because of you. He's very impressed with your mum and dad."

Mari fights back that familiar, uncomfortable feeling whenever she hears someone gush about her parents. It's not exactly pride, not exactly apprehension, just a strange brew of both. She admires them, too, of course, has idolized her mother her entire life, but she wonders about these people, people like Noel—hell, people like *Pierce*—who paint a picture of her parents that probably isn't all that accurate. And she always worries when they meet her, are they thinking of her mother? Are they thinking about what Mari's very existence took from the world?

But it doesn't surprise her that Noel Gordon would be a fan. Her parents were rebels, after all. Not musicians, but writers, philosophers, bohemians. A rare marriage of intellectual equals, a love story of iconoclasts. And Mari's mother dying early had only burnished the mythology. So tragic, so romantic, all of that tripe.

Of course, her father had not been all that unconventional in the end. When he'd learned his daughter was having an affair with a married man, a married man William had welcomed into his home and thought of as a friend, he'd been apoplectic, and she'd gotten the full "never darken my door again" kind of treatment. Running away had seemed like the only option.

But that's all in the past now, and the future is this: spending the summer in Italy at a fancy villa with a bona fide rock star. Who could say no to that?

"What are you two doing, hiding away in here?"

Pierce comes into the kitchen, his shirt half unbuttoned, his hair sticking to his face with sweat, and he gathers Mari up to him, nuzzling her neck.

"We're plotting adventures," Lara tells him, reaching out to stroke his arm even as he pulls Mari closer.

She's always doing that, Lara. Touching him.

Pierce is not faithful, Mari knows that, and she also knows she can't reasonably expect him to be, given that he still has a wife. Sweet, noble Frances, out in some village in Surrey, pining away for him, hoping he'll come to his senses and come back to her.

But he swears it was just one time with Lara, and it was after Billy had died, when Mari had felt lost in her grief, wondering how she was supposed to get out of bed when someone she loved so much was gone forever. Wondering if her baby dying was the universe's way of settling the score, since Mari's birth had killed her mother.

They were dark thoughts, awful thoughts. The chasm she'd fallen into where even Pierce couldn't reach her.

Mari had left them alone in their pain, Pierce had tried to explain, him and Lara. They had only turned to each other because they were both hurting, because they missed her.

Mari has tried to believe it, forgive them, but still.

She wonders.

And as she listens to Lara tell Pierce about the trip, watches him scoop Lara up into his arms, spinning her in that tiny kitchen so that the heels of her boots hit the cabinets, scuffing the paint, Mari lets herself hope that this trip will be what they need. That in Italy, there might actually be space to breathe.

And maybe, she thinks, looking at her journal, there will be space for her own dreams.

Mari Godwick was born famous.

Her father was the noted writer and bohemian William Godwick, and her mother, Marianne Wolsely, had soared to even greater heights as a journalist during the Spanish Civil War. Her dispatches from Seville had captured the attention of a nation, and her one piece of fiction, a short story collection called *Heart's Blood and Other Tales*, sold quite well, but it was her unconventional choices in love that had made her something of a scandal.

Her first notable lover was the painter Rosa Harris, and Marianne's refusal to hide this liaison from the world was seen as bold and uncompromising. After that liaison ended, she was rumored to have had affairs with Hemingway, Prince George, Duke of Kent, and the wife of a prominent MP. Lately, more nuanced scholarship about her life has noted that many of these entanglements have been exaggerated if not invented completely, something that has also been suggested about her daughter Mari and her relationships with what became known as the "Soho Set."

But the most notable connection between Marianne and her daughter was that the day Mari was born, her mother died.

Preeclampsia, a fairly misunderstood condition in 1955, the year of Mari's birth, was the culprit, and later, Mari would say she felt as though they'd been two souls, intertwined for nearly a year in her mother's body, only for one to pass out of being as the other forced her way in.

It was a guilt that Mari would carry all her life. When her only child, a son named William who was fathered by musician Pierce Sheldon, died of a chest infection in 1973,

Mari told friends that it was what she had deserved. This was the kind of self-recrimination she tended toward, especially later in life, and, some say, the reason why she only published one book in her lifetime. *Lilith Rising* was a sensation, and it certainly made Mari comfortable for the rest of her days, but there was always a sense that her success was bittersweet, coming, as it did, on the heels of such a massive personal tragedy.

After she passed away in 1993, several manuscripts were found hidden in her apartment, all completed between 1979 and 1992, all of which would go on to be published posthumously.

Her longtime literary agent, Jeremy Thompson, was as puzzled as anyone else as to why she'd chosen to hide the manuscripts rather than submit them but, as he said to *The Times*, "She was an odd duck, Mari. I knew her for nearly twenty years, but I never felt I actually *knew* her. I'm not sure anyone did."

—*Shadow on the Stair: The Haunted
Life and Loves of Mari Godwick*,
Caroline Leeman, 2015

THE ROVERS WILL
NO MORE GO A'ROVING

On the heels of a sold-out tour of America, the rock group the Rovers shock the music industry and the world by announcing a "prolonged hiatus" while band members focus on "other personal projects." While drummer Sam Collins has already appeared on albums from artists such as Cream and the Byrds, and bassist John Keating performed onstage with the Rolling Stones just last year, all eyes are naturally on front man Noel Gordon and what he might do next.

The youngest son of the Earl of Rochdale, Mr. Gordon has always cut a glamourous (some would say outrageous) figure, frequently compared to Jim Morrison of the Doors and Roger Daltrey of the Who. His velvety baritone and esoteric lyrics have made him a musical superstar, but it's his matinee idol face and frequent high-profile romances that have made him a fixture in newspapers both here in the UK and also across the world.

Currently on his honeymoon on Mustique with the heiress Lady Arabella Wentworth, Mr. Gordon could not be reached for comment, but sources tell us that a solo album is definitely in the works, and one wonders just how much higher Noel Gordon's star might rise.

—*Pop Beats Magazine*, June 1969

CHAPTER THREE

It's surreal that, just two weeks after that lunch in a little café in Asheville, North Carolina, I find myself in Rome.

The flight was uneventful, and I slept through most of it, so being flung into the chaos that is Fiumicino makes me feel like I didn't just leave the country, but possibly the planet.

Chess is already at the house outside Orvieto, and she's left me instructions for how to make my way there. I squint against the bright sun spilling in the windows at baggage claim as I review them on my phone. From the airport, a train to Termini, the station in the city center; from there, another train will take me to Orvieto, where, allegedly, Chess will be waiting for me.

I haven't been overseas in nearly five years, and even then, I was always with Matt. This is my first time navigating a foreign country on my own, and the sense of pride I feel when I manage to get on the right train is probably way out of proportion, but I don't care. For the first time in more than two years, I actually feel like myself again, the cobwebs clearing out, the sense that whatever has been weighing me down is finally lifted.

It's about an hour from Rome to Orvieto, and even though I'm exhausted and the gentle rocking of the train should absolutely put me to sleep, I'm too excited, sitting with my face practically pressed against the window, watching urban sprawl bleed into countryside.

The station we pull into is much smaller than the one in Rome, and far above me, I can see the thick walls that surround the historic part of the city. It looks unbelievably ancient and solid, with only trees and the occasional rooftop visible from down below. I've read about Italy's medieval hill towns, but this is my first time actually seeing one, and I feel tears spring to my eyes as I wrestle my suitcase off the train.

I've done it. After months of being trapped in my house, trapped in my own body, I am somewhere new, and the thrill of it races through my blood like champagne.

I'm even more excited—and relieved—when I see Chess waiting for me just outside the station.

Somehow, she seems to be even blonder than she was in Asheville, and I wonder if the next time I see her, she'll be full platinum. But she's smiling at me, her grin huge, her arms spread wide, and I let myself be swept into her embrace.

"You're here!" she sings out, and then gestures at the car behind her.

It's tiny and red, extremely Italian, and I laugh as I load my suitcase into the miniscule backseat.

"I cannot believe the great Chess Chandler is such a cliché," I tell her, and she looks at me over the tops of her sunglasses, still smiling.

"Look, my best friend is in Italy with me for the summer.

We are going to drive a fucking Fiat, wind in our hair, full *Under the Tuscan Sun* shit, bitch."

That makes me laugh again, and then we're in the car, and she's right—this is exactly how you should do Italy.

The drive winds through the hills, taking us slightly away from Orvieto until we're high enough that I can actually see over those massive walls into the old city itself.

"It's amazing," Chess tells me, following my gaze. "Like an actual fairy tale or something. We can go in this afternoon if you want."

I might, or I might want to do absolutely nothing, and the freedom of that makes me almost giddy.

We drive underneath the bluest sky I've ever seen, past fields and trees, and then Chess turns down a dirt road, the Fiat bumping along in a way it's probably very unused to. This is a car made for the tight streets of Rome, not a dusty track covered in pebbles and potholes, and I think how typically Chess this is, bending even cars to her will.

And then the house comes into view.

"Holy shit, Chess," I murmur, my eyes going wide.

I've looked at photos of Villa Aestas about a hundred times in the past few days, but there's seeing a picture, and then there's seeing the real thing, rising above you like something out of a movie.

It's every dream anyone could have of an Italian villa: a solid but graceful rectangle of butter-colored stone set on the greenest lawn, with bright flowers blooming in every window.

We pull into the curved gravel drive in front. Around the side of the house, I can see the shimmering aquamarine of the pool, and past that, the greener, murkier waters of the pond, lined by tall cypress trees offering pockets of shade at the water's edge.

"It's unreal, right?" she asks, pushing her sunglasses up to get a better look. "The website doesn't do it justice."

It really doesn't. Because it's not just the way the place *looks*. It's how it *feels*.

Peaceful, like a private little universe, tucked away from the world.

I know immediately that this is exactly where I'm supposed to be.

It's a feeling that gets even stronger when Chess opens the heavy oak front door, ushering me into a cool and dim foyer. The floors underfoot are stone, the walls painted the same warm yellow as the outside of the house, and just by the front door, there's an old, scarred table with a vase of bright sunflowers.

"I picked these," Chess tells me, reaching out to stroke the petals. "There's a whole field of them right behind the house. It's like they were determined to make this place as perfectly dreamy and Italian as they could."

And they succeeded. This house doesn't just live up to my fantasies—it exceeds them, wildly.

Another thing that is, I have to admit, perfectly Chess.

"Soooo?" she asks now, lacing her fingers together and lifting her hands under her chin.

"I can't believe someone got murdered in this house," I reply, and she laughs.

"All right, that's your first mention of the murder, you only have four left."

"I'll save them," I promise, because standing in this front hallway right now, light pouring in through an arched window at the top of the stairs, murder is the last thing I'm thinking about. Besides, Chess was right—it sounds like it was more of your typical drugs and rock 'n' roll fiasco of the seventies, not exactly the kind of Gothic story that spooky legends are built around. A musician beaten to death by some lowlife, in an argument that got out of control because everyone involved was high out of their minds. And anyone who was there that night is long dead.

"Besides," Chess adds now, guiding me farther into the house, "people get murdered in all kinds of houses, so why not gorgeous villas?"

She has a point, but it isn't the elegance of the house that I was thinking about. It's that this place exudes a warmth, a serenity that feels totally at odds with someone getting their brains bashed in.

But I don't want to think about any of that right now.

Right now, I want a shower, a glass of wine, and at least two hours of sitting on that patio outside, thinking about absolutely nothing at all.

"Do you want the big tour?" Chess asks, sweeping a hand out in front of her.

I don't, really. I think it might be fun to explore the house completely on my own, finding out its secrets and surprises for myself.

But I can tell that Chess has been looking forward to this, playing Lady of the Manor, so I smile. "Go for it."

She claps her hands, then threads her arm through mine, pulling me along.

It's smaller than I'd thought it would be, cozier. You hear "villa," and you start thinking of some sprawling mansion with wings and secret passageways. But Villa Aestas is homier than that. There's an appropriately grand staircase just past the front door, leading up to a landing with a hallway on either end, bedrooms branching off in both directions. There are at least four bedrooms that I see, and Chess leads me to one on the right, opening a door with a flourish.

"Obviously if you don't like it, you can pick one of the others, but this room felt the most Em-ish to me," she says. She's leaning against the doorframe, smiling her Chess-iest smile, and, as always, she's right.

This bedroom is small, but it faces the pond and the sloping back lawn, and in the distance, I can just make out the walls of Orvieto.

There's a white desk under the window, and the bed is done up in shades of blue, calm against the white walls with their framed prints of bucolic Umbrian scenes. Lace-trimmed curtains float in the breeze. The room is perfect, down to the details, like it's a movie set.

"Admit that I'm good," Chess says, and I turn to her, my throat suddenly tight.

"You're the best," I reply, and I mean it. Not just because she's invited me here, or because she picked out this lovely space for me, but because, for all the weirdness that's happened between us over all the time I've known her, she really, truly is my best friend.

She hugs me again, her grip tight, and then pulls back. "You're going to write so many brilliant words at that desk, I just know it."

I give a slightly watery laugh, rubbing my nose. "You have more faith in me than I do."

Chess shrugs, drifting back toward the door. "I always have."

CHAPTER FOUR

I end up getting that glass of wine and those hours to myself, sitting in a padded lounge chair on the patio, eventually drifting off, awakening to the sun setting and the mouthwatering smell of roast chicken, lemons, and garlic drifting from the open door to the kitchen.

I find Chess there, a dishcloth tucked into her belt as she stirs a pot on the stove, her own glass of wine in one hand. Her phone sits on the counter, and I hear music playing from hidden speakers somewhere in the house. It takes me a minute to pick out the tune, and when I do, I laugh, making her turn around.

"Are you seriously cooking and listening to Avril Lavigne?" I ask her, and she gestures at me with her spoon, dripping some kind of viscous sauce on the stovetop.

"I am listening to my incredibly special 'Em and Chess BFFs Playlist,' thank you *very* much."

She nods at her phone, and I pick it up. Sure enough, she's

got a playlist pulled up called "JessieC+EmmyMac4Eva (1998–2018)" filled with songs that bring back an avalanche of memories from all the years we've known each other, from singing into hairbrushes in her bedroom to drunken karaoke the night before my wedding.

Even the title is nostalgic. "Jessie C" and "Emmy Mac" were old nicknames for each other. I stopped using hers because she never liked people referring to her as any normal offshoot of Jessica, and she'd stopped using mine once I'd become Emily Sheridan instead of Emily McCrae.

But it's nice, seeing those old versions of ourselves side by side again.

Touched, I put the phone back down and push myself onto the counter, feet dangling as I watch her cook. "Why does it end in 2018?" I ask, and she turns, a wrinkle of confusion between her brows.

"Hmm?"

"The playlist," I say. "It starts in 1998, which was the year we met, but it ends, like, five years ago."

"Ah," she says, turning back around. "I made it for our twentieth anniversary party."

Now it's my turn to be confused. "What twentieth anniversary party?"

"The one I was going to throw," Chess replies as the music shifts into something from *High School Musical*. "It was going to be this huge thing, like a *real* anniversary party, but a *friendship* anniversary. I was gonna have it at my place in Kiawah, invite all our friends, family. Everybody."

It sounds sweet, but also slightly unhinged, which is kind of Chess's entire brand. "Why didn't you do it?"

She turns back to me, placing the spoon in a little ceramic cradle on the counter and folding her arms. "Well, I got busy.

That was the year *The Powered Path* came out in paperback, and suddenly everything went . . ."

She waves her hands around because is there any word that can sum up just how nuts things went with that book? Chess had been successful before that, of course. *Things My Mama Never Taught Me* had done really well, and *The Powered Path* hardcover had done even better, but the paperback had really skyrocketed.

That's when Oprah had happened, and Chess had suddenly been on TV, in magazines, the kind of famous that meant people actually recognized her on the street.

"And then *you* were so busy," she continues, then gives me a look out of the side of her eye. "Wasn't that the year Matt started all the Baby Stuff?"

Ah, yes. The Baby Stuff.

That had come later, actually. It started Thanksgiving a couple of years ago when Matt got up at our family dinner, held my hand, and announced to everyone that we had decided to "start trying for a family."

We'd talked about it hypothetically, not in a way that felt all that serious, and I certainly hadn't wanted to *announce* it to anyone. I still remember sitting there, my hand sweaty against Matt's palm, my face red as I thought, *Do my parents really need to know that we're about to start having a lot of sex?*

But that was Matt. Very much a "state your intentions, follow through" kind of guy, and my parents had looked so genuinely happy about the idea, and it just felt easy to go along with it all, I guess. Like Chess, Matt was good at kind of sweeping you up in his plans while making you think it had been your idea all along.

I hadn't known it then, but that was the beginning of the

end. That Thanksgiving dinner with Matt shooting me a look for refilling my wineglass even though I definitely wasn't pregnant yet, and my mom pulling up her Ancestry.com account to see what family names we might want to use, and my brothers joking about who would be the favorite uncle, and me thinking, *This is great, this is what I want, I'm just out of sorts that he announced it so early, that's all.*

Now I shrug off Chess's question, saying, "I also wrote two Petal books that year, so you're right, it was a crazy time."

Chess turns back to the stove, taking a sip of wine. "Anyway, the timing was bad, I guess. Plus, I brought up the idea to Matt, and he was, like, *super* weird about it. I think he felt like I was stepping on his toes or something? Like only he could have an anniversary with you?" She laughs then, her hair brushing her shoulders as she tips her head back. "Do you remember how mad he got at your reception when I joked that he was actually marrying both of us?"

He hadn't actually been *mad*, just . . . irritated, I think. I can still remember how his smile had gone a little hard on his face, how I'd had this sudden knot in my stomach.

What will I do if they don't like each other? I'd wondered when they'd first met. Things with me and Matt had moved pretty quickly, and he and Chess had only hung out a couple of times before the wedding.

But that had ended up being a pointless fear. Even though Chess can be a lot, Matt genuinely liked her. The three of us hanging out had never been awkward, and Matt good-naturedly accepted our in-jokes or references to some teen movie from 2002. Thinking about it now, I realize that I almost miss him.

What a fucking pathetic thought.

Matt is gone now, and Chess is here. *I* am here, and I hop off the counter, going to inspect the stove.

There's the pot Chess was stirring, which I see now is gravy, and there's another sauté pan of asparagus on the back burner. In the oven, I can see a chicken, skin brown and crispy, surrounded by piles of golden chunks of potato, and I straighten up, my eyebrows raised.

"You cooked?" Chess *can* cook, but I've never known her to actually enjoy doing so.

She screws up her face for a second, thinking, and then finally shakes her head. "I really, really want to lie to you and say yes, but actually, the girl who'll be looking after us up here, Giulia, brought it all in. I'm not cooking so much as . . . warming."

I smile, making my way to the blue enamel fridge, opening it to find yet another bottle of wine chilling inside. I top off both our glasses and say, "You know you just used the phrase, 'the girl who'll be looking after us,' right? You know you're now a person who says something like that?"

She rolls her eyes as she licks a spot of gravy off the side of her hand. "That's what she is! She kind of . . . I don't know, comes with the house. Does some light cleaning, brings meals, that kind of thing. Apparently, her family has been working here for generations."

I take that in, gathering up a couple of plates from the cabinets and walking over to the pretty little kitchen table, draped in a floral tablecloth. "Do you think, like, her mom or her grandmother was here when—"

Chess lifts a finger. "Remember," she warns me. "Only four more chances to mention it, do you really want to waste two in one day?"

I grin, shaking my head, and finish setting the table.

We feast on the asparagus, cooked with lemon and olive oil, and the chicken and potatoes, the gravy somehow rich and vibrant all at once, all of it washed down with cold glasses of the Orvieto wine the region is famous for. It's sweeter than I normally drink, but it tastes like summer, and by the time I get up from the table, I'm fuller than I have been in ages, and also more than a little tipsy.

Chess is, too, giggling as she tucks a bottle of limoncello under one arm, two tiny glasses pinched between her fingers, and makes a sweeping gesture toward the door into the hallway.

"Come, let us retire to the drawing room," she says, putting on an overly posh, old-world voice, and I follow behind her, trying not to bump into things. The sun has gone down, and while there are lamps on in the main sitting room we pass, the hall itself is shrouded in shadows.

Chess stops in front of a set of double doors, pushing them open with one elbow. I fumble for the light switch, but as she sets down the limoncello and the glasses, she makes a tsk-tsk noise at me.

"Uh-uh. Hold on."

There's the flick of a lighter, and suddenly a warm pool of light springs up from a tall chest of drawers just by the door. A fat candle in a metal holder splutters, and I watch as Chess goes around the room, lighting more candles. Two more thick pillars are on the mantel just over the fireplace, their light reflected in a gilded mirror, and then a few tea lights on the low table in front of the sofa.

Finally, for the pièce de résistance, she lights a massive candelabra, crystals dripping off of it, making a soft clinking sound as she hefts it on top of a long, low shelf.

I remember seeing this room during Chess's grand tour,

but in the afternoon light, it had been unremarkable—a
smaller sitting room, slightly overstuffed with furniture, not
as pretty as the main salon, its windows facing the front of
the house rather than the prettier view out back.

But now, lit by flickering candlelight, the space is trans-
formed. It feels intimate, but also glamorous, and more than
a little mysterious. The rug underfoot is a little threadbare,
the hardwood floors scuffed, but I like how worn in it feels.
There's something about the drooping sofa with its tasseled
cushions, and the matching wingback chairs done in gold
velvet, bald patches showing in spots. It feels like this room
has seen some things.

"This," Chess says, crossing over to another little cabinet,
"is my favorite room in the house. It's creepy, right?"

I laugh, sinking into one of the chairs, wiggling my toes
against the rug. "Only you would be, like, 'this is creepy, it's
my fave.'"

She throws a smile over her shoulder as she lifts the lid of a
fairly decrepit-looking record player. "Fair, but you're the one
who writes murder books," she reminds me. "So, I thought
you'd appreciate an appropriately Gothic hangout on your
first night."

Once again, Chess gets me in a way that no one else does.
I like that the house can have these different faces, cozy and
soft in the day, a little spooky and grand at night.

Or maybe I'm just more drunk than I thought.

There's a wooden crate next to the cabinet, and Chess riffles
through it now, finally pulling out an album I can't quite make
out. Its cover looks green and faded in the dim light.

"This is very old school," I tell her. "Very freshman year.
You didn't bring pot, did you?"

Chess snorts at that, taking the album from its sleeve. "I

wish. The best I can offer is some CBD oil that tastes like lavender. I'm supposed to be trying it out for the store."

"Store?"

She places the album on the turntable and lifts the arm. "Yeah, Team Chess is thinking of branching out with our retail arm. We sell the books and some merch on the website, but it might be nice to have little pop-up stores. Maybe eventually some permanent brick-and-mortar places, you know?"

I don't know, and moments like this are a cold splash of water on my nostalgic musings about how close we are. Her life is so different than mine it's like we're practically different species at this point, but I nod anyway.

There's a hiss as needle meets record, a pause, and then the opening notes of a song I vaguely recognize.

"What is this?" I ask, and Chess hands me the album cover.

There's a woman on the front of it, sitting on a padded bench, a white guitar in her hands. She's leaning over, turned a little to her right, and her dark curly hair almost obscures her face. Across the top of the cover is the word "Aestas," written in a gentle, curling font.

"That's why they call the place Villa Aestas now," Chess tells me. "It used to be—"

"Villa Rosato," I finish. "I saw that when I was googling."

Chess takes the album cover back, tossing it to the nearby table. "Right. Anyway, Lara Larchmont apparently wrote a lot of this album here, so they decided to rename the villa in honor of it. Do you know that damn thing sold like twenty million copies? And it's good," she adds, gesturing back toward the record player, "but I'd make an actual deal with Satan to sell twenty million copies of anything."

The song shifts into its chorus, and now I know the song. "Golden Chain."

"My mom had this album," I say, and I have an image of her humming in the kitchen as Lara Larchmont sang in the background.

"Everyone's mom had this album," Chess answers with a wave of one arm. "Even *my* mom, and you know she's allergic to things like 'art' and 'feelings.'"

I haven't seen Chess's mom, Nanci, in ages. I doubt Chess has either. They were never close—and, trust me, once *Things My Mama Never Taught Me* came out, any chance of them *ever* being close was shot to hell. But even when we were kids, Chess spent more time at my house than she did at her own. I'd never minded; growing up as the only girl in a house with three brothers meant I liked having someone around who was always on my side, someone to share secrets and whispers with.

And Chess seemed to thrive on the cheerful chaos of my house. It was just her and her mom in their duplex, and the few times I spent the night, I was always struck by how quiet it was, how Nanci would just disappear into her bedroom, leaving me and Chess with the run of the place.

It feels a little like one of those nights now, the two of us alone in this quiet house. But instead of the sad little duplex with its peeling linoleum and secondhand furniture, we're in a *villa*, an Italian villa Chess was able to rent, because despite her kind of dysfunctional and sad childhood, she's done . . . this. All of this.

Sometimes I forget just how impressive that is.

"I thought we should fully embrace the vibe, you know?" Chess says now, smiling in the candlelight. "Especially on the first night."

Chess opens the limoncello, pouring the thick, sunny liquid into the tiny glasses and handing me one. I know I should probably pass—I'm already drunk—but when in Italy, right? So I tip it back, the liquor bright and almost painfully sweet.

Picking up her own glass, Chess flops on the floor, although "flop" isn't an elegant enough word to describe how she folds up her long limbs, then stretches them out again, her cheek resting in her palm as she looks at me.

"You can talk about the murder thing if you want to," she tells me. "I mean, I did bring in the album, it's now fair game."

I wave her off, my head swimming from the wine and jet lag still clouding the edges of my brain. "No. No murder talk in the creepy room."

Chess lifts her glass in acknowledgment, then realizes it's empty. Reaching for the limoncello, she glances over her shoulder at me.

"So, are you feeling any good writing vibes in the house? Any idea what you might want to dive into tomorrow?"

All I'm going to want to dive into tomorrow is the pool, probably. Instead, I say, "Not really sure yet. I mean, I need to finish the next Petal Bloom. I mean, I *really* need to finish it."

"It's pretty late, huh?" Chess asks. As a fellow writer, she gets exactly why the situation is so stressful—which is both a relief, and annoying. I bet Chess has never missed a deadline in her life. Plus, even if she did, it would be no big deal to her financially. But I actually *need* the money that comes along with delivering this manuscript, and I needed it basically yesterday.

When Matt decided to play hardball, I realized I needed an aggressive lawyer, and those, it turns out, are not nearly as cheap as Your Dad's Friend Ben from the Golf Club.

"It is," I say to Chess now, "but everyone understands. The divorce, being sick . . ." I trail off. I can't bring myself to tell her the truth, that even if my editor and agent have been understanding, my checking account is less so. Chess resituates herself on the floor, her second shot of limoncello already gone.

"Do you remember that book we were going to write together? Back in college?"

It's the first time she's brought up the Book in ages, and I lean back in my chair, arms draped over the sides.

"Why didn't we do that?" she continues, screwing up her face.

Because you flaked out, I think, but don't say. *Like you always do.*

That isn't fair, though. Chess's flakiness is actually highly subjective. If it's something she really cares about, like her own books, she's as dedicated and focused as anyone could ever be. But with anything else, there's a big chance she'll just abandon it the second something newer and shinier catches her eye.

It took me a few years into our friendship to recognize the pattern. But when I was fifteen, I was sitting at the kitchen table with my mom, crying my eyes out because Chess was supposed to hang out with me on Halloween, and had instead ditched me to go to a party with her new boyfriend. It wasn't the first time she'd done this kind of thing, and it wouldn't be the last, but this was the first time I'd ever really, truly thought about ending our friendship.

My mom sat across from me, a mug of coffee at her elbow, and sighed, reaching over to take my hand.

"Baby," she said, her Southern accent thick, "here's the thing. This is who Jessica is. It's who she's always going to be. Now, you can either accept that or you can decide that this kind of thing is a deal breaker for you, but what you can't do is keep getting upset over the same thing. She's never gonna *not* do this kind of shit."

I wasn't sure if I'd ever heard my mom deliberately curse before, and that, more than anything else, told me how serious she was.

It had been easier after that, being friends with Chess, and as we sit in this beautiful candlelit room in this beautiful Italian villa, I'm very glad I didn't write her off back then.

"We just got bored," I tell Chess now. A half-truth, but it's as good as any. "And it was college, you know? We had a million other distractions."

"Maybe we should try again while we're here," Chess suggests, and I stare at her, trying to figure out if she's serious.

"Given that I write cozy mysteries and you write self-help, I'm not really sure what that would look like," I tell her. "'Become your best self by committing some light murder in the apple orchard.'"

She laughs. "No, I mean we should resurrect the book we started writing back then. The novel about the girls at boarding school together."

I pour another shot of limoncello so that I don't have to answer right away.

"Think about it," she says, warming to the idea. "It was one thing to write that story when we were teenage girls ourselves, but now? With life experience and shit? We could really do something there, Em."

I think about those nights in Chess's dorm room or the library at UNC, our heads together, each of us throwing out ideas that the other would immediately respond to. We were good at that kind of creative partnership, the whole "Yes, and!" thing, but hours of plotting and talking and gassing each other up didn't actually result in a book.

Which was maybe for the best.

"Can we be honest and admit that the idea was kind of dumb?" I say, and she widens her eyes in mock outrage.

"Dumb? *Dumb?* Um, it had a brilliant title, if you'll recall."

I giggle. "Chess, you wanted to call it *Green*. Just that, nothing else. *Green*. As in 'not easy being.'"

"Because of the double meaning!" she insists. "Their uniforms were green, *and* they were green in the . . . you know, metaphorical sense. Just starting out and all."

I laugh even harder, nearly spilling my drink as I go to set it down.

"Can you seriously not hear how dumb that sounds?"

She pauses, pours another glass.

And then, with a nod of her head, gives in. "Okay, it was really dumb. But!" She reaches out and slaps my knee. "The idea of us writing something together while we're here isn't. So, think about it, Em. Promise?"

I know better than to get my hopes up even if the idea of working on something that isn't Petal Bloom sends little fizzy sparks of excitement racing through me along with all that alcohol. In the morning, Chess will forget we even had this conversation, or she'll get absorbed in whatever "Girl, Straighten Your Hair!"–type manifesto she needs to write next, but for now, in this perfect little room, I give in.

"Promise."

Sun rising over the water/clouds floating so high

A place where I can settle/a home without goodbye

Have I searched for this too long?/Have I finally lost
my way?

Or is this the beginning/of a new and brighter day?

"Dawn,"Lara Larchmont,
from the album *Aestas* (1977)

It's strange, the three of them once again driving through the Italian countryside.

They have a nicer car this time, courtesy of Noel Gordon, who sent Pierce some cash before they left. Apparently, Lara hadn't been exaggerating when she said that Noel was interested in Pierce and his music, and the letters he and Pierce had sent back and forth had quickly been full of the kind of easy affection and camaraderie that usually characterizes old friends.

Not only that, Noel had told Pierce that he had some studio time already booked in London once the summer was over. He had an album that was massively overdue, and the trip to Italy was something of a last-ditch effort to get some songs ready.

That had made something in Mari's chest feel less tight about the entire endeavor. The fact that there was a goal in place, not just an endless stream of parties—plus, a real chance for Pierce to break through to a new level at Noel's side. Now, as she sits in the passenger seat, the warm breeze blowing in through the window, Mari tilts her head back to gaze up at the sky and breathes in deep.

It's a bright, cloudless blue that feels uniquely Italian, and the sun is already turning the skin of her forearm a slight peach, bringing up freckles that Pierce will later trace with one delicate finger, telling her she has constellations written on her.

Mari pulls her arm back in from the window, twisting around in her seat to look at Lara.

She'd fallen asleep earlier, but she's awake now, her dark eyes wide, taking everything in.

Mari remembers that from their last trip, too. Lara always seemed to be watching, waiting, afraid to miss one single second, and now, as they begin climbing the steep road up to Orvieto, she leans forward, as excited as a little kid.

"Look at it!" she breathes, fingers clutching the back of Mari's seat.

The town is worthy of the reaction. Set high on a hill, Orvieto is surrounded by a massive wall and in the city center itself, there's a cathedral, its spires reaching into all that blue.

Mari wonders if they'll be able to see it from the house.

Pierce lays a hand on her knee, shaking her leg. "Happy, darling?" he asks, looking over at her, and Mari smiles back, nodding.

She is, actually. Happy.

For the first time in ages.

Pierce leans out the window, the wind ruffling his curly brown hair as he smacks his hand against the side of the car. "My girl is happy, Italy!" he yells, and Mari laughs, tugging him back into the car.

"The villagers are going to come after you with pitchforks now, you nutter," she tells him, and he gives an easy shrug, his blue eyes bright.

"Wouldn't be the first time."

Pierce actually does seem to thrive on people's dirty looks, on whispers behind hands, Mari thinks. It cements his idea of himself as a rebel, the iconoclast who turned his back on his conservative family for a life of adventure and music and art. His blood isn't quite as blue as Noel's, his defection not quite as shocking, but there's still money there, a baronet in the family tree, and a big Georgian mansion in the countryside. All of it, Pierce has told her, is deeply boring and stultifying, a life he couldn't imagine leading.

His willingness to go his own way had seemed so brave when he'd first told her about his family. But sometimes, Mari thinks about his parents, how Pierce is their only child, and what it must feel like to be so thoroughly, irrevocably left behind.

The car follows a long dusty road through the hills, finally turning onto an even narrower dirt track, and finally, the villa comes into view.

"Oh my fucking *god*," Lara murmurs from the backseat, and Mari blinks, equally stunned.

It's . . . perfect. Even lovelier than she'd let herself imagine. Warm and yellow in the sunlight, surrounded by green and flowers, a jewel box of a house tucked into a lush, beautiful setting. As Mari gets out of the car, it's all she can do not to jump up and down like a little kid.

Lara doesn't hold back, though, grabbing Mari's arm and doing just that, her curls bouncing as she says, "It's perfect! Oh, Mari, isn't it *perfect*?"

But then the front door opens, and Mari turns toward it, shading her eyes with her hands as Noel Gordon strolls out onto the lawn.

It's surreal, watching a man whose face she's seen on posters, in newspapers, smirking out from album covers at the record store, from the wall of her own childhood bedroom, walk toward her, his arms open, his smile wide.

He is both everything she imagined and nothing she expected, all at once.

Noel wears an old-fashioned velvet dressing gown over a pair of black jeans, no shoes, the sides of that ridiculous robe flapping open to reveal his bare chest. His hair is dark, curling over one brow in a way that has to be purposeful, and as he gets closer, Mari can see that he limps slightly.

She remembers reading about that now, some accident when he was young, but it doesn't slow him down. If anything, it just adds to the weird halo of glamour that seems to surround him.

"So, you've found me, Sheldon," he calls to Pierce, who rushes forward. Mari thinks he'll envelop the other man in a hug—Pierce has always been very easy with his affection—but he catches himself at the last moment, instead grabbing Noel's hand and pumping away in the world's most enthusiastic handshake.

"This place is unreal, mate," he says to Noel. "Thank you for letting us bum around it with you."

Noel smiles, waving his free hand. "Been bored off my tits out here on my own. Needed some fresh blood."

He looks at Mari then, and she can already see it, that assessment she gets from so many people. They look at her, and they see how much she resembles her mother, how she has her father's red hair. And sometimes, she thinks, they look at her and wonder what it is about her that made Pierce leave his wife and family behind.

Then his eyes slide over to Lara.

Even though Noel Gordon is a stranger, Mari feels a strange kinship for him in that moment because his expression says exactly what he's thinking. A sentiment she's felt herself.

Ah, yes. You're here.

How many times has she had that sinking sensation in her chest, coming home from a café or food shopping, only to find Lara perched on the sofa next to Pierce, her chin in her hand, a sly smile playing across her face?

Too many.

And now, here is someone who finally understands what it's like to wish Lara were anywhere else, and even though Mari knows she should feel a sense of outrage—or at the very least, some sympathy for her obviously besotted stepsister—she just feels a kind of fierce gladness.

It's not just her. She's not just jealous or small-minded or, god forbid, *bourgeois* as Pierce sometimes likes to accuse her of being.

"And I see Miss Janet has made the trip safely," Noel says, his smile twisting a little, and at her side, Mari feels Lara pause.

Janet is Lara's real name, a name she hasn't used in several years, deciding at fifteen to rechristen herself "Lara," after a summer obsession with *Doctor Zhivago*.

And, Lara had reasoned, lying on her stomach on Mari's bed, stockinged feet kicking in the air, *it sounds better with Larchmont. Lara Larchmont. It'll look so good on posters, don't you think?*

Mari hadn't asked what kinds of posters Lara planned on gracing—that changed frequently. Actress, singer, model . . . whatever Lara had decided was the most glamorous identity that week.

Now her stepsister shakes a finger at Noel, her smile bright even as Mari sees the uncertainty in her eyes. "Naughty Noel," she says. "You know I hate that nickname."

"Not so much a nickname as your actual name, but why quibble?" Noel replies, throwing his hands wide, and Lara laughs.

Mari does, too, even though she's not sure why.

"This is my sister," Lara says, all jittery energy as she bops up behind Mari, wrapping her arms around Mari's waist in a way she has never once done before.

"Stepsister, isn't it?" Noel counters, smiling a little at Mari, who stands there frozen between Lara and her lover.

"Oh fine, get technical," Lara says. Her voice has changed in that way it does, her accent becoming posher, her vowels more rounded. She lets go of Mari, stepping around to stand next to her. Pushing herself up on the balls of her feet, she grins at Noel and adds in a fake whisper, "You'll probably end up falling in love with her."

"Lara," Mari mutters, her face going hot. Lara gets like this when she's feeling insecure, pushing herself to higher and higher levels of outrageousness. Mari may be used to it, but she doesn't want it here, not in this lovely space where she had hoped to free herself of all this bullshit.

Noel only laughs. "She has enough to deal with in one musician, wouldn't you say, Mari?"

He turns his attention to Pierce, still standing there with his hands clasped in front of him, his face glowing. "Hope you've brought some songs with you, my friend. My well feels quite tapped at the moment, so I'd like to actually hear someone else's music instead of my own insufferable shite."

Pierce nods quickly, his hair falling into his eyes as he steps forward. "Fuck yeah, man, I got a ton of stuff I can play for you. And, like, maybe you could add to it or something?"

"Collaborate?" Noel asks, raising his eyebrows, and before Pierce can answer, Mari interjects, "His stuff is amazing. Musically speaking. Your lyrics might be a little tighter, but what Pierce can do with a guitar . . ."

Noel swings his head to look at her. Like Pierce, he has blue eyes, but his are darker, and Mari can see that they're blood-shot, violet circles underneath.

Stepping forward, Pierce raises his hands. "Oh, I don't know about all that. I mean, she's my old lady, you know, she's gotta say that stuff."

He grins at Noel, and Mari is about to argue, but then Lara is there again, having pulled her own guitar case out of the car.

"I have some songs, too, Noel," she tells him. "I've been writing, like you suggested, and I really think—"

"Lara, you barely play, babe," Pierce cuts her off with a laugh, and even Mari can't feel too sorry for Lara right now. The guitar is merely the latest hobby Lara had picked up, and it's true, she seemed to spend more time picking out which guitar to buy than she actually spent using it.

"I've been playing for nearly a year now. I've taken lessons and everything," she insists, which is news to Mari. The only lessons she's ever known Lara to take were the same wretched piano lessons Mari's stepmother forced them both to take, and Lara managed to wheedle out of those months before Mari did.

Noel ignores Lara, and turns back toward the house.

"Johnnie!" he yells. "Stop being awkward and come say hello to our guests!"

Mari had thought Noel was here alone, was fairly certain he'd just said he was by himself, but sure enough, another man comes out the front door, squinting a little in the sunlight, running a hand over his shaggy black hair.

He's actually dressed, wearing a faded T-shirt and jeans, a pair of battered moccasins on his feet, and as he approaches, Mari notices that he's taller than Noel, and possibly even more handsome.

"Johnnie here," Noel says, slapping the man on the back, "will be serving as our entertainment director, as it were." He smirks a little and Mari wonders what he means even as Johnnie shrugs, giving a sheepish smile.

"Hi," he says, offering his hand first to Mari, which she likes. It was all beginning to feel a little Boys Club to her, what with Noel and Pierce immediately attempting to impress each other.

"Hullo. I'm Mari," she says, and he smiles, revealing a slightly crooked front tooth. Mari likes that tooth, too, likes that it breaks up the otherwise symmetrical perfection of Johnnie's face.

"Mistress Mary, quite contrary," Noel sings to himself, and then he surprises her by suddenly putting an arm around her shoulders, pulling her close.

"Like I said, I've needed fresh blood around here." The smile he gives her seems genuine, and Mari once again tries to wrap her mind around the idea that the voice that sang "Autumn Sun" resides in the throat just inches from her face right now.

Then he reaches out his other arm, embracing Pierce as well, pulling both of them toward the house as Lara and Johnnie trail behind.

"Come, my new compatriots!" Noel nearly shouts. "Welcome to Villa Rosato, and the beginning of it all!"

Mari rolls her eyes, but when she glances at Pierce across Noel's body, he's got the look of someone experiencing religious ecstasy.

This place will be good for him, Mari thinks. *Noel will make him focus on actually producing something.* She looks up at the villa, the windows winking in the sunlight. *And it'll be good for me, too.*

Later, she'll look back at this moment and wonder why

there was no warning, no sense of the horrors that would unfold in that house.

But on that bright June afternoon in 1974, Mari just basks in the promise that here, in this beautiful place, things might finally be different.

Victoria hadn't actually wanted to come to Surrey.

She'd liked their house in London. There was smog, yes, but she even liked that. And she enjoyed the bustle of city life. It made her feel like she was part of something, a single cell in a bigger organism.

In the country, she worried that she might feel her solitude more. Under skies so wide, so clear of anything save clouds, it might be easier to remember that, in fact, she was quite alone. Even within her own family.

It had always been that way.

But as she got out of the car on that bright summer morning and faced Somerton House for the first time, she felt her spirits lift. On a rainy, cold day, the kind that characterized English autumns and winters, she might not have been so enthused.

The house was old, for one thing. Her stepfather had said that the original bits—a kitchen no one used, one of the outbuildings—dated from the 1300s. The rest of the house had grown up around those parts like a snail's shell, curling around itself.

A main staircase built in 1508.

Drawing rooms from the 1700s.

A series of turrets and fanciful stonework added sometime in the early reign of the queen Victoria for which the style had been named.

It was a dark house, a place that seemed not to sit upon a hill so much as crouch on it, but Victoria loved it all the same, from the moment she emerged from the backseat of her mother's Renault.

Tall grass scratched against her calves. There had been a gravel drive once. She could still make out the pebbles and a *kind of rough, semicircular shape. But nature had taken it back over the years, and that was another thing Victoria loved about Somerton House. It was wild.*

"Lord, it's ghastly," her mother said, tilting her head back to look up at the place, and Victoria made a sharp tsk-tsk sound.

"Mama," she chided. "You'll hurt its feelings."

Her mother only shook her head, an indulgent smile crinkling her eyes. "You are an odd girl, my Vicky."

She hated that name and had chosen the much more sophisticated "Victoria" three years ago, when she turned thirteen, but she didn't want to start another argument, not today.

Instead, she ran ahead of her mother and her stepfather, who was just now getting out from behind the wheel of the car. He hated the Renault, probably because it had belonged to Victoria's father, and he hated most everything that had ever been Frank Stuart's.

Including Victoria herself.

"Slow down," he called to her, but she didn't listen.

The steps leading up to the grand front door were wide, covered in patches of green and gray, and she made a game of skipping over them, her sneakers slapping on the stone.

And then the front door was before her.

Scarred and looking older than the stone that surrounded it, the massive oak entrance had a lion's head for a knocker, and wide knobs made of a dark metal.

If only, she will think a thousand times after. If only we had never come here, if only we had stayed in London, if only I had never walked through that door . . .

But ifs are pointless.

She did come there, they had not stayed in London.

She had walked through that door.

—*Lilith Rising,* Mari Godwick, 1976

CHAPTER FIVE

I wake up the next morning with the mother of all headaches, just like I'd feared.

The wine that had tasted like peaches and honey on my tongue last night tastes like furry garbage this morning, and I wince as I get out of bed. I'd stumbled up here sometime way past midnight, drunk and giddy and too exhausted to even appreciate how comfortable the bed was, how the sheets smelled like flowers and sunshine. I vow to myself that it was just a First Night Celebration thing, and I'll be more careful with the wine—and the limoncello—for the rest of the trip. I mean, I just got back to feeling relatively normal, the last thing I want is to wake up like *this* every morning.

The hottest shower in the world and some very intense teeth-brushing helps get rid of the worst hangover symptoms, and by the time I'm dressed and heading downstairs in search of coffee, I feel slightly more human again.

"Chess?" I call out, keeping my voice pitched fairly low

in case she's still sleeping it off. But the rooms downstairs are quiet, and when I make my way into the kitchen, I see that it's already almost noon.

Thankfully, the house comes equipped with one of those fancy pod coffee machines, and I make myself a cup, drifting over to the kitchen table where I see there's a note from Chess scrawled on a pink legal pad.

Going to run some errands and try to get whatever fucking goblin is currently hammering inside my brain out of there. Giulia left sandwich stuff in the fridge XOXO Infinity!

I'm still not quite up to Sandwich Level, so I take my coffee into the back sitting room. It's a bit more modern than where we hung out last night, the floors shining, the sofa a little newer, and I sit down with a grateful sigh, propping my bare feet on the coffee table.

I tilt my head back as a soft breeze blows in through the open French doors. I should probably open my laptop today, give Petal and Dex at least an hour of my time, but for now, I'm happy to just sit in the quiet.

My phone beeps in my pocket.

Well, the relative quiet.

I pull out my cell to see that I have a missed call and two text messages.

All are from Matt.

I frown.

We're not technically divorced yet, but since he moved out, we've really only communicated through lawyers. The idea of trying to make small talk with a man I once thought was going to be the father of my children is too depressing, so I've been happy—well, not exactly *happy*, but resigned—to simply close down the lines of communication.

And now, just as I'm settling into what is supposed to be a relaxing, rejuvenating getaway, here he is.

I have no intention of calling back, but I do read the texts.

Just checking to make sure you got there okay.

How the fuck does he even know I'm away?

But then I remember. The night before I left, I posted on Instagram. Just an old shot of me and Chess back in high school, our arms around each other, cheeks pressed together, smiles wide.

"Off to Italy for a *whole summer* with this one! Here's to over two decades of friendship and all the pasta we can eat."

It had gotten the usual comments: "Italia! Have fun!" "Is Dex coming back in Book 10?????" "If Dex isn't back, WE RIOT," and a new addition, "Holy shit u know Chess Chandler??"

But now, when I open the app, I see there's a new comment. Matt's profile picture (updated from the shot of us walking down the aisle at our wedding to him gazing off toward a sunset, aviators shading his eyes) appears next to the words: "Hope you and your 'bestie' enjoy yourselves."

It's the first time he's commented on any post of mine in over a year. Honestly, even before the separation, Matt wasn't big on providing social media validation. Not that this is all that validating. I don't know if those quotation marks are meant to be sarcastic or if he's just making sure no one would ever think he'd use the word "bestie" unironically.

I delete the comment, but decide to answer his text.

I did.

He's not getting a "thanks!" from me or even an emoji.

My phone pings again almost immediately, and I glance down.

Guess you must have finally turned in the next Petal book.

Ah. Of course. This isn't about checking in on me, this is about checking in on my *money*.

My throat goes tight, angry tears stinging my eyes, and I can't believe that I've only been here twenty-four hours, and he's already ruining this for me.

Chess is paying, I type, and then delete it. Why the fuck should I give any kind of answer, any kind of excuse?

As I stand there, wondering if I should reply at all, another text pops up.

I'm not being an asshole. I'm just glad you're working.

Right, because if I'm working, he's getting paid.

Except you ARE an asshole, I type back.

An asshole who left his sick wife saying, "This whole thing is just more than I bargained for, Emily." An asshole who posts pictures of yourself shirtless at the beach in your new town, just in case people weren't getting the message that you'd finally ditched me and were officially single while also trying to own something I spent *years* making. You. Are. An. Asshole. TRUST ME.

I stare at the wall of text I've typed, and my heartbeat speeds up at the thought of pressing Send. I imagine those words zinging their way across the ocean, punching him right in his smug face as he lies in his bed in Myrtle Beach.

It would feel good, I know. Really good. Fucking *great* actually.

But no. I'm in Italy. Matt's not.

And Matt doesn't get to be in Italy, not even if he's only in my head.

I delete everything I typed, and, after a pause, I go ahead and delete his messages.

There.

But I still feel unsettled.

Suddenly, I remember that when Chess was giving her big tour, she'd nodded to one of the bedrooms. "They're using that as kind of a library, I think. Tons of books in there."

That's what I'll do. I'll find something to read, then change into my swimsuit and spend the rest of the day lounging by the pool, while Matt has to go to his stupid office and do boring accountant shit.

The thought immediately makes me more cheerful, and I practically bound up the stairs until I reach the door Chess pointed out.

It's still technically a bedroom—there's a narrow twin bed, shoved up against one wall, with a lace bedspread that's not quite as nice as the other bedding in the house.

Bookshelves haphazardly line the other long wall. They look like an assortment of flea market finds or estate sale treasures, and while the effect might be disordered and sloppy elsewhere, like most things at Villa Aestas, it somehow comes across as homey and comfortable.

I've never been able to resist a bookcase in a rental house—I used to tell Matt that you could always tell who were the real readers, and who were the people who just thought of books as another form of décor, filling the shelves of their beach house or their mountain cabin with curated hardcovers.

And then there are bookcases like this, stuffed with paperbacks left behind by various travelers over the years.

I crouch down, my eyes scanning the titles. There are several books in Italian, some I've never heard of, some translations of big English language best sellers, at least half a dozen guidebooks, one with brightly colored Post-it Notes sticking out from half the pages. I spot a couple of thicker books about art history, and then a whole row of Henry James novels.

I'm just reaching for *The Portrait of a Lady* when something else catches my eye.

The spine is so warped, I can barely make out the title, white creases scarring the dark purple, the shiny foil letters dulled with age and use, but the curlicue "L" is unmissable.

Lilith Rising.

I pull the book out from the shelf, surprised at just how thin it is, and study the cover.

It's your typical seventies trash, all that deep purple, the silver foil, the haunted and overly large eyes of the girl with the long, straight blond hair, one bloody hand raised like she's reaching out to the reader.

The pages are yellowed and curling slightly around the edges, and I imagine how many times this book has been read in this house. Maybe out by the pool, the spine cracked and folded around so that the reader can hold it in one hand, chlorine and rosé eventually dotting the pages.

I turn the book over, my eyes drifting over the cover copy, every bit as purple as the cover itself, zeroing in on the tiny little bio of Mari Godwick at the bottom.

Born in England, Mari Godwick lives in Edinburgh, Scotland. Lilith Rising *is her first novel.*

That's it.

No mention of her famous parents or her famous stepsister or her famously dead boyfriend.

No picture, either, and I reach for my phone.

There aren't that many photos of her online, and the most

prevalent one seems to have accompanied her obituary, a simple and serious shot of a delicate-looking woman in her late forties with reddish hair pulled back from her face, her eyes dark, her lips pressed together in something that isn't quite a smile.

Scrolling down further, I finally find what I'm looking for, a picture of Mari when she was nineteen. The summer she stayed here.

The photograph is black and white. She's standing outside what looks to be an Italian courthouse, her small, pale face set off by a high-necked black dress and a huge pair of Jackie O–style sunglasses. Her head is down, one arm raised toward the camera, a desperate attempt to block the flash. It's a surprisingly eerie echo of the cover of *Lilith Rising*, that hand reaching out, covered in blood.

"Ooh, are we snooping?"

I look up, startled, to see Chess in the doorway. She's wearing leggings and a sports bra, her hair pulled back from her face in a sweaty ponytail. She must've gotten a run in around her errands. Chess does love to multitask.

"Finding something to read," I tell her, holding up the book.

She looks not even the slightest bit worse for wear from last night, and takes the book from me, eyebrows raised.

"Well, this is a whole lot," she says. "I'm going to send a picture of this to my editor, tell her it's what I want the paperback of *Swipe Right on Life!* to look like."

"You'd look good with the seventies hair," I reply and she winks at me.

"The bloody hand might be harder to sell my publisher on."

"Tell them it's the blood of the patriarchy," I reply, and

she breaks into a high, giddy laugh that I used to assume was fake but now I know is the real thing.

"So, you've never read it?" she asks, sounding surprised.

I shake my head. "Just saw the movie. Sarabeth Collins's house, remember? Sleepover for her twelfth birthday party."

Chess shakes her head, putting *Lilith Rising* back on the top of the bookcase. "I didn't get invited to that one, clearly."

Except she did, I'm sure of it. I didn't know Sarabeth that well, and I was a shy kid. There was no way I would've gone if Chess hadn't been there, too. But it's not worth contradicting her.

"Well, it was on TV that night, and we missed, like, the first twenty minutes, but we watched the rest of it, and even though we made fun of it the entire time, I don't think any of us actually slept afterward."

I'd never watched the movie again, and more than twenty years later, I have only hazy memories of the plot. I remember the lead actress, her face covered in blood à la Sissy Spacek in *Carrie*, and I remember these shots of the house, this big, looming Victorian mansion against a very blue sky. That had made it scarier, I'd thought. Awful shit was supposed to happen in the dark, late at night. But when Victoria kills her family, she does it in the middle of the day, the blood almost garishly red in the sunlight.

"Maybe this can be my pool book," I add, and Chess wrinkles her nose.

"Kind of dark, don't you think?"

I shrug. "Might be neat. I mean, we listened to *Aestas* the other night, why not read the book that was written here, too?"

"Because *Aestas* is gorgeous and vibey, and this book has

literal blood on the cover and the movie scared you so badly you wouldn't sleep in your own sleeping bag."

I laugh, but what she's just said snags in my brain. She's right, I hadn't slept in my own sleeping bag that night. I'd curled up on someone else's. I thought it was Chess's but she just said she wasn't there.

I almost push her on it, but shake it off. What does it matter if she was there or not, if she remembers or not?

Still, I can't help but feel momentarily strange.

Disoriented.

It reminds me of those long months when I was dizzy all the time, my stomach lurching, and every doctor telling me there was nothing there, nothing wrong with me at all, and I shove the paperback back onto the shelf, suddenly wanting nothing more to do with *Lilith Rising*.

"You're right," I tell her. "No murder talk, no creepy books. I'm gonna go dig up an issue of *Town and Country* on my iPad instead."

"That is such a solid plan," Chess agrees as we leave the room. "And I am going to have a shower and then get to work."

"Perfect," I say, pulling the door closed behind me. "But first, can we go back to the fact that your next book is called *Swipe Right on Life*?"

She laughs, throwing her head back in that way she does. "The title was my publisher's idea, and it's gonna sell fifty bajillion copies, so you're not allowed to make fun of it."

As we head downstairs, we continue teasing each other ("It really bothers *me* that your alliterative titles are in alphabetical order, but you don't see me bringing *that* up, Emily Sheridan." "Okay, but at least none of my titles enthusiastically reference dating apps"), and just like last night, it's as if no time has passed at all. Like we've been in each other's pockets, in each other's lives, every day for years.

I knew this trip would be good for us.

And if I feel a little sting that, just as I'd predicted, Chess doesn't bring up the idea of us writing something together again, I do my best to ignore it.

CHAPTER SIX

"Petal still in peril?"

I look over the top of my laptop at Chess. We're sitting in the formal dining room, a room we haven't eaten in once in the week since we've been at Villa Aestas, but which we have repurposed as a sort of working space.

Well, Chess is working. Earbuds in, tiny cup of espresso at her elbow, her fingers clacking away on her extremely expensive and whisper-thin laptop. I don't think she's stopped typing from the moment we sat down.

Meanwhile, I have . . . opened a Word document.

And we've been in here for nearly two hours.

"Always," I reply, not adding that I'm beginning to think I'm the one actually in peril these days. If I can't finish this book while we're here, I'm not sure what I'm going to do. I'd thought getting out of my house, situating myself in a brand-new space, would be all the jump-start I'd need to finally finish this damn thing, but so far, no good. I have maybe two workable chapters, and just got an email from my editor, Caleb, this morning with a less-than-gentle nudge asking how the book was coming along.

Worse, there was an email from my new fancy attorney's bookkeeper, a reminder that I still owe part of last month's bill and a link to how I can "easily pay and catch up!"

No book, no money, I remind myself, but I've never worked well under stress, so that's not exactly the most helpful thought.

Not for the first time, I wonder if I should just tell Chess what's going on with Matt and the divorce. Just how much Matt is looking to take from me. She'd understand, I know she would, and she'd hate him as much as I did for it.

But then it would just be another thing in the Litany of Things Going Wrong in My Life, and I'm tired of being that friend. The sick one. The divorced one. The one fighting to hold on to what, to Chess, is probably a negligible amount of money.

Poor Emily.

Chess stops typing and looks up at me, her head tilted to one side. "Are you just not feeling it?" she asks, because of course she saw through my chipper response, of course she knows I've been over here reading celebrity gossip for the past hour or so.

Sighing, I lean back, the ancient dining room chair creaking. "I don't know," I tell her. "I first started working on the books when I was living with my parents and feeling really stuck. They were an escape, and now . . . now it's like I need an escape from them."

That sounds overly dramatic out loud, so I shake my head. "Or maybe the series has just run out of steam, you know? Nine books is a lot. Maybe it doesn't really merit a tenth."

"Plus, Dex is Matt, so writing him must blow."

Surprised, I close my laptop, leaning my elbows on the table. "You could tell?"

Chess gives me a look that's somewhere between affection and pity. "Sweetheart," is all she says, and I roll my eyes at myself, burying my face in my hands.

"It was so obvious, wasn't it?"

"You were in love," Chess replies. I can't see her, but I can hear the shrug in her voice. "I mean, I never got it, but you clearly were."

That makes me look up. She's still typing, her eyes now on the screen, but the earbuds are out. She's wearing another one of the seemingly endless linen outfits she brought here, not a wrinkle in sight. Maybe rich people have some special kind of linen the rest of us plebes don't have access to. That's the only explanation I can think of.

"I thought you liked Matt," I say. "I mean, you two talked on the phone and texted and stuff. You even took him *golfing* in Kiawah, even though you hate golfing."

It had actually been surprising how quickly Matt and Chess had become friends. A good kind of surprising, like it was something I hadn't even known I could hope for. It was nice seeing two people who were so important to me take an interest in each other. It made me feel . . . I don't know, special I guess. It helped that they had things in common. They both cared way too much about college football, resulting in flurries of texts on Saturdays in the fall. And they were both foodies, both admirers of slick cars.

But sometimes I thought their connection was even deeper than that. They were alike at a molecular level, too. Both ambitious, driven. Sometimes more than a little self-centered. And like Chess, Matt moved through the world like everything was going to fall into place for him—and maybe because of that, it did.

Thing is, while that's a great trait in someone you love and who loves you, it's pretty fucking terrifying in someone who is now pitted against you.

Chess pauses again. I can hear her manicured nail tapping against her laptop. Finally she sighs and says, "I did like him."

Her green eyes meet mine across the table. "But I didn't think he was right for you."

"Maybe you should have said something," I tell her. "Could've saved me some heartache, and also several thousands of dollars."

"Would you have listened?"

I think back to when I first met Matt. It wasn't a grand moment or an adorable meet-cute, not the kind of thing they make rom-coms about, but that had made it, and him, feel all the more real and grown-up. He worked at the same accounting firm as my dad, and when I'd occasionally go in to help with phones or filing, he was always there, smiling at me from his desk, smelling good when he passed by, remembering that if he grabbed me a coffee, I liked almond milk.

I'd been struggling at home, driftless. Matt seemed so sure of who he was and what he was doing—another way he reminded me of Chess. And even though I hated to admit it, he *was* the one who'd seen me reading stacks and stacks of cozy mysteries and said, "I bet you could write one of those."

Like I said, it's not exactly heady stuff, but it had been . . . lovely. Easy. Matt was steady, he smiled quicker than anybody I knew, and he had a sixth sense for when I needed something. I'd be working away, thinking that a cup of tea might be nice, and boom, there it would be at my elbow. And

I liked that my parents adored him. How even my oldest brother, Brandon, who liked basically no one, still thought Matt was "a good dude."

Maybe it's a little pathetic that at twenty-three, I still wanted my family's approval, but it had mattered to me. Brandon and my middle brother, Stephen, were both lawyers, my other brother, Tyler, was in med school, and I was still at home, still figuring it out. So it felt good, seeing the way their faces lit up whenever I brought Matt over.

And I liked being part of a twosome.

Matt and Emily.

Emily and Matt.

"I wouldn't have," I admit, and Chess gives a firm nod.

"Anyways, you're both better off now," Chess says, returning to her work, eyes drifting back to the screen, and I give an angry bark of laughter.

"Okay, but we don't actually give a fuck if Matt is 'better off' or not, right? We hope Matt loses his hair and becomes the first person to contract a fatal case of chlamydia."

Chess stops typing and looks up at me, a mix of pity and disappointment on her face.

"If you want to receive the good things the universe has for you, Em, you can't have ugly thoughts blocking the path. We have to let go of pain and resentment if we want the gifts we deserve."

I stare at her, waiting for her to break character, for her serious expression to melt into a typically sly Chess Chandler smile that lets me know all this is bullshit, that *she* knows it's bullshit, just the stuff she sells to the public. Not to me, not to her best friend.

But there's no break.

She watches me with this oddly benevolent expression, like she's waiting for me to tear up or have some kind of epiphany.

"Well, thank you for that advice," I say slowly. "Anything else? Although I should warn you if the next thing you ask me to do involves the words 'helter-skelter,' I am out of here."

Chess's mouth thins, and if the skin of her forehead could wrinkle, it would. "I'm serious, Em. You have to let go of this shit."

She turns back to her computer, typing even faster now. "And for the record," she continues, "I'm actually pretty good at giving advice. I *actually* kind of know what I'm talking about. Or maybe you think ten million people are wrong, I don't know!"

"I know you're good at this kind of thing," I say, stung and honestly a little surprised at how pissed she is. "I just didn't realize it was . . ."

"What?" she asks. The typing stops.

"Real."

Now it's her turn to stare at me. We hold each other's gaze for about three heartbeats, and then she just shakes her head a little. "Okay," is all she says, and I sigh, putting both palms on the table and pushing myself up from my chair.

"I think I need a break," I say, and Chess may be irritated with me, but at least she doesn't use the opening I just gave her to point out that I haven't actually done enough work to require a break.

"Giulia is bringing lunch in about an hour," is all she says in response, and I nod, leaving her to her furious typing.

Problem is, once I'm out of the dining room, I'm once again unsure what to do with myself. I could take the car into Orvieto—we still haven't done that, happy to hide ourselves away in the villa—but that would require going back into the dining room and asking Chess where the keys are, and we clearly need a little space from each other right now. I'm already a little waterlogged from consecutive afternoons spent by the pool, and obviously writing is not on the agenda.

Instead, I find myself drifting back upstairs to the little library and picking up *Lilith Rising* from where I left it on top of the shelf.

The cover looks even more lurid today, and I snort softly. Thirty-five years old, almost thirty-six, and I'm about to hole up with a scary book because my friend hurt my feelings.

I find a good spot for that kind of Peak Seventh Grade Wallowing, a window seat tucked into the upstairs hallway, and I fold myself up, an undeniable thrill running through my fingertips as I turn to the first page.

Houses remember.

"Good opening line," I murmur. "Well done, Mari." Opening lines are important, after all, which makes them the hardest part of the book sometimes. And Mari came up with that one when she was just nineteen.

I keep reading.

Lilith Rising is a good, old-fashioned haunted house book, so it builds up that dread about the setting right away, and I'm deep into Chapter Two before it clicks.

Somerton House sat on a small rise overlooking a quaint and peaceful village, and Victoria liked to spend afternoons on the window seat at the top of the stairs, watching the lawn slope into trees, watching the trees give way to rooftops.

She was there on the summer afternoon it all began, sitting on that same seat with its faded green cushion, a small tear in the left corner, stuffing spilling out in a way that made her think uncomfortably of wounds. It was raining, as it had been nearly every day that week, and Victoria watched the water slick down the glass as (with a diamond ring pilfered from her mother's jewelry box just that morning) she stealthily scratched a "V" in the right corner of the furthermost pane.

I put the book down, a chill rippling through me. The cushion I'm sitting on isn't green, and it definitely isn't torn— for the kind of prices people paid to stay here, I doubt anything that isn't pristinely Shabby Chic is allowed. But the view from the window does look over the lawn, and the lawn does eventually become trees, and past those, I can make out the tops of a few buildings.

This is Italy, though, not the English countryside, and the description isn't super specific. Still, looking at the view from this window and reading the view described in the book, I keep imagining Mari Godwick sitting in this same spot almost fifty years ago, a notebook on her raised knees, scribbling down the story that will one day become one of the most famous horror novels in the world.

I lift the book again, ready to read on, and as I do, my eyes drift to the windowpane.

And there it is.

I put *Lilith Rising* back on the cushion, leaning forward.

At first, it just looks like a flaw, a smudge even, but I reach out and touch the corner of the pane with my finger, tracing the shape etched there.

Not a *V*.

An *M*.

"Do you like it?"

Mari sits at the end of the bed, her cotton floral nightgown sliding off one shoulder as the last note Pierce played seems to hover in the air between them.

He's reclining against the headboard, guitar cradled in his lap, his hair a wreck, and Mari thinks she's never been more in love with him. Not even that first night he kissed her in the back garden of her father's house.

By then, he'd admitted that he was married, and she had known that this was wrong and probably headed for disaster. But she hadn't cared.

And in moments like this, when it's just the two of them in their perfect cocoon, she doesn't regret any of it.

"It's gorgeous," she tells him now, crawling forward on her knees and placing her hands on either side of his face. "Absolutely gorgeous."

Pierce smiles, leaning in to kiss her softly. "You think everything I play is gorgeous."

"Because it is," she replies, and then she's scooting closer, wishing the guitar weren't between them.

Luckily, Pierce must want the same thing because she hears the twang of the strings as he places it on the floor, and then his arms are around her, their bodies pressed close.

Italy has been good for them, just like she'd hoped. A bedroom at the end of a long hall, not next to anyone else, no worry that Lara could hear them from her spot on the sofa on the other side of the thin walls of their flat. A comfortable bed, and *time*. That was the thing Mari craved the most, the thing she felt she and Pierce never had enough of, *had* never had enough of.

From the very first, every moment had been illicit and stolen, and while that had been exciting, she's grateful for the luxury of togetherness.

"I've missed you," Pierce murmurs against her neck, pushing the strap of her nightgown down, and she presses her forehead to his.

"I've been here the whole time."

He looks up at her, his eyes so blue in that pale and serious face. "Have you?" he asks.

She knows he's talking about Billy. How losing their baby turned her into a ghost for months on end. But that memory belongs to cold gray England, not to this sunny bedroom in Italy, and she pushes it away even as she pulls Pierce closer.

"All right now, plenty of time for that later!"

There's a loud rapping at the door, and Mari looks over her shoulder to see Noel standing there in the doorway.

"It's not even noon, you heathens," he says, and Mari scowls at him, pulling her nightgown back up her shoulder.

"Closed doors mean something, Noel," she says, and he gives one of those elegant shrugs she's seen so many times over the past few weeks since they arrived.

"Not in my house they don't."

"It's not your house," she reminds him, but Pierce is already getting up from the bed, reaching for the pair of worn jeans crumpled on the floor.

He's naked, but Pierce has never been the slightest bit modest. And why should he be when he looks like a marble statue come to life? All pale skin and hard muscle, and Mari's eyes can't help but drift longingly over him.

But when she glances back at the door, her face suddenly hot, she sees that Noel is also looking.

He doesn't even try to hide his interest, his gaze frankly assessing, the corner of his mouth ticking up.

And when he notices Mari watching him, that smirk blooms in full.

Winking at her, he once again thumps the door. "*Allons-y*, Sheldon! I'm actually in the mood to make music for fucking once."

Pierce finishes buttoning up his jeans and shoots Mari a sheepish look, pressing a kiss to her forehead before dashing out the door, guitar in tow.

Mari sits in the middle of the mattress, the sheets still warm from Pierce's body, and wraps her arms around her knees, thinking about that look Noel gave Pierce, wishing the feeling unfurling in her was something as simple as jealousy or irritation.

It's not, though. It's something altogether more interesting and complicated than that, and Mari tucks it away, a thought to poke at later.

She showers and puts on one of her favorite dresses, a lilac A-line with a gauzy white scarf around the waist, then heads downstairs, expecting to hear music. She hopes Pierce plays Noel the song he played for her this morning. The melody was gorgeous, and what Noel could do with it, lyrically . . .

If Pierce could actually produce a song, or several, with Noel Gordon, if Pierce could be a part of Noel's comeback, their entire world would change. There would be money, there would be opportunities, and there would be that precious commodity again, *time*. They wouldn't have to hustle to simply make ends meet, and Pierce wouldn't have to say yes to every gig on the off chance that the right person from the right record company might be in the audience.

Noel Gordon can do that for them.

But there's no music playing when she goes downstairs. In fact, there's no one around at all. She's standing in the front hallway when she hears a distant shout from outside.

It's a warm day, the sun blanketing the lawn, and Mari immediately sees the source of the noise. It's Noel, standing up in a little rowboat out on the pond, declaiming something while Pierce sits on the bench, oars across his lap, laughing up at him.

So much for music, apparently.

There's a small dock out over the pond, and Mari can see Lara sitting at the end of it, dangling her feet over the murky green water. As Mari watches, Lara calls something out to the two men in the boat, her hands cupped around her mouth, but either they can't hear her or they just ignore her.

Lara's hands drop. So do her shoulders just the littlest bit, and Mari feels that tug in her gut, that feeling that she needs to go out there, sit with Lara, make her feel less awkward and alone.

But Jesus Christ, she doesn't want to.

It had become almost immediately clear that whatever Lara thought her relationship to Noel was, Noel did not see it the same way. They weren't sharing a room, for one thing, Lara tucked away upstairs with Pierce, Mari, and Johnnie while Noel claimed the largest bedroom downstairs as his lair. Mari doesn't doubt that Lara still occasionally finds her way into that room and into Noel's bed, but she gets the sense that it's more out of convenience on Noel's part than any real desire.

And it makes her sad how even that seems to be enough for Lara.

"Mari!"

She turns to see Johnnie sitting on the lawn, his long legs stretched out in front of him. He waves at her cheerfully, and, relieved, she goes to sit beside him.

The grass prickles her legs through the sundress she's wearing, and she shades her eyes with one hand, wishing she'd brought some sunglasses.

Reading her mind, Johnnie pulls his own pair off his face, handing them to her. "Here ya go," he says, and she takes the glasses with an embarrassed little laugh.

"You don't have to," she says even as she slides them on her face, and he shrugs.

"Want to."

She's been at Villa Rosato for two weeks now, and Johnnie remains something of a mystery. He has a guitar—Mari has seen him with it, although she hasn't heard him play—and she still wonders what Noel meant by "entertainment director."

And while Noel has called him his friend, the relationship between them seems more contentious than anything else. Noel loves his barbs and quips, but the ones he throws at Johnnie seem especially pointed, that current of cruelty she picks up when he speaks to Lara shooting through each word.

She thinks again about Noel's eyes on Pierce's body this morning and feels her face flush. Is that it, then? Is Johnnie Noel's lover?

But then she's gotten used to these sorts of men. Boys, really. She used to see them at her father's house, and she sees them in her flat now. Eternal outsiders, drifting on the edge

of a group, but never firmly inside of it. Drawn to the life-
style of art and freedom (and yes, also sex and drugs). There
one week, gone the next. Johnnie has that air about him, that
slightly hazy quality like she could blink and he'd suddenly
vanish.

There's another shout from the pond, this one from Pierce
as the boat tilts precipitously to one side. Noel is still standing,
his arms spread wide, his head tilted back to the sky. He's
wearing a pair of sunglasses with bright blue frames, a cigarette clenched between his teeth, his smile positively wolfish.
Mari sighs.

"He came and got Pierce out of bed so they could write,"
she tells Johnnie. Gesturing at the cavorting on the pond, she
needlessly adds, "But this doesn't really look like writing to
me."

Johnnie nods, clearly weighing his words. "He's not always
like this," he finally says.

When Mari only looks at him, he laughs, pushing his dark
hair out of his eyes. "Okay, he is, but the thing with Noel is
that there are always . . . levels, you know? General baseline
of Noel-ness. Some days he's at a four, others at a ten."

Mari understands that well enough. Pierce is always
Pierce—dreamy, passionate, in love with the world—but there
are times when those qualities seem more overwhelming than
others, or somehow out of balance.

"Is he—" Mari starts, and then stops, her tongue thick in
her dry mouth. "That is, are . . . are the two of you—"

"Are we shagging?" Johnnie asks, squinting at her, and
Mari hopes he assumes that the pinkness of her cheeks is due
to the sun.

Some rebel you've turned out to be, she chides herself. *Can't even
ask a simple question if it involves sex.*

"Well, I wasn't going to put it so bluntly, but I guess that's what I was asking, yes," she says, drawing her knees up and tugging her dress over them.

Johnnie laughs, reaching up to ruffle his hair, so black it's nearly blue in the sunlight. "We're friends. Kind of."

"Why only kind of?" she asks, noting that this is not really an answer to what she asked. Out on the pond, Noel shucks off the flowing white shirt he was wearing, letting it drop carelessly into the water.

"He doesn't trust me," Johnnie says. He nods out at the pond. "Thinks I'm some sort of spy."

Mari laughs. "A spy?" she repeats, incredulous. "For whom?"

Johnnie shrugs. "Depends on the day, really. Sometimes it's for the record company or Tom, his manager. Sometimes it's for his ex. The day before you lot turned up, he went on *quite* the epic rant, accusing me of phoning Arabella in the middle of the night, reporting back on what he's doing. I told him, 'Mate, I've never met your missus, and even if I had, I doubt she'd be all that interested in hearing that you're drinking yourself to death and fucking Italian birds.'"

Mari actually has met Noel's ex-wife. Or rather, not-yet-ex-wife, because as far as she's heard, there's no divorce, just a sort of extended separation, with Noel in Europe, and Arabella living with her parents in their country pile in Devonshire.

She was pretty, Arabella, if desperately serious. Mari had only exchanged some pleasantries with her at a party in Mayfair, the sort of thing that she and Pierce were usually not invited to, but one of Pierce's old friends from Eton had insisted they come. All in all, it had been a boring night, Pierce sliding back into the person he must've been before she met him: rich, slightly posh, drinking too much, and talking too loudly.

Mari had hung on the edges of the room, and that's where she'd found Arabella Gordon. She remembered wondering how on earth two such different people had ever decided to get married, but now that she knows Noel a little better, it makes sense in a strange way. He'd probably needed the calm solidity that had been radiating off the petite brunette, and Arabella . . . well, who wouldn't want to be the one to tame the wild Noel Gordon?

Hadn't taken, of course.

Looking at Noel now, draped at the end of the rowboat, shirtless and very clearly flirting with Pierce, Mari wonders how Arabella could have ever thought it would. "S'ppose the next thing will be that I'm working for the papers," Johnnie continues, leaning back on his hands. "Or the government. He comes up with some wild shit, let me tell you. If he put half as much thought into his music as he does into wondering who's keen to fuck him over, he'd have three albums out already."

Lara has perched herself on the end of the pier now, her bare feet dangling in the water. She's singing something Mari vaguely recognizes, a Judy Collins song Lara was obsessed with a few months ago. Lara's always had a lovely voice, pretty and clear, strong enough that Pierce has invited her onstage a few times to sing with him.

The song carries across the grass, and even though Lara's giving a good performance of someone singing solely for the pleasure of it, it's clear this is another attempt at drawing Noel's attention.

It's not working, from what Mari can tell, and next to her, Johnnie makes a sound of disgust, ruffling his hand over his hair as he sits up. "Anyway, this is the first time I've got you to myself since you got here, don't want to talk about bloody Noel."

Surprised, Mari looks over at him and realizes for the first time that his face is a bit pink, too, even beneath his tan.

"Is it completely inappropriate to tell you how gorgeous your hair is in the sunlight?" he asks.

That was the last thing she expected him to say, and now she searches Johnnie's handsome face for some sign that he's just taking the piss, but his expression is so serious it almost breaks her heart.

She's suddenly aware of how young he is.

He's still older than you, she reminds herself, but she's not sure anyone has ever felt as old at nineteen as she does now. She seems to have already lived a thousand lifetimes, has lost her family, lost a child, and it's aged her. Maybe not in her face, but her soul feels heavier, and she can see from Johnnie's face that his soul is as light as air.

It's nice, having a sweet boy look at her, paying her compliments about something as mundane as her hair.

The first night she'd met Pierce, when he'd come by her father's house and ended up staying for hours, talking music and art and philosophy, Mari had walked him to the door, her heart beating so hard she was sure he could see it, already so infatuated with him she could barely see straight.

They had paused there just outside the house, cloaked in shadows, and Pierce had cradled her face in his palm, his eyes moving over her face. "How have I gone this long without knowing you?" he'd murmured, and she'd felt that, too. That every moment up until that one had been wasted, but now they'd found each other and life could truly begin.

Pierce still says things like that to her, and while they thrill her in their own way, she realizes she's missed this kind of mindless flirting, the kind that girls her age are supposed to engage in.

Girls her age *should* be sitting in the grass with charming boys, hearing how pretty their hair is. Girls shouldn't be sneaking out of the house in the middle of the night with married men, running off to Europe, holding a baby that coughs and coughs and burns so hot. . . .

It's a dark memory for such a bright day, so she does her best to shake it off.

"Thank you," she says to Johnnie, giving him a little smile. "And you may, by the way. Tell me my hair is pretty."

"Gorgeous," he corrects her, and there it is, that slightly cocky, winning smile. "I said it was gorgeous."

"That's fine, too," she says. And even though there's no real racing pulse, no frisson of sexual tension, despite how handsome Johnnie is, that little moment by the pond warms her for the rest of the day.

Later that evening, after they've all finished dinner and begun to drift to their own corners of the house, Mari picks up her notebook from where she'd left it in the front drawing room to see a small piece of paper sticking out.

The edges are ragged, and with a little bit of dismay, she realizes the page was torn from this same notebook, leaving a jagged place halfway through the mostly blank pages.

The window seat, the note reads. *In the glass, at the bottom.—J*

Curious, she climbs to the second floor. There's only one window seat in the house, and it's in the upstairs hallway, halfway between the room she shares with Pierce and the staircase. It's a cozy spot, one she's used for reading several times already, even though the cushion is torn and every time she gets up, she seems to have little bits of stuffing stuck to her legs.

It's dark in the hallway. The villa has electricity, but there are no lamps up here, certainly no overhead lights. There are candles all over the place, though, piles of thin tapers messily stacked on top of end tables, tucked into corners of bookcases, stuffed into drawers, matchbooks usually close at hand.

Mari moves to one of the little tables lining the hallway now, and sure enough, there's a candlestick and a matchbox from some club in Rome.

Setting her notebook down on the table, she feels like a Gothic heroine as she lights the candle, laughing at her own reflection in the window.

Her face looks so white and so serious, her red hair drifting around her shoulder, the flame flickering, and she leans down, careful to keep her hair away from the fire.

It takes her a minute to find it, but then she sees it, the four carefully etched marks in the glass.

An *M*.

It's sweet, Mari thinks.

It's simple.

Her fingers trace the shape as she imagines Johnnie sitting up here, scratching it into the glass with . . . what? Probably a razor blade, a pocketknife.

But as she looks at it, she imagines something else, something more romantic. A ring, maybe. A diamond ring, stolen from a jewelry box.

And then she catches sight of her own face in the window again. A girl. A girl in a window seat, scratching an initial with a stolen ring.

Mari places the candle in one of the brass sconces lining the hallway, picks up her notebook, and arranges herself on the window seat.

She had left the pad with those two words scrawled across it—*Houses remember*—back in London, but she writes them again now, and this time, they don't sit there alone on the paper. Other words follow. There's a house, and there's a girl. Victoria. She's come to this house with her family for the summer, and she doesn't know it yet, but this will be the summer that changes everything. Although, maybe she does sense it. Maybe that's why she scratches her initial on the glass, wanting to leave her mark on this place that will leave its mark on her.

When Mari gets into bed, it's nearly three in the morning, and she has ten pages of her notebook filled, and something buzzing, fizzing inside her chest that wasn't there until now.

The next day, Johnnie finds her out near the pool, her notebook on her lap, her pen scratching across the paper.

"So?" he asks her, and she startles, her brain still stuck in the fields of England, in Victoria's world, not her own.

It takes her a second to come back to herself, but by then, Johnnie is already losing some of his bright smile, his feet shifting awkwardly. He wants to sit on the end of her chair, she thinks, but isn't sure if he'd be welcome.

"Did you see it?" he asks. "In the window?"

She'd actually forgotten about it. Not the letter itself—that had started her writing, after all—but the intent behind it, who actually did it and why. From the moment she'd started to write, that little detail had become *hers*, infused with the meaning that *she* wanted to give it, and she wonders if this is how Pierce and Noel feel when they write songs.

Powerful. In control. Possessive.

"I did," she says to Johnnie now, making herself smile even as her fingers itch to make her pen move again. "It was really sweet, Johnnie, thank you."

"Sweet," he repeats. It's the wrong thing to say, clearly, but she can't make herself take it back.

It's a fucking initial carved into glass, she thinks, irritation making her uncharitable. *Pierce blew up his entire life and mine so we could be together, did you* really *think that one letter would impress me?*

But still, she keeps smiling and he eventually nods, sort of shuffles off, and finally, Mari is alone again.

Well, she amends as she starts to write. *Not really alone.*

She has Victoria now, after all.

[INTRO MUSIC FADES OUT]

Bex: Hiiii, my lovelies! Okay, so as you may have noticed, our music selection was a little different today. That was your first hint. A hint about what we're gonna talk about on this fine evening. Or morning or afternoon, I guess, I don't know when you're listening to us blather on.

Kali: I mean, the title of this episode pretty much tells them what we're talking about, so . . .

Bex: I know! But I was trying to be mysterious, *god*.

Kali: Sorry!

Bex: Always fucking up my attempt at setting a mood, Thompson, I swear.

Kali: I'm just pointing out that the very nature of podcasting doesn't really allow for surprises when it comes to the subject of said podcast.

Bex: [pause] Okay, that's fair. Anyway! What you just heard was a snippet from a song called "Sister Mine," by one Lara Larchmont, and it's from the album *Aestas*.

Kali: If you have never heard or seen the album *Aestas*, please go to your mom or grandmother's house right now, because it's there. Promise.

Bex: If you ever came home from fifth grade and found your mom listening to music and crying in her den, it was probably *Aestas*.

Kali: [laughs] Who did not come home from fifth grade to find their mom crying in the den, I ask you?

Bex: [laughs] Well, now that we've made things sufficiently dark, let's continue with the official breakdown, shall we? [clears throat] Here we go, the formal bit. "In the nearly fifty years since the so-called 'Villa Rosato Horror'"—

Kali: Jesus Christ, did people really call it that?

Bex: They did! Everyone was, like, extremely extra in the seventies, I guess. Anyway! "In the nearly fifty years since the so-called 'Villa Rosato Horror,' there have been other, more shocking crimes involving famous people, enough so that the events of July 29, 1974, are almost forgotten. There were no splashy prestige TV miniseries about it or true-crime classics written detailing what happened outside of Orvieto that summer.

MAYBE it's because the murder itself was so grubby and unglamorous, or maybe it's because the people involved all went on to much bigger things. Mari Godwick wrote *Lilith Rising*, one of the most famous horror novels of all time"—

Kali: Scary as shit.

Bex: And Lara Larchmont's *Aestas* is a folk-rock classic on par with *Tapestry*.

Kali: Sad as shit, as established.

Bex: [laughs] And of course Noel Gordon, despite being dead for decades, is still one of the most recognizable rock stars in the world.

Kali: Hot as shit.

Bᴇx: Facts.

Kᴀʟɪ: No printers, just fax.

Bᴇx: [laughs, clears throat again] "But the Villa Rosato Horror, or, as some insist it should be called, the Villa Rosato Tragedy, is worth revisiting. The major players all agreed they could barely remember that night, and the accused murderer swore he was innocent. There were lurid tales of sex, drugs, and rock 'n' roll mixed in with darker rumors of the occult."

Kᴀʟɪ: Oh yeah, people in the seventies and eighties fucking *loved* to think the devil was involved.

Bᴇx: Loved! It! Could not get enough of that devil guy.

Kᴀʟɪ: And Mari wrote a devil book.

Bᴇx: Oh my god, you are stepping on me again, we're gonna get to that!

Kᴀʟɪ: I prematurely deviled, and I'm sorry.

Bᴇx: You should be! Okay, let me finish with my big line and thesis of today's episode: "With all that tension, all that drama in one house, is it really so far-fetched to think that maybe the Italian courts didn't get this one right?"

Kᴀʟɪ: Ooooh.

Bᴇx: I know! I'm making big claims right up front!

Kᴀʟɪ: I am intrigued by your thesis, and wish to know more.

Bᴇx: And so you shall. So, as always, let's start with the victim and the ten-second backstory. Victim! One Pierce Sheldon, age twenty-three, musician, apparently really talented, but something of a douche.

KALI: What level of Summer's Eve are we on here?

BEX: Extra strength, for sure. In 1971, he's married, he's already got a kid, and then he meets Mari Godwick because he . . . I don't fucking know, he just meets her, and, like, he is *sprung*. Just immediately sprung, totally crazy about her, and she feels the same way about him because she is *sixteen fucking years old*.

KALI: Ew.

BEX: I mean, I, too, would have run off with a married man when I was sixteen provided that married man was, like, on a fucking CW show or something. Tenth-grade me, absolutely risking it all for Jensen Ackles, so I get it for Mari, but still, Pierce, ya gross.

KALI: I kind of like this actually. It'll be less sad when he dies at least? Won't bum out our listeners too much?

BEX: Exactly. Also, not only did he leave his wife and, like, abscond to Europe with a literal child, he also took her stepsister with them! Who was *also* sixteen! Pierce! What the fuck!

KALI: I get that we can't exactly endorse murder on this show, but I'm not gonna lie, hearing about this dude makes me feel . . . a little murder-y?

BEX: For. Sure. Which is now where our murderer comes in.

KALI: Our *alleged* murderer.

BEX: Right, our alleg—but he was convicted? So, I don't think we have to say alleged?

KALI: Good point. Our *convicted* murderer, then.

BEX: Yes, our *convicted* murderer, one John Dorchester who apparently everyone called Johnnie.

KALI: Awww, Johnnie. Like he was in the T-Birds.

BEX: [laughs] Yes, Johnnie. Poor Johnnie. This was a bad summer for you, bro!

KALI: Just a real shit show of a summer vacation for good ol' Johnnie.

—transcript of Episode 206 of
Two Girls, One Murder: "When in Rome (Don't Do Murder)"

CHAPTER SEVEN

"You have to admit, long as we've been friends, this is a first for us."

I pull one earbud out of my ear, pausing the podcast I was listening to. "What?"

Chess sits next to me on a wooden bench seat, draped in yet more bizarrely unwrinkled linen. Her hair frames her face, setting off a pair of jade statement earrings, and I wish I'd thrown on something a little nicer than the cotton floral jumpsuit and ballet flats I'd chosen.

"I said," Chess says, reaching over to take out my other earbud, "This is a first! In our friendship."

I look around me as we climb higher and higher toward the walled part of Orvieto. We'd decided that after nearly two weeks bumming around the villa and the local country-side, it was finally time to tackle the city itself.

"Doing touristy things?" I ask. "Because we did Panama City Beach for spring break in 2006, although I can't blame you for not remembering that given the sheer amount of Jose Cuervo consumed."

Nudging my foot with the toe of one leather sandal, Chess pushes her sunglasses up on top of her head. "I'm referring to *this*," she says, gesturing out the window. "Riding a funicular."

"That is true," I agree, nodding. "Whole new mode of transport for us."

"Planes, trains, automobiles, and funiculars," Chess adds, and I laugh.

"Maybe you can use that as one of your new book titles. *Ride That Funicular, Girl!*"

"*A Funicular That Only Goes Up.*"

"*Girls Just Wanna Have Funiculars.*"

Chess laughs at that, a real laugh, and I lean against her for a second, feeling relieved. Things had mostly gone back to normal after that tense moment at the table the other day, but I've felt the memory of it hanging there between us, a dark cloud neither of us wants to mention. Today is the first day I've finally started to feel like we're back on track, back to being Em and Chess.

"So, what have you been listening to so intently?" she asks now, gesturing at my phone, and I sheepishly hold it up.

"Murder podcast."

She reads the title—*Two Girls, One Murder*—and rolls her eyes. "Oh my god, I know those women. We were at the same women in tech conference once. Completely obnoxious, *deeply* L.A."

I'm not sure what that actually means—the L.A. part, that is, I get the obnoxious bit—but I nod along anyway. "They're not always my favorites," I say, "but there are only a couple of podcasts about the murder at the villa, and this one is a lot better than the three-part series by Fedora Dude that I told you about."

Chess's earrings jingle as she swings her head to look at me. "That's two," she says, holding up two fingers. "You are now halfway through your allotted murder mentions."

Laughing, I wrap my own fingers around hers, pulling her hand down as the funicular shudders to a stop. "You're going to have to give me some leeway on it because it's actually super interesting, Chess."

"Super macabre," she counters, and I can't argue with that.

I don't tell her that I already finished reading *Lilith Rising*, that I actually read it all in one day, and that ever since I saw that *M* carved into the window upstairs, I've been thinking about the book and the woman who wrote it.

"Think of it this way," I tell Chess as we step off the funicular and into a picturesque piazza. "We're now part of the history of this house, and that whole thing was *also* part of the history of the house, so it's almost like we owe it to . . . I don't know, fate or history or something to learn more about other people who stayed there."

Chess gives me a skeptical look. "I like how you've summed up a brutal murder with"—she makes air quotes—"'that whole thing.'"

Then she turns, taking in the view around us, making me stop and appreciate it, too. It's another sunny day, all electric-blue sky and puffy white clouds, and from up here, the entire valley below spreads before us.

I rest my arms against an ornate metal railing, taking a deep breath, and next to me, Chess does the same. "Best idea," she says, and I nod.

"Best."

The day is the best, too. We wander the city, which is every bit as quaint and medieval as I'd hoped it would be, quintessentially Italian, but so different from the hustle and bustle of Rome. Cobblestone streets crook and curve up hills, the buildings close enough together in some places to almost blot out the sky.

Chess and I stop at a little trattoria adorned with window boxes of bright pink flowers, sitting in a cozy corner inside to devour a pasta dish I can barely pronounce, but know that I'll probably dream about for the rest of my life.

We also split two bottles of wine between us, so by the time we're back out in the square, the massive duomo towering over us, we are both in a very good mood.

Chess pauses in front of the church, tilting her head back to look at it. It's huge, almost overpowering in the small square, and I realize that anywhere you went in the area, your eyes would be drawn back to it over and over again. It's that big, and also that beautiful. Graceful spires, stained glass windows, gilded mosaics . . .

"Take a picture of me," Chess commands, handing me her phone.

She poses herself on the wide steps leading up to the doors, and I see it, the instant she transforms from my friend Chess into Chess Chandler ☺.

It's almost eerie, really, the subtle change that comes over her. You'd never guess that ten minutes ago, she was draining a wineglass and laughingly telling me a story about the last guy she dated trying to go down on her in the greenroom at one of her events.

The Chess looking soulfully at the camera now would never tell that story. She'd never *have* that story because this

Chess would have been sitting alone in that greenroom, drinking tea and journaling her feelings. Thinking Big Thoughts About the Universe.

I take the picture, then a couple more so that she can pick the best one and then hand her phone back to her.

"I expect at least a two-paragraph caption on this one," I tell her. "Be sure to use the word 'spirit' at least twice, okay?"

The last picture she'd posted on her official Instagram had been of the field behind the villa at sunrise, and my eyes had actually glazed over at all the New Age speak in the caption, stuff about truth and light and "the inner core."

Chess gives me a tight smile, and her movements as she puts the phone back in her purse are a little stiff.

Apparently, we can talk shit and tease each other about some stuff, but the Chess Chandler brand is a sore spot.

Which is why you keep poking at it, a little voice in my head says.

A voice I choose to ignore.

"So, what now?" I ask, still looking up at the cathedral. "We've done window-shopping, we've done boozy lunch, we've done god . . . what else should we explore here in Orvieto?"

"Let's just wander for a little while," Chess replies, sliding her sunglasses back on. "I tend to find the best stuff that way."

Once again, the tension between us gradually eases. The more we walk and talk, the more quintessentially Italian things we see that make us stop and gasp.

We're about to make our way back to the Piazza Cahen and the funicular station when we pass a short line of people outside a round stone building, and Chess draws up short.

"These people clearly know something we don't," she

says, and a young woman with bright red hair and a battered leather bag slung across her body turns around.

"It's the Pozzo di San Patrizio," she says, and it's clear she's a fellow American. "St. Patrick's Well."

"People line up to see a well?" I ask, and she shrugs.

"It's apparently a really famous well? I don't know, I'm just hitting the guidebook highlights."

She opens her bag, and I see she's actually got several travel guides packed in there, their spines cracked with use, names of countries stamped on their covers in bold letters. AUSTRA-LIA, THAILAND, VIETNAM, ITALY.

Riffling through them, she picks out a smaller, thinner book, barely a book at all, more like a slightly thicker brochure, and hands it to me.

It's got the Duomo di Orvieto on the front, and "Day Trips in Orvieto" written across the top. "You can have it," she says. "I'm headed out to Florence tomorrow."

"Thanks," I reply, turning around to show the book to Chess, but she's got her phone out, thumbs moving across the screen at a furious pace, and I look back at the travel guide, flipping it open to the part about the well.

Begun in 1527 and completed in 1537, Pozzo di San Patrizio is a marvel of Renaissance engineering. Double helix staircases allowed for easier access and constant traffic both down into the well and up from the well. . . .

My eyes skip over other details about the well's dimensions, the sophistication of its architecture, the number of windows inside allowing in light. That's the kind of stuff Matt would've been interested in, I'm sure, but he's not here, and I am, so I'm not reading up on Renaissance building practices.

In fact, I'm thinking Chess and I can just skip this alto-gether when I see something a little further down the page.

The well's name comes from the legend of St. Patrick's Purgatory in Ireland, a cave that was so deep, it was said to reach to the underworld.

Something about that description seems familiar to me, and I wrack my brain, trying to remember where I had read it. Recently.

I fish in my bag, pulling out my copy of *Lilith Rising*. I don't know why I've been carrying it around with me like some kind of totem, but I like having it close at hand.

Now I page through it, looking for the scene I'm thinking about.

I find it about a third of the way through the book, in Chapter Six.

"There's a cave in Ireland that reaches down so deep, you can cross into the underworld."

Colin murmured the words against Victoria's throat, and she swallowed hard, reaching out to tangle her fingers with his.

"Have you seen it?" she asked. She felt like she was always asking him things, desperate for any hint of the life he'd had before he'd come to the village. She liked imagining it even though it also made something in her stomach twist. A Colin without her. The man he'd been before.

The man he might be again.

That thought terrified her even more than stories about caves and hell, and she pressed herself closer to him in the warm dark of the barn.

"No," he replied. He had his head propped in his hand, looking down at her. Even in the dim light, his eyes were bright blue. "But I'd go there if I could. I'd take you there."

"I'd go with you," she told him, and she meant it more than she'd ever meant anything before.

A kiss, salty with sweat, hot with promise.

"I would," Victoria insisted. "I'd follow you anywhere."

"Even into hell?"

Colin was watching her carefully, like her answer really mattered to him, which was funny to Victoria, because what other answer was there?

"Yes."

I scan the rest of the pages, but there's nothing more about the cave, no reference to this particular well at all, and I'm more than a little disappointed. I don't know why I'm enjoying it so much, finding these little hints in *Lilith Rising* that connect to Orvieto, but there's something satisfying about it.

Something exciting.

The line has started moving, and the redheaded girl is already inside. But when I turn to Chess, I see that she's on her phone, turned slightly away from me.

I wait until she's done with her call, and am about to suggest we check out the well when she gives me an exaggerated frown. "So, I'm the worst, but that was Steven, and, apparently, he needs a couple of sample chapters from the new book for their foreign rights guy, and he needs them, like, ASAP. And of course, they're only on my computer, so I need to get back to the villa and send them by this evening in New York. But you can stay!" she quickly offers. "Get your well on!"

Steven is Chess's agent, a man I've only met once but who struck me as a terrifying human and probably a fantastic agent. My own agent, Rose, is a much better human, but only an okay agent, a trade-off I've mostly been fine with.

For a second I think about staying, and then shake my head.

Weirdly, I want to get back to the villa, too.

And for the first time in months, I want to write.

To: Rose@ThePetersonAgency.com
From: EmilyLSheridan@PetalBloomBooks.net
Subject: Don't Kill Me (New Book?)

Hi, Rose! Greetings from beautiful Italy! Like I'd hoped, this change of scenery is really doing me so much good. How much? Well, I'm actually writing again! You might be the only person MORE excited than I am about that fact. ☺

The only issue is that I'm not working on Petal right now. (I know it's still due, and thank you so much for getting me the extra time on that!) I don't know how much you know about Mari Godwick and the murder of Pierce Sheldon, but it turns out the house we're staying in is the very one where that happened. Now, this is obviously a GOLD MINE for a mystery writer, even one who usually writes cozies, and I've gotten really interested in the case. Not only that, I think there are some interesting links to be made between the murder here in 1974 and Mari's famous horror novel, *Lilith Rising*, that came out in 1976. I know that would be a VERY big change of pace for me in terms of what I write, but I genuinely feel like there's something really cool here, something that has the potential to be big, especially with how popular true crime is these days.

Once I have something more concrete, i.e., pages, I'll send them your way, but I just wanted to loop you in on what I was doing, and also make sure you won't murder me if I send you a new book that's *not* Petal10.

Best,
Emily

"Christ, I'm bored."

Noel doesn't say it so much as declare it, flopping back onto the low sofa in the drawing room, his face turned up to the ceiling as though he were addressing the chandelier. It's a rainy night at the villa after a rainy afternoon, and a rainy morning before that. Which means they've all been trapped inside together for too long.

They need the space, Mari quickly realized, in order for the delicate ecosystem they'd built here to thrive. She'd spent most of the day lying listlessly in bed, looking over the pages she'd written, wondering why that voice that had seemed so vibrant just a week ago had suddenly stopped speaking.

Victoria's story seems to have come to an abrupt halt, stranding her in the scene where she first meets the village reverend she'll eventually fall in love with, and nothing Mari has done—long walks to think, glasses of wine to lower her inhibitions—has worked. The project has, like so many before it, stalled completely.

"Aren't the rest of you?" Noel asks when no one replies to his announcement, and when he drops his chin to his chest, scanning the room, Mari feels his eyes land on her.

She's curled on the sofa opposite him, her notebook by her side just in case Victoria regains her voice.

"No," she says, flatly. At her feet, Pierce laughs, resting his cheek against her knee. His guitar sits idle next to him, a notebook open but no words written.

"Mari is never bored," he tells Noel. "Whole bloody party going on in that head of hers."

It's a compliment, or meant to be one; Mari knows that, but it still irritates her when he pulls this shit, talking about her like she's not there. And he's doing it much more than usual around Noel. He's eager to impress, she thinks to herself.

"We could go on a little adventure?" Lara suggests. As usual, she's perched near Noel, not quite sitting next to him because if she gets too close, he might move away, and then her shame would be on display for all to see.

"What about Rome?" Lara continues.

That's another tic she's picked up, this constant questioning. Everything ends with a slight rise in her voice.

"Rome would also be boring," Noel says, dismissing her with a wave. "And besides, I'm paying for this bloody place, I'm not going to put you all up in Rome, too."

He draws the *O* out, the word drawled—*Rooohhhhhhme*—just in case Lara didn't know he was mocking her, Mari supposes.

"You *could* try to write some music," Mari says. "Which I believe was the point of this entire trip."

It's frustrating, watching Noel and Pierce nearly get stuck in on something only to grow distracted when Noel wants to go for a drive or take the rowboat out or swim in the pool or do any of a dozen things that won't bring him or Pierce—or Mari, for that matter—any closer to their goals.

And there's that studio space waiting back in London, that golden chance for Pierce that seems to be slipping further and further away.

Lately, Mari has begun to wonder whether, if Noel can propel Pierce to greater heights, it means that the inverse is true, too. Should this all fall apart, is Pierce going to be hit by the shrapnel of Noel's failure?

But Noel just ignores her, like she'd known he would.

"We oughta go into Orvieto," Johnnie says. "The old part."

Tilting his head back, Noel fixes Johnnie with a look. "And see what, exactly? A church? Some old ladies selling bread?"

Unlike Lara, Johnnie never flinches from Noel's barbs, merely shaking them off like he does everything else. He'd clearly been a bit wounded by Mari not immediately throwing herself at him over the etched glass, but on the whole, he seems to have recovered, and she's relieved. There are already too many romantic complications in this house without adding Johnnie's crush on her into the mix.

He glances over at her now, his gaze warm, then turns his attention back to Noel. "Supposedly, they've got a well that goes down into hell."

Noel perks up at that. "Really?"

"Well," Johnnie amends, "it's named after some place in Ireland that goes down into hell, but it's still pretty fucking deep."

Scowling, Noel sinks further into the sofa. "Think I'll pass on seeing a very deep hole in the ground, mate. I'm not quite *that* bored yet."

Johnnie may not mind Noel's jibes, but it's clear he enjoyed those few seconds when Noel actually appeared interested in something he had to say, so he tries again. "Also, the lady who runs the shop down the hill told me this villa is meant to be haunted. Apparently someone topped themselves up here back in the fifteen hundreds."

"Whoever this unfortunate person was, I feel a kinship,"

Noel says, sighing dramatically as he tips his head back, and Mari can't bite her tongue any longer.

"Yes, what a hardship, staying in a gorgeous villa with all the food and drink you could want and no shortage of beautiful things to look at. However have you coped thus far, milord?"

It's a nickname she's given him over the past week, a pointed reminder that for all his decadence and rock-star pretensions, he's still the son of an earl, and Mari suspects he loves it and hates it in equal measure.

Lara shoots her a dirty look, but Noel only laughs.

"Now, see? Pierce is right. Mari is neither bored *nor* boring."

His gaze slides to Lara, upper lip curling slightly. "Some of you should clearly take notes."

The hurt that flashes over Lara's face is gone as quickly as it appeared, but Mari catches it. She feels sorry for her stepsister, truly she does, but she also can't deny the primal satisfaction she feels, seeing Lara taken down a few notches. Mari knows she should be ashamed of herself, but she isn't.

Noel stands, slapping his hands against his thighs. He's once again thrown that garish dressing gown on over a pair of black jeans and nothing else, the rings on his fingers glinting in the candlelight. "I've changed my mind," he announces, dark hair flopping over his brow. "Come, Sheldon, let's give Mistress Mary what she's commanded."

Pierce stands up, guitar in hand, his gaze fixed on Noel, face bright. His free hand absentmindedly brushes over Mari's hair as he goes to where Noel has set up his guitar near the window. They'd dragged over a couple of wooden chairs from somewhere else in the house a few days ago when they'd sworn they were going to write, only to get distracted by . . . lord, Mari can't even remember.

There are so many distractions at Villa Rosato.

But now, finally, they're sitting down, Pierce's notebook is open on his knee, and Noel is actually listening to him.

Lara crosses the room to flop onto Mari's sofa, leaning her head against Mari's shoulder. "Aren't they beautiful?" she says dreamily, her eyes fixed on Pierce and Noel. Pierce is already strumming his guitar, Noel nodding along, watching the placement of Pierce's fingers.

And they are beautiful, but it irks Mari, that dreamy wonder in Lara's voice.

"I've started writing a little myself."

It's Johnnie, who has taken a seat on her other side, his thigh pressed against hers, and Mari frowns in confusion.

"I saw you were writing," Johnnie goes on, gesturing to the notebook on the other side of Lara. "And I thought I might try it. I play music, too, you know. Brought my guitar, but Noel never wants me to play with him, so maybe writing could be something I'm—"

"Right." Mari cuts him off, her gaze drawn back to the two men in front of her, and though she knows she's being a little rude, she doesn't care, not right now. Right now, she wants to watch what she's sure is history being made. The beginning of something great.

She feels Johnnie's eyes on the side of her face, but she doesn't turn to meet his gaze, and after a moment, he gets up with a sigh.

Mari hears the creak of the door, hears his footsteps as he leaves, a muted slam coming from somewhere upstairs.

"What's his problem?" Lara asks in a low voice. Pierce is

still playing, but he's just repeating the same two chords, and Noel is shaking his head, reaching over to scratch something in Pierce's notebook.

"Johnnie?" she answers, her eyes still on Pierce. "I don't know."

"He's hot for you," Lara whispers, and Mari frowns.

"He is not," she says, even though she knows that he is, and Lara laughs, her head tipping back. It's a real laugh, her real voice. She's not playing a part for Noel or for Pierce right now, and Mari remembers that there was a time when she actually really liked spending time with her stepsister. Back when they were girls, sharing the same bedroom, sleeping in twin beds and whispering secrets in the dark.

"I have eyes, Mare," Lara says, nudging her. "And he clearly has taste."

She snuggles in close to Mari again, all easy affection because that's Lara. Mari has always felt her own prickliness acutely, knows that she's not easy to talk to or really get to know. Lara, though . . . it's all out there with Lara, and there are moments, like now, that Mari is glad for it.

Still, Mari wishes things were different with her and Lara. That they could just be sisters, sisters who love each other, sisters who aren't vying for the same thing.

For the same man.

But that was always their way, wasn't it? Before Pierce, it was Mari's father. Lara had been twelve, nearly thirteen, when her mother had married William Godwick, but that hadn't stopped her from calling him "Papa," from running to him every evening when he got home to regale him with some story from school or a new book she'd read or an album she'd listened to.

Mari had always thought it was a little sad, how eager Lara

had been for William's attention, but then her father always indulged it, always smiled fondly at Lara in a way he never did at Mari, no matter her accomplishments.

Maybe Lara was simply easier to love because she wasn't a living reminder of the woman William had loved and lost. Or maybe it's something in Mari herself that makes men she loves, be they father or lover, look for something else in Lara.

That's over, she tells herself. *They both promised you it would never happen again, and, besides, Lara's clearly hung up on Noel now.*

But when Mari glances over at Lara, it's not Noel she's watching with those dark eyes.

And Pierce stares back. Not for long, and his eyes almost immediately slide to Mari, but his fingers nearly miss the note. Suddenly Lara's skin feels uncomfortably warm and damp next to hers.

She's thinking about going up to bed when something in Pierce's playing shifts. The song becomes less hesitant, more solid, and then Noel finally picks up his own guitar.

The candles flicker and make eerie shapes on the wall while outside, the rain continues to pour down, thunder rattling the panes of glass in the windows. The storm that had not so long ago made her feel claustrophobic and trapped now makes the room seem cozy and close in a good way. Like their own universe.

Then Noel starts to play, and Mari instantly understands.

All the drugs and the women and the men, all the wild, dark rumors, all of that is both a distraction from and an off-shoot of what this man can do with his guitar, his voice, and his words.

His elegant fingers move over the strings, and later, Mari will try to recall the exact melody of this song. Noel will never play it again, certainly never record it, and years after this night, when she asks him about it, he'll swear to not remember even playing.

But Mari will remember, and this song will stay with her.

Noel begins to sing in that low voice she's heard a thousand times on the radio. It's different in person, though, and her heart seems to beat both a little harder and a little slower in her chest.

This, she understands, is the Noel people fall in love with.

And then there's another soft chord as Pierce picks up his guitar again, too. He finds the harmonies easily, Noel lifting his head to give the other man a surprisingly kind smile. Pierce practically glows in response, and the song continues, lifting, falling, raising goose bumps on Mari's arms.

When it ends, there's no sound except the patter of the rain on the windows, and Mari's own breathing in her ears.

"That was gorgeous," Lara enthuses, and not even her bright energy can quite puncture the moment, which feels heavy with meaning, with . . . something that Mari can't quite put a finger on.

They play more songs, that night, Noel and Pierce. Songs of Noel's, including Mari's favorite, "Autumn Sun." They play songs they each like, Pierce's sweet voice lending unexpected depth to lighter tunes like "I Wanna Hold Your Hand," Noel's famous velvet baritone turning "California Dreamin'" wry and less wistful.

Eventually Lara gets up from the sofa, clearly intending for Noel to follow.

He doesn't, of course, and there's another muffled slamming of a door upstairs, but by then, Mari is drowsy and happy, content to watch Pierce and this man he admires so much create music in the candlelight.

She's not sure when she falls asleep exactly. The music

makes everything soft and hazy, lulling her into dreams. Mari's never been a fan of drugs, barely drinks more than a glass or two of wine, but she thinks this is what those kinds of altered escapes must feel like, this slow slide, like slipping into a warm bath.

When she wakes up, the music has stopped, and she opens her eyes to see Pierce and Noel are now standing, their guitars abandoned.

It takes her a moment to make sense of what she's seeing. Noel's mouth on Pierce's, Pierce's hand almost tentative on Noel's waist underneath that dressing gown. Pierce has always seemed so tall to her, but Noel is taller, his grip surprisingly strong in Pierce's soft brown hair.

When they part, Pierce's face is flushed, his throat moving as he swallows hard, and when he looks over at Mari, she waits for the guilt to flash across his face, for outrage to rise in her.

But Pierce only watches her, his gaze steady and warm, and there's no anger in her at all, she realizes. Only a sort of vague disappointment that they've stopped.

Then Pierce turns toward her even as his hand never leaves Noel's waist. "Come here, Mari," he says, his voice soft, and she gets up from the sofa, wondering if she's still dreaming.

Noel is watching her, too, smirking lazily, but she can sense the tension in him, and when she gets closer, she sees that he's actually trembling.

It melts something within her, and she leans forward, the threadbare carpet under her bare feet, the candles burning all around them.

In the mirror just over the fireplace, Mari sees the three of them, watches as Pierce comes to stand behind her, kissing the place where neck meets shoulder, his hands skating down her bare arms.

She doesn't look like herself, or maybe it's that she finally looks like herself, her eyes half-lidded, her lips parted, cheeks flushed.

Noel moves to stand in front of her, his hand once again going to Pierce's hair over her shoulder, but he's looking at her, and she wonders what he's seeing.

"In for a penny, in for a pound, Mistress Mary," he murmurs, and Mari rises up on her tiptoes, pressing her lips to his.

His kiss is different from Pierce's, the only one she has to compare it to. There hadn't been anyone before him, no quick snogs behind the school, no fumbles at school dances. She had always thought it was because, somehow, she knew she was waiting for Pierce.

But she likes this, likes the firmness of Noel's mouth, the forthrightness of it all, his hand on her neck, his tongue against hers, and as she leans closer, Lara's face is there in her mind for a moment.

We're even now, she thinks, but just as quickly, she's shoving that thought away because she doesn't want Lara here, a part of this moment.

This isn't about evening the score. This is about what Mari wants, and right now, she wants this.

This, finally, is a version of Pierce's ideal world that might get to include her as well.

Thunder rattles the house, the storm growing even stronger, and Mari gives in.

SHE WAKES TO another slamming door, but this one is close.

Too close.

It's past noon, she knows immediately, and the rain has stopped. The light that pours through the windows is bright, illuminating everything that had been shadowy and dim the night before.

Mari is on the floor by the fireplace, a chenille blanket covering her from the waist down, her head pillowed on Pierce's chest. He's sleeping like he always does, like a little kid, his arms thrown over his head, his face peaceful.

Noel is a warm weight at her back. His arm lays heavily across her, palm resting on Pierce's bare stomach, and Mari takes a deep breath, looking up at the ceiling.

She waits for regret to come, but there isn't any. It's done, after all, there's no taking it back.

And, she thinks, with a smile that threatens to turn into a laugh, what's the point of going to a villa in Italy with a notorious rock star if you don't let yourself go a little wild?

But that doesn't mean there aren't consequences, and as she gingerly disentangles herself and finds her discarded dress, she knows she needs to deal with them as soon as possible.

A part of her had hoped the person at the door might be Elena. The girl might be a little scandalized, but it would give her a story for her family and the rest of the town for donkey's years, so the damage there would be fairly minimal.

Johnnie might be hurt, and she regretted that, but he also had no claim on her, so that was easily handled.

But, of course, it's not Elena or Johnnie.

She finds Lara sitting on the end of the diving board, her knees drawn up to her chest, her shoulders hitching, and Mari steels herself as she approaches.

"Lara," she starts, but Lara whirls on her before she can say anything else.

"Why him?" her stepsister demands, and Mari, who was ready to be conciliatory about the whole thing, feels anger flare in her chest.

"Why him?" she repeats, and Lara has the gall to nod, her head bobbing.

"You know how I feel about Noel. You know, and you did . . . whatever that was anyway."

"I'm fairly sure you knew how I felt about Pierce when you fucked him," Mari fires back, her arms tight across her chest. "So please do not pull this wounded act now, Lara. Besides, last night was just . . ."

Images unspool in her mind, and she tries very hard to keep any of what she's thinking off her face.

"It was a bit of fun. A little wildness. Nothing more."

"That makes it *worse*," Lara cries, standing up on the diving board, her hands balled into fists at her sides. It would be a much more dramatic gesture, the kind of thing that begged for a plaintive "Don't jump!" from Mari, but of course, Lara is standing over six feet of beautiful turquoise water, and Mari can't help the laugh that bursts out of her.

It's just so . . . typically *Lara*, so overwrought but ultimately pointless and silly, and Mari is so, so tired of this particular drama that she and her stepsister keep playing out.

She shrugs at Lara and throws her hands up. "I really don't see how it is, but—"

"Because I love Pierce," Lara says, and now Mari doesn't feel like laughing at all. "I love him, but he loves you!" Lara goes on. "So, I tried to love Noel instead, but you couldn't even let me have that."

"*Noel* won't even let you have that," Mari reminds her, but Lara just makes a disgusted sound, marching down the diving board and back onto the patio. The door slams again, and Mari wonders if all the hinges in the villa will need to be replaced at the end of the summer.

Tipping her head back, she looks up, where clouds are

already beginning to form, promising yet another evening trapped inside the house, trapped with Lara and her feelings.

Mari can't help it. She opens her mouth wide and screams, literally screams at the sky, a howl of frustration that hurts her throat, but at least relieves some of the pressure in her chest.

That done, she flops into one of the chairs next to the pool, the metal screeching against the stone.

"Christ, I hope that wasn't a comment on last night's performance."

She whips her head around to see Noel standing in the doorway that leads into the kitchen. He's wearing sunglasses and carrying a mug of coffee, the chenille blanket that had been covering Mari earlier now wrapped around his waist, and he makes his careful way out to where she sits, taking the chair next to her and sinking into it with a sigh.

Mari guesses she should feel differently about Noel now that he's made her come, but it's just that same mix of faint disbelief that she's talking to *Noel Gordon*, mixed with an almost begrudging fondness—plus the slightest tinge of annoyance.

Which is a relief, actually. It would be disastrous to feel anything more for this man.

She wonders if Pierce knows that.

But then Pierce's tastes have always run to women. To girls, really. Mari was sixteen when she met him, and his wife, Frances, was only fifteen when he took her from her boarding school in the north of England and crossed into Scotland to marry her.

He worships Noel, and clearly enjoyed himself last night, but Mari instinctively understands that what Pierce was after was experience and novelty, and now that he's had them, last night will probably not be repeated.

Which is undoubtedly for the best.

Noel blows out a breath over the top of his coffee, his long legs stretched in front of him, feet crossed at the ankles. "What's that thing you're writing?" he asks her, and Mari startles.

"What?"

"That journal you're always carrying around. You left it on the sofa last night, and I had a gander this morning."

"You read my journal?"

He shrugs, completely unapologetic. "I was hoping to find moony sonnets about me, so imagine my surprise to see Mistress Mary is writing a novel."

She flushes red. "You shouldn't have done that."

"But I did. And it's honestly quite good, which I find extremely annoying given that you're already young and beautiful. Being talented on top of that just isn't fair."

Mari doesn't reply, and Noel clears his throat. "This is the part where you're supposed to point out that I also have all these attributes."

That makes her laugh against her will, and he smiles again, affectionately nudging her foot with his own. "I am serious, though. You've got something there. I hope you'll follow it wherever it leads."

Those few pages, still unfinished, call to her, and Mari allows herself a small smile.

"I hope I will, too."

There were always rumors about just how involved the five young people at Villa Rosato were that summer. Of the five, Noel Gordon was the eldest, and he was only twenty-six. Pierce Sheldon was twenty-three, Johnnie Dorchester a mere twenty, and Mari Godwick and Lara Larchmont were both still teenagers, just nineteen in the summer of 1974. They were also all part of a set that ran fast and loose when it came to sexual partners and mores. Pierce had already left one wife, as had Noel, and both men had been involved with Lara Larchmont at different times.

But it's also tempting to make things more illicit than they actually were, especially when it comes to rock royalty. It's equally possible that none of the rumors were true at all, and that the romantic configurations at Villa Rosato were fairly tame. None of the survivors ever indicated differently.

While Noel Gordon and Mari Godwick remained close for the remainder of the former's short life, Mari never discussed the events of that summer, not even in her private diaries, which her literary agent donated to the University of Edinburgh after her death in 1993. There is only one entry dealing with Noel Gordon, and it is found on a page labeled March 22, 1980. It says simply, "Noel is dead. How can Noel be dead?"

Intriguingly, there was a bit after that that had been scratched out in a flurry of black ink, but X-ray technology done on the diary revealed the words, "It's not fair that I'm the only one left."

— *The Rock Star, the Writer, and the Murdered Musician: The Strange Saga of Villa Rosato*, A. Burton, longformcrime.net

The first thing you notice about Lara Larchmont is how normal she looks.

There's none of the mystique of a Stevie Nicks, nor the arresting beauty of a Linda Ronstadt. There's just a dark-haired girl of about medium height with brown eyes and a smile that's a little crooked, but completely charming. As she welcomes me into her London flat, I think she could be a girl you went to school with, a friend from down the street.

A friend whose debut album has sold well over a million copies, mind you, but other than the poshness of her Belgrave address and the gorgeous furnishings in her flat, you'd have no way of knowing that . . .

There is only one topic completely off-limits with Larchmont: the events of July 29, 1974. Everyone knows the story. It was one of rock music's biggest scandals, a dark and lurid tale of sex, drugs, and murder involving one of the most famous men in rock, Noel Gordon—a man Lara was, it was rumored, pregnant by that summer, though given that she very demonstrably does not have a child, who can say how accurate that rumor was?

The murder of Pierce Sheldon reverberated through rock circles, and both Lara and her stepsister, the writer Mari Godwick, were swept up in it. The swift conviction of John Dorchester, a hanger-on and drug dealer who had accompanied Gordon to Italy that summer, did nothing to stem interest in the story, and his suicide in an Umbrian prison just six months after said conviction only fueled more tawdry conspiracies.

Five years later, though, most of that has died down,

eclipsed by the success of Mari Godwick's sensational novel *Lilith Rising* and Lara's *Aestas*.

And it is *Aestas* that provides me my one chance at getting a hint of Lara's feelings about Villa Rosato and the summer that saw the gruesome murder of Pierce Sheldon.

I wait to bring it up until nearly the end of the interview when the sun has set outside and the tea we were drinking has been replaced with two vodka tonics.

"Why the title?"

Larchmont's dark eyes narrow slightly.

"Pardon?" she asks, but I don't think it's a question. I think she's trying to give me a way out. I probably should have taken it, but I press on.

"*Aestas* means summer in Latin," I say. "And you wrote these songs in Italy in the summer of 1974."

It's the closest I'll get to mentioning the events that happened at Villa Rosato, and there is something in the way Lara Larchmont looks at me in that moment that makes me feel slightly ashamed—slightly grubby—for even bringing it up.

"I did," she finally says. "But the title of the album was really inspired by Camus. You know, 'I found there was, inside me, an invincible summer,' all that."

Since she was gracious enough to let me slide in something so personal, I return the favor and don't press. And honestly, there is something of the invincible summer about Lara Larchmont. Her smiles are easy, her eyes warm, and she seems untouched by all that darkness in a way that the other survivors of Villa Rosato are not. Photographs of Noel Gordon taken just this past summer in Venice reveal a man whose legendary beauty is fading (and whose equally legendary talent is being squandered), and there's always been a whiff of the tragic around Mari Godwick, despite her literary success.

But Lara Larchmont still walks in the sun.

I mention this later to an acquaintance, a writer who'll remain nameless but was friendly with Larchmont and her set in the early seventies, and is still a force to be reckoned with in music journalism now.

To my surprise, he disagrees, shaking his head vehemently. "No, that summer ate her the fuck up, too, man. She's just better at hiding it than the rest of them."

—"Invincible Summer:
The Rise and Rise of Lara Larchmont,"
Rolling Stone, November 1979

CHAPTER EIGHT

Ten thousand words.

I look at the number at the bottom of the page on my laptop again, and no, I'm not imagining it.

In the past three days, I've written ten thousand words, which is more than I've written in the last eight months combined.

Granted, not a one of those ten thousand words is about Petal Bloom, a fact that probably won't thrill my editor, and certainly doesn't help my bank account, but for the first time in ages, I actually feel like me again. Writer me, losing herself for hours at her laptop, slipping into some kind of jet stream only I can feel.

The only problem is I'm not sure what it is I'm writing exactly.

The name of the document is "TheVillaBook.doc" but it's not about the villa, really. Or not just about the villa. It's part biography of Mari Godwick, part true crime dealing with the murder of Pierce Sheldon, and part personal narrative—my Italian summer, post-divorce, where instead of eating, praying, and loving, I became interested in the link between a horror classic and the real-life horror that unfolded at the villa where I was staying.

It's not like anything I've ever written before, but there's *something* there, I'm sure of it, and even Rose seemed cautiously optimistic when she replied to my email, reminding me that I should still make the next Petal Bloom book the priority, but that she was just glad I seemed excited about writing again.

And I am. As excited as I can remember being in a long time.

A couple of years ago, just after Matt made his big baby announcement at Thanksgiving, I'd been between Petal books, and decided to try my hand at something different, something darker, edgier. I think there had been a part of me afraid that if I didn't start it then, I might never do it, that I'd get too busy with life, with a baby, with the other Petal books still under contract.

It was never a book, never anything more than a quickly sketched-out premise about twin sisters in North Carolina, one of them a murderer, but which one? Still, I'd loved working on it, stayed up late just to spend more time with those characters, made playlists and Pinterest boards, thought about them when I was driving, when I was at the gym.

I always thought that's why Matt's reaction had been so lukewarm when he read the few chapters I'd written. He hadn't liked how much it had consumed me, kept asking if I "really thought this was the best time to veer from the course," and of course, it's hard to try for a baby when your wife is practically glued to her laptop.

But maybe Matt had seen something in the pages that I hadn't because when I'd sent them off to Rose, she'd come back with a very kind, very gentle reminder that I still had two more Petal books under contract, and the thriller market was so crowded.

You're so good at what you do! she'd said over the phone. *Do you know how hard it is to write cozies? Anyone can write these kinds of dark, twisted books. Think of this as a fun little exercise you did to get limbered up to work on Petal #7, okay?*

It shouldn't have hit that hard. Books were a business, after all, and Rose was smart, and probably right, and whatever that book might have been, it was now sitting on a flash drive that I'd misplaced somewhere in the house.

Besides, right after that was when I'd started feeling sick, so it was probably for the best I hadn't started some big new project then, but I still thought of it sometimes, still wished I could slip back into the flow I'd felt working on it.

And today I had.

Closing the laptop, I stand up and stretch, looking out my bedroom window to see Chess outside on the lawn. She's sitting on a striped blanket, her laptop perched on her knees, and even though her sunhat means I can't see her face, I can see that, for once, her fingers aren't flying over the keyboard.

They're just sort of . . . hovering.

I know that position well, but Chess always seems to be barreling through her book, so it's weird seeing her just sitting there, tortured by the blinking cursor.

Tires crunch on the gravel out front, and I turn away from the window, heading downstairs.

As I'd thought, it's Giulia, coming in with a load of groceries, and she brightens when she sees me.

"Buongiorno, signorina!" she calls out. Giulia is a little older than us, probably in her mid-forties, and she always seems to be in the best mood any person has ever been in.

I gesture to the open door, her car beyond.

"Let me help you with that."

She gives me a grateful nod, and we quickly get the remaining food inside.

I always enjoy Giulia's visits. Maybe it's because she's always so sunny and easy to talk to, or maybe I just need a little conversation that isn't with Chess. In any case, I'm glad she's here this morning because I've been meaning to ask her about something.

"Giulia," I ask, sitting down at the kitchen table and pulling an orange out of the big bowl of fruit, "Was someone from your family working here in 1974?"

Giulia pauses as she unloads the bag and turns to look over her shoulder at me, a smile curling her lips. "Ooh, are you one of them?" she asks in her accented English, and I laugh, digging my nails into the skin of the orange.

"One of who?"

"The true crime people," she says. "With your podcasts and your Netflix."

I shake my head, still smiling. "No. Or, I mean, I wasn't? Maybe I am now?"

She nods, turning back to the bag. "That's how it happens, I think."

"It's just interesting," I say, wondering if I'm trying to convince her or myself. "And weird that no one really talks about it that much anymore given that it involved famous people."

Giulia moves to the fridge, her ponytail swinging. "It's a good thing people forgot it. I like working here, and I want nice people like you and Signorina Chandler. Not weirdos who come here for murder."

Fair enough. Villa Aestas is a peaceful, pretty place that doesn't deserve to be tainted by one bad night fifty years ago.

I'm just about to get up from the table when Giulia adds, "But to answer your question, yes."

She closes the fridge with a thunk and turns around. "My aunt Elena was working here that summer. She actually testified at the trial. Made her a little famous for a time."

Giulia sighs, her hand going to her bangs. "Ruined her life, though. Made her think she was somebody when really she was just a part of a somebody's story."

Part of a somebody's story. It's a twisty turn of phrase, one I immediately like, and I tell myself to remember it later.

"Is she still in Orvieto?" I ask, and Giulia shakes her head.

"No, she moved to Rome for a bit in the late seventies, and by 1985, she was dead." She taps her nose, mimes taking a big sniff. "Drugs."

"I'm sorry," I say, instantly wishing I hadn't brought it up, but Giulia only shrugs again.

"I told you, it ruined her life. Took it in the end."

Wagging one finger in my direction, Giulia narrows her eyes at me. "So, you leave all that alone," she tells me. "It's like a curse, that story."

She's joking, being playfully stern, but I think there's something a little sincere behind it. And given that everyone involved in that summer is now dead, Elena included, I can't really disagree with her.

Doesn't mean I'm going to stop writing about it, though. Not with those ten thousand words sitting on my computer and my brain actually feeling like it's firing on all cylinders for once.

The door from the back patio opens, and Chess comes in, her laptop tucked under her arm, a rose-gold Hydro Flask in her other hand. "What are you two gossiping about?" she asks, and Giulia laughs, gathering up her purse.

"She wanted to know all about the *muuuuurder*," she replies, wiggling her fingers like claws, and Chess shoots me an indulgent look that makes my teeth itch.

"Are you still thinking about that?" she asks.

"I'm writing about it, actually," I say. "Already have a couple of chapters."

I don't know why I tell her, and it's not technically true, anyway—what I've got so far is mostly freeform, nothing organized into sections yet. But saying it out loud makes it feel real, and I want desperately for this to be *real*. An actual book, a thing I've made.

I see the way Chess takes that in, and I nod at her laptop. "How's your work coming?"

"Great!" she chirps, too fast and too bright.

Giulia looks between us for a second, and then offers her own too-bright smile.

"You should be set for the next few days, I think. Call me if you need anything else."

We thank her, and then she's gone, her little blue car traveling back down the hill, leaving me and Chess alone again.

Chess sits at the table across from me and unscrews the top of her flask. "So, tell me about it," she says before taking a drink of water. "What you're working on."

I make myself lean back, casual, as I pull a section from the orange. "It's kind of a mix of things. Little bit about the murder, little bit about *Lilith Rising*, little bit about me."

Her eyebrows go up. "About you? So, it's like a memoir?"

"Not exactly."

"Then, what exactly?"

I laugh, but it sounds shrill. "I don't know yet, Chess. It's still in the early stages, but I'm having fun with it at least. And wasn't that the point of this trip? To get some writing done?"

She acknowledges that with a nod, then folds her arms on the table, leaning in closer. "I'm just surprised, is all. I never thought you'd want to do nonfiction."

Neither had I. I've always liked my stories fictional, preferred inventing characters and situations rather than just reporting them as they happened, but this was different. This felt like . . . unearthing something. Exorcising it, maybe.

Ooh, that was a good word for it, especially considering the subject matter of *Lilith Rising*. I should remember that, try to work it into the book.

My fingers were already itching to return to my laptop, brain whirring in that way that tells me I have an excellent few hours of writing ahead of me.

I get up from the table, but as I do, Chess stands, too. "God, do you remember when I took that fiction writing class with you junior year? What was that dickhead professor's name?"

"Dr. Burke," I say immediately, not adding that A, she wasn't a dickhead, and B, I remember her name because she's in the acknowledgments of the first Petal Bloom mystery. She was the first person who ever told me I might be able to make a living at writing, and it was her voice I heard in my head when I sat down and started that first book, *An Evil Evening*.

"Dr. Burke," she repeats, nodding. "Who hated me."

"She didn't hate you," I say, "she was just tough on your stories."

Chess rolls her eyes. "She told me, and I quote, 'If you're

this interested in yourself, Miss Chandler, maybe you should move to memoir rather than fiction.'"

I don't remember that, but it does sound like something Dr. Burke would've said. Especially to Chess, who seemed to push her buttons for some reason. That was around the time we were working on *Green*, and Chess had decided she wanted to take a creative writing class with me, that if we were writing for the same teacher at the same time, it would help our collaboration or something.

Except that Chess had ended up with a C while I made an A, and it wasn't long after that *Green* was abandoned.

I wonder why she's bringing it up now.

"Well, you took that advice," I remind her. "And sold a gazillion copies and made a gazillion dollars, so maybe you should send Dr. Burke a thank-you note."

She snorts at that. "Maybe. Anyway, if you need any help, let me know," she says, and her voice is breezy, but there's something in her eyes that doesn't match that tone. "This is my deal, after all. The nonfiction thing. I'm happy to read what you've got, give some tips, whatever you need."

"Thanks," I tell her, "but it's really nothing I'd want anyone to read yet. It might not be anything at all."

A lie. It's something, I know it is.

And it's not that I don't want anyone to read it.

It's that I don't want *Chess* to read it, specifically—and I can't really explain why.

"So, what is the book even about?"

It's two days later, and Chess and I are back in our favorite room in the house, the small sitting room with its soft sofas and crystal candelabras. Tonight's wine of choice is a red, a Sangiovese that Giulia brought for us, and it's sliding over my tongue like velvet as I study Chess on the other sofa.

"*Lilith Rising*," she clarifies. "I know, I know—you don't even have a book yet, right?"

What I have is 21,863 words that I now know in my heart are absolutely a book, but I make myself shake my head. "No, I'm still just in the exploratory stage. But you really want to know about *Lilith Rising*?"

Chess is slouched on the sofa, her feet on the coffee table, the toenails a bright coral, and she lifts her glass like a toast. "If my best friend is obsessed with something, I wanna know about it. Like when you got super into those dragon books in ninth grade, and made me read the little stories you were writing about them."

I laugh at the memory. "You never even read the dragon books."

"And I'm probably not going to read *Lilith Rising,* but I still want you to tell me about it. I know it's all demons and possession and stuff, but—"

"It's more than that," I tell her, and she immediately holds up a hand.

"Okay, sorry to insult your new favorite book. Please continue."

I throw one of the tiny decorative pillows at her, and she dodges nimbly, her wine sloshing, but not spilling. She's laughing, and she once again looks like the Chess I knew years ago. Less polished, less perfect, her hair in a messy bun, dressed in an old T-shirt and pajama pants with watermelons on them instead of one of her Guru in Italy looks.

Maybe that's why I let down my guard a little.

"All right, so *Lilith Rising* is about this teenage girl, Victoria Stuart, who moves with her family to a big old manor

in the English countryside called Somerton House. And everything is perfect and bucolic and summery, and the house isn't
even super creepy, and you're, like, 'Oh, okay, so maybe this
isn't gonna be so bad!' But then she meets this priest, and
they fall in love."

"Hot," Chess acknowledges, and I nod.

"Also, timely. This book came out right after *The Thorn
Birds*, so everyone was very into that. But this priest is evil."

"Not exactly a shocking plot twist."

I forgot how fun it can be to talk with Chess like this, like
bouncing a ball back and forth, both of us somehow always
knowing the right thing to say to each other. I've never experienced that kind of intellectual chemistry with anyone else.
Not even Matt.

"No," I agree, "but that's kind of the point of the book.
By the end, you're not sure who was the corrupting influence,
him or Victoria. And he's dead, so she's the only one telling
the story, and obviously she's putting herself in the best possible light. But . . ."

I sit up, warming to my story, feeling excited all over
again. "That's what's so cool about the book. Horror was
pretty straightforward at the time. This person is bad, they
do a bad thing, or this house is bad, it makes people do a bad
thing. But *Lilith Rising* is just really ambiguous. Was there
even a demon? Is Victoria making up a story to explain why
she does all this violent shit? Or did she just want to kill her
family, kill the priest who seduced her, and blame it on some
outside force?"

"That is kind of fucking cool," Chess says, propping her
ankle on her knee, her foot jiggling, the light catching on a
thin gold anklet she's wearing.

"It's very fucking cool," I assure her. "Plus, at the end of it, she wins! Sure, they ship her off to a hospital for a while, but then in the last chapter, she's been released and is living back in the house that she loved, and all the other assholes are dead. And so of course, male critics were, like, 'this is bleak as shit.'"

"And female critics were, like, 'actually, this rules'?" Chess supplies.

I nod. "Exactly. And that's why *Lilith Rising* is considered a masterpiece of feminist horror."

Chess claps, careful not to spill her wine, and I lift my glass to her. "It's no TED Talk, I know, but I've hit the high notes for you."

Chess grins at that. "And you think there are more connections between the book and the house than just 'she wrote it here.'"

A little of my tipsy enthusiasm fades. Now we're back on my story, and I'm probably imagining it, but there's something so . . . avid in Chess's eyes as she studies me.

"I think there could be," is all I say.

I don't tell her what I've really been thinking, which is that Mari Godwick wasn't just writing a book inspired by this house and people she knew. She was actually trying to tell us something, something more about what happened that summer. Was Pierce Sheldon's death really as simple as a drugged-up argument between two men that went too far? And if it was, why were the survivors so secretive about it for the rest of their lives?

"Your brain is working, I can tell," Chess says, and no, I'm not imagining it, the hungry expression on her face. Suddenly, I think of the past few days and try to remember if I've seen Chess working at all.

She was out most of yesterday, and then the day before,

I saw her reading at the pool. I've been so absorbed in my own stuff that I haven't really been paying attention.

And then something in her voice goes sly as she says, "And you're a dirty rotten liar, because you absolutely have a book."

I blink at her, my stomach lurching. "What?"

She's very drunk, I realize now, way more than me, and she's giggling as she sits up. "Okay, don't be mad, Emmy . . ."

Emmy.

It's always "Em," unless Chess suspects she's fucked up. That means she *knows* I'll be mad.

"But"—she places both hands on her knees, watching me—"the other day, you left your laptop open when you ran out to the store, and I was just passing by, and maybe I had a *teensy* little peek."

Holding her thumb and index finger close together, she gives me what I'm sure she thinks is an endearing squint.

"You read it?" I ask, holding very still, and she drops her hand, some of the silliness immediately falling away from her.

"It's not like it was some password-protected document, Em. It was just up on your computer, and you've been so weird about all of it that I mostly wanted to check and make sure it wasn't a hundred pages of 'All Work and No Play Makes Emily a Dull Girl.' I was looking out for you."

"You were snooping," I counter, and she rolls her eyes, throwing up her hands.

"You're being so dramatic, oh my god. I just read through what you were working on because it was *there* on an *open laptop*. And it's really fucking good, Em! That's why I wanted to tell you, so that I could *compliment* you, and now you're making, like, a federal case out of it."

"I'm not," I argue, standing up off the sofa, my shins

bumping the coffee table. Chess sits there, her arms crossed now, her expression petulant, and it could be sixth grade again, the time I found her flipping idly through my diary in my bedroom after I'd gone downstairs to get us some snacks.

"You are," she insists. "And honestly, I'm the one who should be kind of pissed at *you*."

Chess Logic is occasionally baffling, but this is particularly confusing. "Um, why?"

"Because you've been holding out on me!" She sits forward again, her forearms on her knees. "You were all, 'Oh, it's just some ideas, it's nothing really,' and then it's actually this *amazing* thing about books, and stories, and murder, and life and, like, how do you not see it?"

She slaps the coffee table. "*This* is it, Em. Fuck *Green*, and any of our other stupid ideas, *this* is the book we were meant to write together."

I stand there, staring at her, surprised by the sudden rush of anger that surges through me.

"What?"

"This is nonfic, Em, and it's a whole other world than your little garden party murder books. This is the kind of stuff that's on NPR. Reviewed in the *Times*. It's a *big* idea."

"And it's mine," I say, the words rushing out before I can even think about them, the feeling almost primal.

This is *mine*.

"I know that," she says, waving a hand. "But, Em, my name on this could take it even further. And I have some ideas, too, you know, ideas about how we can broaden the story, make it apply to more women. . . ."

Her eyes are bright now, and I can see it all taking hold of her the same way it's taken hold of me. I also think of how quickly she gets bored. How this will just end up being another thing she throws herself into only to dump it when it gets too hard or too boring.

But what scares me more is . . . what if she doesn't?

"No," I hear myself say, and she rocks back on the sofa, almost gaping at me. "I don't want to cowrite this, I . . . I want to keep working on it. By myself."

Silence.

The tick of the ormolu clock, the creaking of the house.

My breaths, sawing in and out of my lungs.

And then Chess speaks.

"Fine. It was just an idea."

I nod, telling myself to unclench. "And in the future, please don't go through my things."

She gives the most extravagant eye roll I've ever seen. "There was no *going through*!"

"I'm just saying, I wish you hadn't done it," I continue, talking over her, my voice louder, and Chess stands up, too, grabbing her empty glass.

"Okay, well, I did, and I'm sorry, and now I'm going to bed, so please, feel free to work on your precious book without worrying that one word of it will reach my unworthy eyeballs."

"Now who's being dramatic?" I call after her, but she's already stomping up the stairs, probably muttering under her breath about what a bitch I am.

I sit back down on the sofa with a sigh. Maybe this is why Chess and I haven't spent that much time together in the past few years. Put us in the same room for too long, we fall back into old patterns, old fights.

But it still bothers me, the thought of her scrolling through what I'm working on, not asking, just taking.

Like she always does.

I should go to bed and hope that by tomorrow, she'll have sobered up and maybe I'll get an actual apology.

Jesus, if all those fans of hers who think she's the most enlightened being since Gwyneth Paltrow's vagina could have seen her tonight, I think as I stand up.

Powered Path, my ass.

To: Steven@ConclaveLit.com
From: Chess@ChessChandler.com
Subject: [no subject]

S-

Almost done with the excruciatingly titled *Swipe Right on Life!*, so using this time in Italy to think about what's next.

I really feel like there are only so many times you can advise women to journal their feelings or start every day with lemon water and cleansing breaths, and we don't want to go stale. I know the next big thing in wellness seems to be selling $500 vibrators, but I'm not sure that path is for me.

What I've been thinking about is—and this will sound nuts, but I swear to you, it's brilliant—something in the true crime sphere. But not the usual kind of thing, four hundred pages about some dead white girl from Nebraska, I'm talking something a little more elevated, a little more sophisticated.

The villa where I'm staying was the scene of a pretty famous murder in 1974 that involved a bunch of artist types—rock stars, writers, that kind of thing. One of the men was murdered by another guy, blah blah blah, we don't care so much about the murder. But! The *women* staying here ended up producing two really important works of twentieth-century art. We get *Lilith Rising,* a famous feminist horror novel, and *Aestas*, which is basically *Tapestry,* but sadder. What if the next book focuses on them and that summer? The ways in which adversity can spur women to creation? How toxic men hold women back from reaching their full artistic potential?

This is amazing, right? You're dying and imagining putting "National Book Award–Winning" in front of my name, aren't you?

Will talk soon!
Chess

"Fancy getting out of here for a bit?"

Mari has been sitting by the lake, her tears hidden by sunglasses, and she wipes quickly at her cheeks as she looks up at Johnnie.

She's surprised to see him, given that he's been keeping his distance ever since that night in the study. Maybe Lara told him what she saw, or maybe he'd just sussed it out on his own, but Mari sensed that he knew something had happened between her, Noel, and Pierce, and that it had hurt him.

There hasn't been a repeat of that one mad night, but Lara is still upset and Noel is snapping at her too much, which in turn makes Pierce angry. (*God forbid he miss leaping to Lara's defense,* Mari has thought more than once.)

And Johnnie . . .

Johnnie had seemed to be slipping further and further away from all of them, lost in a haze that Mari had not quite understood until she'd seen Pierce emerge from Johnnie's room, holding a small packet.

You didn't know? he'd asked when Mari had questioned Pierce. *That's why he's here. He's Noel's dealer, and Noel didn't want to be stuck in Italy without . . . resources. Why did you think he was here?*

I thought they were friends, she'd replied, and Pierce had laughed in that way he did, smoothing her hair back to kiss her fore-head.

My innocent girl, he'd said, and then his eyes had heated, and he'd taken her to bed, and she'd forgotten how much she hated it when he called her things like that.

But now Johnnie looks like he did the first day they arrived, bright and happy, his skin golden in the sunlight, and if he sees she's been crying, he doesn't mention it.

"Where did you have in mind?"

"Needed to go into town," he says, nodding in the direction of Orvieto. "Thought you might like to come along."

Mari thinks about that packet in Pierce's hand again and wonders if that's the reason for Johnnie's errand. But she hasn't been writing, and the tension in the house has started to give her a headache.

And it's Billy's birthday.

Or it would be his birthday, if he had lived.

He would be two, an idea that is almost impossible to contemplate. He was only nine months old when he died, a baby still, chubby and sweet in her arms. What would he be like at two? Would his blond hair have darkened to Pierce's brown or reddened like her own? What words would he be saying?

All of it hurts to think about, hurts in a way she can hardly bear, and it hurts all the more to know that Pierce doesn't re-member the date.

She'd waited this morning for him to say something, even to simply catch her eye or pull her into his arms wordlessly.

But nothing.

So yes, the idea of zipping down the mountain in the ridic-ulous sports car Noel lets Johnnie drive, feeling the wind and summer sun on her skin, is appealing enough to make her put aside any misgivings about why Johnnie might need to go into town. What *resources* he might be bringing back to the villa for Noel to use.

"I would, actually," she tells him, and he offers a hand, pulling her to her feet. His palm is warm against hers, bicep flexing beneath the tight sleeve of his Jefferson Airplane T-shirt, and when she's upright, he doesn't let go right away, pulling her just the littlest bit closer.

Testing the waters, maybe, seeing how she'll respond, but Mari just pulls her hand back from his with a flustered sort of laugh, and he gives an easy shrug, hands shoved in his back pockets.

"You all right?" he asks as they make their way across the lawn, and Mari looks over at him sharply. He *had* noticed her red eyes. He had, and Pierce hadn't.

For a moment, she thinks about lying. Saying she's fine, or even making up some other less-tragic reason to have been crying by the lake.

She surprises herself by telling him the truth.

"I had a baby. Billy," she tells him, wrapping her arms around her body. "Two years ago. He was born two years ago today."

Johnnie stops, turning toward her, his brows drawn together, but he doesn't say anything, and that makes it easier for Mari to go on. "He got sick," she continues. "When Pierce was on tour with the Faire last year. We . . . we thought it was just a cold. All babies get them, you know?"

Billy's body in her arms, hot against her chest, his breathing wet and ragged, and there was no money for a doctor's visit, everything they had was keeping them on the road, and didn't she see, didn't she understand, they were so *close*, they couldn't leave the tour now, and Billy was strong, Billy was always healthy, Billy was going to be *fine*, just like everything was always going to be fine . . .

Until it wasn't.

"He died," she says. She is struck, as she always is, by how small those words are, how simple. How they sum up what happened and don't come anywhere close to capturing the horror, all at once.

She doesn't tell Johnnie about the rest of it: the grief that ate her alive, the long days she can't even remember now. How she'd wanted nothing more than to go home, but how even the death of her child hadn't softened her father's heart toward her.

How she'd learned then that her home was with Pierce—with Pierce and with Lara, both—for good.

"I'm sorry," Johnnie says now, because what else can he say? But when Mari looks up at him, she sees his expression is serious, his eyes warm behind his sunglasses, and she's thankful for that.

When he's not high or trying too hard to impress her or Noel, he's a good guy, Johnnie. Later, this is a memory that will break her heart a thousand times over.

In the moment, though, she just smiles and nods. "Anyways," she says, heading toward Noel's car, "I could use an outing today."

There's more Johnnie would like to say, she can tell, and she doesn't miss the strange look he shoots at the house in the direction of the bedroom she shares with Pierce.

They reach the car, and Johnnie opens her door for her before sliding into the driver's side, keys already in the ignition.

He's just put the car in reverse when the front door suddenly flies open, and Noel is there, wearing a pair of jeans that Mari thinks might be Pierce's and one of those flowy white shirts he seems to have an endless supply of. Before she even has time to make sense of what's happening, he's opening the car door behind Mari and flinging himself into the backseat with a dramatic sigh.

"Where are we going?" he asks, but before Johnnie can answer, he waves a hand. "Fuck it, I don't care. Tell me you're going to drive this car off a cliff and I'd still rather be here than in that house."

Johnnie glances over at Mari, frowning slightly even as he continues to pull the car out of the driveway, and she looks back toward the villa

It's stupid, that sudden surge of panic she feels, that silly, childish urge to ask Johnnie to stop the car, to let her go back inside. All so that Pierce and Lara won't be alone in the house together.

She almost gives in to it. Her hand actually moves to the door handle, her lips part, and then she catches Noel's gaze in the rearview mirror.

He's watching her, waiting to see what she'll do, the tiniest smile playing along his lips.

Is that why he'd suddenly decided to join them? Is he playing one of his weird little fucking games?

In that case, Mari isn't going to give him the satisfaction.

She places her hands in her lap and faces forward, and if she hears a snicker from the backseat, she ignores it.

JOHNNIE HAD WARNED Noel to stay in the car lest he start some kind of riot, but Noel had insisted on walking the streets of Orvieto with them. He's plopped Mari's hat on his head, pulling the floppy brim low, and with Johnnie's sunglasses covering most of his face, he's actually fairly well disguised.

Or maybe it's that Noel's fame is beginning to fade. Because while heads do turn in their direction as they make their way through the narrow streets, Mari suspects it has more to do with Noel's ridiculous getup than the locals actually recognizing that there's an international celebrity in their midst.

"I'm not disrupting a planned romantic interlude, am I?" he asks Mari in a low voice as Johnnie walks slightly ahead of them, and Mari shoots him a look.

"Even if you were, would you care?" she asks, and he chuckles.

"I'm merely teasing, Mistress Mary. It's very clear your heart belongs only to Pierce. Shame John-o there hasn't quite picked up on that yet."

Mari watches Johnnie ahead of them, sees the way eyes linger on his tall form, and shakes her head. "You're wrong about him."

"Am I? He's been glaring daggers at Sheldon for the past week."

Mari had noticed that, too, but she thought it might be more about Noel than about her. She still didn't understand the nature of Johnnie and Noel's relationship, and now, as Johnnie glances back at them, his eyes once again straying to Noel, she wonders again whether there's more to the story than Pierce had suggested.

Noel reaches down, grabbing her hand and tugging hard, nearly pulling her off her feet. "Come on," he says, and then cups a hand around his mouth and shouts, "John-o! See you back at the car, mate!"

Johnnie stops, his handsome face creasing with confusion. "Where are you going?" he calls back, and Noel holds up his and Mari's clasped hands, shaking them.

"To hell!" he calls back, and then he's pulling Mari down a twisting street.

The day has turned slightly chillier, clouds piling up thick and gray, when Noel brings them to a stop in front of a squat, circular building.

"Pozzo di San Patrizio!" Noel exclaims, sleeves falling back as he gestures up at the building, and Mari remembers Johnnie mentioning this.

The well named after a place in Ireland and said to spiral down into hell.

A shiver races down her spine that has nothing to do with the weather.

"Shall we descend?" Noel asks her, reaching for the door, but before he can open it, a man in some sort of uniform rushes forward, a rush of Italian spilling from his lips.

Mari can only pick up the odd word, but she knows they're being told to bugger off, and she's about to suggest they do just that, but then she sees the moment the man recognizes Noel.

"The Rovers!" he says in a thick Italian accent. "Rovers!"

Noel smiles, but it's a little tight around the edges as he nods, and then makes an elaborate gesture back at Mari that has the guard—if that's what he is—chuckling and nodding in that way that men do, and has Mari rolling her eyes.

But the door is opened, and she follows Noel into cool darkness.

It smells metallic, like earth and stone and water. Shafts of sunlight shine through narrow windows carved along the top of the spiraling path that descends into the side of the mountain. She can hear a slow drip, the slap of her sandals, and she wonders how many feet have walked this same sloping ramp, wearing grooves in the rock. How many people, long since dead, made this same descent. The thought seems morbid, but it comforts her, oddly. Especially today.

People are never just gone, after all. There are always marks, always signs.

"I have to say, this is substantially less dreary than I expected." Noel's words echo around them, and Mari snorts, poking him in the back.

"Less dreary than you'd *hoped*," she corrects him. In the fading light, she can see him grin as he replies, "Guilty."

It's growing darker as they walk farther, the sound of water louder now, and Mari looks around, letting her fingers graze the cold walls.

"Do you think this really could reach all the way to hell?" Mari asks absentmindedly, and from just ahead and below, she hears Noel laugh.

"Depends on if you believe in hell, I suppose. I, for one, very sincerely and very obviously hope there is not one, but maybe we should cut this walk short just in case."

"You just don't want to walk all the way back up to the top."

"If you were a man, I'd call you out for that."

Mari's laugh sounds too loud in this solemn place, but she doesn't mind. She's feeling better now, a little lighter. Her mind has started drifting back to Victoria, back to the book. Maybe she can use this spot, somehow. Is there a well at Somerton? Could it be a place where—

"Didn't your mother write about Hell? Something about a demon?" Noel suddenly says, and Mari is so surprised, she nearly stumbles down the steps.

Noel pauses, turning to look back at her. "Is it gauche to bring up someone's dead mother whilst journeying into the underworld?"

Recovering herself, Mari shrugs. "Probably, but when has a fear of being gauche ever stopped you from anything, milord?"

Noel laughs and turns back around, taking the steps a little slower now. Mari trails behind, her fingers brushing the stone as she says, "And yes. She did. Although the entire point of that story was that Lilith wasn't a demon at all, just a wronged woman."

Mari hasn't read her mother's writing in a while. When she was younger, she'd gobbled it up in secret, spending hours in the library with her mother's one book in her hands, her fingers tracing the words. Mari's father had kept Marianne's writing in the house, of course, multiple editions of the book of short stories, all her articles cut out and carefully preserved in an oxblood leather album, but Mari had never asked to see them. She'd always felt that doing so would just remind her father that she was the reason his brilliant, talented wife was dead.

Not that he needed such a reminder, of course. She knew that now. But that's how it had worked in her childish brain, and so Mari just had that one library copy, read and reread and finally, shamefully, pilfered in her satchel to be hidden under the mattress in her bedroom.

The same copy has come with her to Orvieto because it goes with her everywhere, even though it's been some time since she's opened it. Still, she likes having it near, likes the cracked spine and the title, *Heart's Blood and Other Stories,* in faded gold foil on the green fabric cover.

"The First Wife" was the shortest story in Marianne's collection, almost more like a poem, really, a metaphorical, lyrical take on the legend of Lilith, said to be Adam's wife before Eve. But Lilith had been made of the same earth as Adam rather than made from him, and she hadn't been obedient, which of course made her wicked.

Marianne clearly hadn't thought so, and neither did Mari. In fact, she remembered the first time she'd read that story, sitting there at the long table behind the rows of books by old dead men, and thought how thrilling it was, having a mother who would write something like this.

It had caused a minor scandal on publication, Mari had later learned, throwing churches and priests all in a tizzy. Thinking of it now, Mari knows she'll want to reread it once they get back to the house. Maybe immersing herself in her mother's words will bring Victoria's voice back to her.

"Listen, Mari," Noel suddenly says, stopping so abruptly she nearly runs into his back. He turns around, looking up at her since she's still on a step above him.

"I was only teasing about Johnnie earlier, but . . . truly, you're not interested, are you?"

Mari's brain is still on her mother, on "The First Wife," so it takes her a moment to even understand what Noel is talking about, and even once she does, she's confused.

"Because if you are, that's certainly your prerogative," he hurries on, "and let me not to the marriage of true minds—"

Rolling her eyes, Mari gives him another shove, this one slightly harder.

"Piss off."

Noel gives an exaggerated grimace, but Mari thinks he's actually a bit relieved, some of the tension leaving his shoulders. "Okay, so you don't reciprocate young Johnnie's feelings then. I didn't think you did, but you're a very hard girl to read, Mistress Mary. Still waters and all that."

Coming from him, Mari suspects that's a compliment, but

she's still slightly bemused. "What does it matter to you if I did?" she asked, and he glances up at her, one eyebrow raised.

"For one, there's quite enough sexual intrigue in the house already, don't you think? And two . . . well, to be frank, if you want to step out on Sheldon, you could do much better."

For a moment, Mari wonders if this is Noel making some sort of play for her himself. They haven't talked about what happened that night, and Noel's behavior toward her hasn't changed. But she suspects that if he were declaring himself, he'd be a great deal more forward about it. "I couldn't 'step out' on Pierce," she tells him. "It isn't like that with us, we're . . . open. Free. Which you should know better than most, frankly."

Noel makes a rude noise at that. "Please. Sheldon may tell you that, may certainly practice that for himself, but something tells me that if you were ever to act on any attraction or desire without him present, it might be another story."

Mari has sometimes thought that herself, but she doesn't want to give Noel the satisfaction of agreeing.

"In any case," she says now, "I'm not interested in Johnnie. Or anyone besides Pierce."

"Wound to the ego, balm to the mind," Noel replies, then sighs, shaking his head. "He's a good lad, Johnnie. Sweet and loyal. Bit like a spaniel, really. Sadly, a rubbish musician."

"I haven't heard him play," Mari replies, and Noel flicks that away with an elegant gesture.

"You haven't missed anything, believe me. He's desperate to get in on the studio time I have booked when we're back in London, but he just doesn't have what it takes. I keep him around because he's gorgeous to look at, and he has a surprising talent for finding any kind of . . . let us say, *recreational substance* a man might desire, no matter where one is in the world. Last year, he managed to get hashish in the *Outer fucking Hebrides*. Otherworldly, I tell you. Honestly, I thought about letting him play on the album just as a reward for that alone, but Sheldon is right—if one element is out of place, the whole thing falls apart."

Mari's first reaction is relief that Pierce and Noel have been talking about music at all. But then she thinks about how kind Johnnie was to her earlier, and her heart aches for him. She knows what it's like to want something and feel like it's close, but just out of reach. How much it must sting, watching Noel and Pierce play together and being shut out. To see Noel turn his attention to Pierce, to give Pierce the opportunity that Johnnie himself has been craving.

The well, which had felt magical and soothing earlier, now feels too small, too narrow, and Mari is intensely aware of the layers of rock and soil above her, around her, below her.

She turns and begins trudging back up the stairs, her breath harsh in her ears, her eyes fixed on her sandals, and she doesn't see Johnnie sitting on one of the steps until she nearly trips over him, a startled, "Oh!" flying from her lips as her hands land awkwardly on his knees.

He's holding himself stiffly, and Mari knows, immediately, that he heard every word Noel said. Maybe it didn't come as a surprise, but thinking a thing and having it confirmed are different beasts, as she well knows.

"Johnnie," she breathes, and he stands up quickly, his hands taking hers as he helps her up onto the next step.

"What did you think of hell?" he asks, and tries to give her that bright smile she's used to, but it falters just the littlest bit.

"Hellish," she replies, trying to match his fake cheer as Noel comes up behind her, slightly wary.

"John-o," he says, but Johnnie only smiles at him, too.

"Got everything," he tells Noel, patting his pockets with a knowing look. "We should be set for the next week or so at least."

"Good man," Noel says, clapping him on the shoulder, and if Mari sees something flicker in Johnnie's eyes, she blames it on the light.

CHAPTER NINE

The next morning, Chess is waiting for me.

She's wearing a bright red sundress over the striped bikini I've seen her wearing at the pool, and there's a massive picnic basket on the kitchen table, a big gingham ribbon tied around the handle.

"What's all this?" I ask her, and she comes forward, enveloping me in a hug.

"*Please* let me take you on a fabulous adventure today and assuage my guilt for being such a 'See You Next Tuesday' last night."

This is another classic Chess move, the Extravagant Apology.

Thing is, I'm always susceptible to it, desperate to get back to "normal." Although part of me is starting to realize—maybe this is just who we are with each other, who we've always been. Maybe this *is* our normal. We push each other, and, inevitably, we fight. Maybe I need to start remembering that.

"I like that you don't use the C word anymore," I tell her.

"It's bad for the general image, but please know I use it in my head on the regular."

I laugh again, then nod at the basket, which looks stuffed to the brim. "So, you're taking me on a picnic?"

"It felt like the one big summer in Italy cliché we hadn't checked off yet," she says, and I can't argue there.

It's not long before we're situated by the pond on a big blanket, Chess pulling out white plates with little strawberries on them, the sun shining down on us. We're under one of the trees, so there's a nice bit of shade, and I lean back on one elbow, looking out over the pond. The water is a dark, murky green, but it's pretty to look at with its small dock, a decrepit rowboat tied to one post.

"In the spirit of honesty, this is yet another thing I didn't actually make, just paid for," Chess tells me as she starts unloading cured meats and wrapped cheeses onto the blanket, followed by two bottles of Orvieto wine.

After last night, I decide to pass on the wine, but I open a chilled bottle of mineral water and take a couple of pieces of bread.

For a long while, we just sit in silence, looking out over the water. It's another perfect day in a perfect place, which makes it easy to forget last night's ugliness. Soon we're chatting like normal again, laughing and joking, back to being Em and Chess.

"How goes *Swipe Right on Life*?" I ask, and she tears off another hunk of bread, wrapping it around a little piece of mozzarella.

"It goes. It slowed down for a while there, but I'm finally feeling a little more inspired. It's just that there's only so many ways to say, 'let go of your shit.'" She sighs, pushing her sunglasses on top of her head.

"Maybe that's what you should call it instead," I tell her. "'Let Go of Your Shit.' I'd buy that before 'Swipe Right on Life.'"

She laughs, then gives me a sly look from the corner of her eye. "Speaking of 'swiping right' . . ."

I look back out at the lake where something under the water sends up bubbles, ripples dimpling the glassy surface.

This is a conversation I've had before. With my friend Taylor, with my mom, hell, even with my hairstylist, but I don't want to have it now.

"No."

"Why such a hard no?"

I draw my legs up, wrapping my arms around my knees. "Once your husband has cheated on you while you were at your absolute lowest and then leaves you, it makes the idea of opening yourself up to any man, ever again, kind of lose its appeal."

Chess is quiet, the only sound the twittering of birds and the wind through the trees for a few beats before she says, "You never really told me about all that. Matt cheating."

"It's not exactly my favorite subject," I reply, but I wonder if it might feel good to actually talk about it.

"I never knew anything for sure," I continue, my eyes still on the pond. "There wasn't some big moment where I caught him in bed with someone, nothing that Lifetime movie. He just . . . started getting distant. And then his phone suddenly had a lock code on it, and . . . I don't know. It's like I could just *sense* someone else in the house, in our relationship, even when it was just the two of us."

Those had been the worst days. Sick, my mind permanently fogged, certain there was another woman . . .

"Then I finally had the *Love, Actually* moment, and I knew," I finish up, and Chess turns to face me, crossing her legs on the blanket.

"What does *that* mean?"

I laugh, even though the discovery was not remotely funny at the time. "Oh, you know. Found a piece of jewelry hidden away in his sock drawer. A bracelet. My birthday comes around, there's a box, but it's perfume, not a bracelet, and when I look again in his drawer, the bracelet is gone."

"Oh fuck, Em."

"Yup."

A month ago, that memory would have lanced through me like a knife. Now it's just a dull kind of ache, and I turn to face Chess.

"I was so mad at her, whoever she is, for so long. I kept conjuring up these imaginary women, or remembering some lady he worked with, even picturing the barista at the coffee shop he liked. But now I feel like I probably owe her a fruit basket, whoever she was."

Chess shakes her head, sunlight glinting off her hair.

"Only you, Em," she says. "Only you would say something like that."

"I'm serious!" I insist. "If things hadn't fallen apart with Matt, I wouldn't be here now."

I take her hand, squeezing it.

She squeezes back, then adds, "You also wouldn't be a third of the way into a brand-new book that's totally going to revitalize your career."

I smile, but it's tight and not exactly genuine. I'm willing

to get over last night, but I still don't like Chess bringing up
the book, and I still wish she hadn't read any of it.

"I don't know about that," I say now, settling back on the
blanket. "I'm still not sure what it even is. Sometimes it feels
like a memoir, sometimes it feels like a biography of Mari."
I shrug. "Maybe it's just an experiment. Something I need to
get out of my system."

"No harm in that," Chess says. And then she adds, "She
actually came back here, you know."

My head jerks around. "Mari?"

Chess nods. "You're not the only one who knows how to
google, Em. After I read your extremely very good pages and
started thinking we could work on it together—which I totally get now is a no-go, don't worry about it—I was curious."

There's a sour taste in my mouth, and my stomach knots
thinking about Chess sitting there on the sofa, scrolling through
articles about Mari. This is *my* thing, even though I know
that sounds ridiculous. You can't claim a person or a subject
like that. I really should be flattered that my bestselling best
friend is so interested in my work.

"When did Mari come back?" I ask, and Chess tilts her
face toward the sky.

"In 1993."

The year she died. Was that why she'd returned? For one
final goodbye?

But why bother coming back to a place where something
so terrible had happened to her?

Chess stretches out on the blanket, her hands behind her
head. "Go on," she says, indulgent. "I know you're dying to
run inside and get your research on."

I am, but I make myself sit there for another ten minutes,

sipping my water and eating cheese while Chess naps, and I don't *run* back to the house.

I just walk very fast.

There's not much online about Mari's second visit to Villa Rosato, just a throwaway line in one article about the murder—yes, she came back here the summer before she died; no, she didn't stay long, only for a week.

I close my laptop. Something tickles at the back of my brain, the same way it did that day in Orvieto with the well.

There's a bit toward the end of *Lilith Rising* where Victoria hides her diary, right before she's sent away, afraid it might be used against her.

I flip to that part of the book now.

There wasn't much time, but Victoria knew she had to hide the diary. If she didn't, if someone found it, it would damn her.

She knew she should burn it, but she couldn't make herself destroy it. Instead, she tucked it away in a special spot.

Where even from far away, it would remain close to her.

That's it. From there, Victoria is ushered away, and there's no explicit reference to where she puts the diary, just that vague description that reads more like a riddle than anything else. How could it be close to her if she was far away?

But a thought occurs to me, electric enough that I jump to my feet.

It's probably nothing, I keep telling myself as I walk upstairs. *You've found connections between the book and the house, but that doesn't mean everything is some kind of clue.*

But just like before, there's this sensation, almost like a hand guiding me, and I move toward the window seat.

The *M* etched in the glass seems to be watching me as I lift the cushion off the bench, feeling stupid even as my heart races and my palms sweat.

There's just a flat wooden surface, and when I pull at the edge, nothing happens. I hadn't really expected the entire seat to lift up, revealing a treasure trove, but I'm still a little disappointed.

But it was silly to think that Mari would've left anything here back in 1993. She probably just came for some kind of closure in her final days.

Except that I kept returning to that same thorny issue. This was the spot where her boyfriend had been horribly murdered—wasn't that closure enough? Why revisit the scene of the crime, literally?

But after she died, several unpublished books—everything she had written since *Lilith Rising*—had been found hidden around her apartment.

So, maybe it wasn't completely crazy to think Mari came back here to hide one last thing. Maybe I just misinterpreted the riddle.

That's when I spot it.

The window seat isn't completely flush with the wall, and at some point, someone had added a thin piece of wood to fill in the gap. It's painted the same shade of white, so the seam is barely visible, but it's there.

I grasp the end of the board and gently pull.

At first, it seems as solid as the rest of the seat, but then there's a slight give, and suddenly there's a thin piece of wood in my hand.

Gingerly, I slide my hand inside the gap between the wall and the bench, visions of something lurching out of the dark to bite my fingers, my heart pounding in my ears, but there's no sharp sting, no pain.

There's just the rustle of paper.

Mouth dry, I pull out a folded stack of yellow paper and when I open it, I see each line filled in a neat, economical scrawl.

And at the top, the words that make me lift a trembling hand to my mouth.

Mari—London, 1974.

The scream doesn't just wake her.

It sends Mari hurtling into consciousness, her brain rattling in her skull. She'd always thought it was a cliché, that moment of someone sitting straight up in bed, heart pounding, but that's where she is now, hand pressed to her chest as she searches the room for the source of that sound.

She's sees almost immediately that it's Pierce. They'd fallen asleep peacefully enough earlier, wrapped up in each other, sweat still drying on their skin, but now he's out of bed, crouched naked in one corner of the room, his hands over his ears, his eyes wild.

And he's still screaming, screaming and screaming, the sound so loud that Mari is forced to get out of bed and go to him, grabbing his wrists as she tries to wake him.

"Pierce!" she says, her voice sharp. "Pierce!"

She can hear footsteps in the hall, and then Lara's voice at the door. "What is it? What's wrong?"

"Nothing!" Mari calls back, even though Pierce is still whimpering at her feet, blinking like he's trying to clear his head.

"Go back to bed!" Mari adds, and she kneels down in front of Pierce. He's covered in sweat, almost glowing in the moonlight spilling through the window, and Mari brushes his hair back from his face.

The rain has returned and with it, the oppressiveness of the house, a feeling that seems to affect Pierce more than any of them, and Mari sometimes has the crazy thought that maybe they were the ones causing it, that all their tension and weird energy was spinning out and up into the sky.

"It's all right, love," Mari says, and she's assailed by the memory of holding Billy as he burned like an ember against her chest, shushing him and speaking the same words into his damp hair.

It's all right, love.

They're not words anyone has ever said to her.

"I . . . I was dreaming," Pierce gulps out, his hand shaking as he reaches up to grab Mari's wrist. "But it was real, Mare, it was so . . . so fucking *real.* . . ."

She doesn't bother reminding him that this is why they'd agreed that while booze is fine, he should lay off the drugs. They always mess with his mind like this, make him see things or hear things or have these horrible nightmares he can never shake. He'll be ruined for days now, she knows. No music, no writing.

"What was in the dream?" she asks, trying to make her voice soothing and steady. He looks at her, his face somehow going even whiter in the moonlight.

"You," he says, and then she shakes his head again, pulling his hand back from hers. "You were covered in blood. Reaching out. And it was . . . it was like you were so tall, and I was so small, I was crouching at your feet."

Pierce breaks off then, putting his face in his hands. "It was so fucking wild. I was looking up at you and all that blood and thinking, *she's inevitable, she's inevitable,* like this fucking *drumbeat.* . . ."

Mari lifts his face again, looking into his eyes. "It was just a dream, Pierce. See? Look. No blood." She holds up both her hands. "Just me."

He gives another shuddering sigh, leaning forward to rest his head against her breasts, and she keeps stroking his hair, feeling his sweat and tears soaking through her nightgown.

When he seems calmer, she can't stop herself from saying, "And, you know, Pierce, that line you said? 'She's inevitable'?"

Pulling back, Pierce blinks at her, and she goes on, her heartbeat speeding up. "That's really good. It's so cool and could be foreboding, but could also be romantic. . . ."

His brow furrows. "What are you getting at?"

"I just think it's a line you should use. Like in a song."

Pierce pushes her away, his hands on her arms, his movements shaky as he stands. "No way," he says on a breathless kind of laugh. "I just want to forget that shit and go to bed."

But Mari doesn't want to forget it.

She's still thinking about it long after Pierce goes back to sleep, breathing softly beside her, and when she can't lie there anymore, she gets up, goes to her notebook and the little desk under the window.

Victoria's story has been frozen in amber for weeks now, but suddenly Mari feels it coming back to life.

She's inevitable.

Pierce's vision of Mari covered in blood comes back to her as she starts to write.

She's inevitable.

Victoria, covered in blood. Whose blood? It doesn't matter, not yet. She'll figure that out.

The well, the cave into hell. There's something there, maybe. Something, too, in the shopkeeper's story about a suicide in this house. Years and years ago, but everyone in the town still remembers.

Houses remember.

Now the line makes more sense to her, now she knows how to use it.

Not a love story at all.

Or yes, a love story, but there's horror inside of it. There's death and loss, blood and sweat. Just as there is in every love story, after all.

Mari's pen moves faster and faster as the story starts taking shape.

By the time the sun rises, she knows the book she's writing and she understands why she couldn't write it before.

It needed Pierce's dream to show her the path.

Pierce wakes up, eventually, presses a kiss to the top of her head, but thankfully doesn't bother her, drifting out of the room with his guitar in hand.

After a moment, she hears him begin to play in another room, and that seems to make her write even faster. She likes it, this sense of them both creating at the same time, near each other, but not together. Her writing inspiring his playing, his playing inspiring her writing.

It's the life she's wanted for them since the moment she climbed out that window in North London three years ago.

Finally, her hand cramping and her shoulders aching, she pauses, stretches.

Pierce is still playing, but it's not a song she's heard from him before. It's sweet and sour at the same time, the notes dancing, and it makes her get up from her desk and go in search of him.

But when she steps out into the hallway, she realizes the music is coming from behind Lara's cracked bedroom door.

Pierce is with her.

Pierce is playing for her.

Mari makes herself cross the narrow hallway, pushing the door open.

Lara's room is nearly identical to the one Mari shares with Pierce, just smaller and done in shades of green instead of blue. There's the same window, the same small desk under it, and the bed is pushed against the same far wall.

But it's only Lara sitting on that bed now, her guitar in her lap. Pierce is nowhere to be found. It takes Mari a moment to realize that it's actually Lara who has been playing this entire time.

It was Lara's music filling her head as she wrote, spurring her on, and Mari isn't sure how to feel about that.

The song stops as Lara registers Mari in the door, and Mari can tell she's been crying again. Her face is red and puffy, her eyes wet, and when Mari comes closer, she can see splattered teardrops on the sheet music Lara has been writing on.

"That was beautiful," Mari tells her, and Lara lifts her chin, her gaze meeting Mari's.

"I've been trying to tell you all that I'm good," she says. "You just never listen."

Lara is right. She hasn't listened. Neither of them have listened to each other.

Mari has spent such a long time feeling wronged by Lara that it never occurred to her that Lara was being wronged, too.

Just in a different way.

She approaches the bed cautiously, the way you'd try to get close to a skittish animal, but Lara scoots over, making room for her, the strings of her guitar twanging softly as she adjusts it.

"Play me something else," Mari says, and Lara looks at her for a long beat before nodding, her hands falling back to the guitar.

This song is sad, too, the melody in a minor key, and Lara hums as she plays, but doesn't sing. Even with just that, Mari can tell her voice is pretty, that it suits the music she's making.

Aestas will eventually be heard everywhere. In other bedrooms, in cars. In the background at parties, and in quiet living rooms, in movies, in commercials. People will play it when they're in a good mood, but it's the heartbroken that it's written for, and they're the ones who'll play it the most.

But the first time any songs from *Aestas* are played for an audience, it's here in this small bedroom in Umbria, with two sisters—because they know in their hearts that's what they are, no matter their parentage—finally beginning to understand each other.

When the last note fades out, Mari realizes she's crying, her own tears joining Lara's on the sheet music.

"I wrote that after Billy," Lara says quietly, and Mari closes her eyes because somehow, she'd already known that. The sadness weeping out of the song was familiar to her even without words.

"I miss him, too," Lara says, and for the first time Mari lets herself remember the good parts of it all, before her son got sick. When he was a sweet, rosy-cheeked baby there in their little flat, and she can see Lara holding him, dancing around the kitchen with him in her arms, his little face alight with joy and with love.

Lara had loved him. Lara had lost him. All this time, she's been reaching out to Pierce, waiting for him to join her in her grief instead of wishing it away.

She should've reached out to Lara, too, but her hurt and her anger was too raw. It was justified, and she can't feel guilty about it, but even at nineteen, she's learned the world isn't as cut-and-dried as all of that.

Mari entwines her fingers with Lara's and rests her head on her sister's shoulder.

"You're the one who should be making an album here," Mari tells her, and then squeezes their joined hands. "You're the one who's *going* to write an album here. And I'm going to write my book, and by this time next year, I'll be a famous author, and you'll be a star. Bigger than Carly Simon. Bigger than Joni Mitchell. You watch."

She thinks Lara is chuckling at first, amused by Mari's grandiose plans, but then Lara sucks in a watery breath, and Mari realizes she's crying again.

"What is it?" she asks, lifting her head to look at Lara.

And that's when Lara gives another wrenching sob and says, "Mare. I'm pregnant."

"It would've been better not to love him," I tell her
through my tears./

But my sister's a plain-speaker, voicing all my fears./

"Not better. Just easier."/

The simplest words I've ever heard./

And they cut me to the quick like only she can./

"Not better. Just easier."/

A silk glove on an iron hand.

—"Night Owl," Lara Larchmont,
from *Aestas,* 1977

CHAPTER TEN

Mari's papers are burning a hole under my mattress.

Since that afternoon three days ago, I've read them at least half a dozen times, hardly believing they're real.

Or, I guess I should say, I've read most of them. I've held off on what appears to be the last chapter. I'd skimmed it, of course. That was the first thing I did when I'd realized what I'd found, desperate to read Mari's version of Pierce's murder.

But the pages end before that, stopping when Pierce is very much alive. I'd decided to save that last chapter, wanting to experience that summer with Mari, as she experienced it. Wanting to savor this treasure for as long as possible.

Because that's what it feels like—an illicit treasure, hidden underneath my bed.

If I can prove that *this* is the definitive account of what happened the summer of 1974, as written by one of the main people involved, and that my original idea about *Lilith Rising* holding clues to the events of that summer was right . . .

It'll be huge.

Which is why it's vital that Chess doesn't know what I've found.

But I think she's beginning to suspect something.

We've gone back into Orvieto, craving an outing after several consecutive days holed up at the villa. The skies are cloudy today, making the walled city appear more foreboding than the first time we visited. In the heavy heat, the closeness of the buildings is less charming, the duomo more overwhelming.

I sip from one of the bottles of mineral water Chess brought for us as I pretend to gaze into shop windows, my brain a million miles away, back with Mari and Pierce and Noel.

"You have been a very busy bee this week," Chess says, bumping my hip as I turn away from the window. Overhead, the hanging baskets of red flowers are very bright against all the gray.

"I feel like I've barely seen you, but I hear you, clickety-clicking all the time."

I thought I was doing a better job of hiding how much I was working, but clearly not.

For a moment, I struggle with how to answer, and then the perfect excuse comes to me.

Making myself look as sheepish as I can, I say, "I'm actually back on Petal."

Chess stops, her leather bag swinging on her shoulder. "Wait, seriously?"

I nod. "The book about Mari and the villa wasn't really going anywhere, and then it occurred to me that just like *I* needed a change of scenery, maybe Petal did, too. So I threw out what I'd been working on before and started a whole new draft. Petal in Italy, solving the case of the poisoned cappuccino."

"I *love* it," Chess replies, squeezing my arm, and the obvious relief on her face tells me more than anything how pleased she is that I've put the villa project aside.

But why? Is it because nonfiction is supposed to be her thing, and she wanted me to stay out of her lane? Was she worried I might actually write something that eclipsed even the great Chess Chandler?

Or, I make myself consider as we walk farther down the street, maybe I was imagining all of this, assuming the worst about Chess. Maybe she is just genuinely happy I'm writing again, that I'll be able to deliver the book that's due and get the payment that I *definitely* need.

How is it that someone can bring out the very best and the very worst of you all at once?

Pushing that thought away, I pull out my phone to check the time. Instead, I see I have missed calls.

Four of them.

All from Matt.

I frown, and Chess moves closer to me. "What is it?"

"Matt," I tell her, and she snorts.

"What does he want?"

I shake my head, checking my texts to see two from him.

Hi. Know you're busy, but really needed to talk to you about something.

Give me a call when you can.

More paperwork, probably. Some new wrinkle in the divorce proceedings, some extra money his lawyers have figured out how to squeeze out of me.

I know I have to call him back, but not now. Not *here*. I don't like the idea of him here, invading this place that's just mine.

Well, mine and Chess's.

"I'm sure it's nothing," I tell her now, and I put the phone back, resolved to put Matt out of my mind for the rest of the afternoon.

Chess watches me for a beat, and then folds her arms over her chest.

"Em, this is an Ostrich Moment."

I stare at her, wondering if I've suddenly had a stroke, but she's just watching me expectantly and suddenly I realize this has to be something from one of her books, something I've missed, apparently.

"An Ostrich Moment," I repeat, and yes, I can practically hear the trademark appearing next to it now.

Chess steps forward, taking my hands in hers, rooting us to the spot even as other tourists are forced to walk around us.

"You want to stick your head in the sand, and make this all go away. But the thing is, it's not going to. The sand doesn't *fix* the problem, it just *hides* it."

I know there are women who would pay thousands to get their own personal Chess Chandler Therapy Session, but right now, I really wish I were getting Chess my friend, not Chess the Guru.

Even though I know she's probably right.

"So, you're saying I should call Matt."

She squeezes my hands. "Get it over with. We'll head back to the house, and you'll call him. Find out what he wants, and I promise you, whatever it is, it won't be that bad. It'll take, like, fifteen minutes max, and then, instead of agonizing over what he *might* want, you'll know. And then you'll come into the kitchen and meet me, and you'll have a cocktail roughly the size of your head, and everything will be fine."

The thing with Chess is, when she says something, you believe it.

Which is why I find myself in my bedroom at the villa half an hour later, dialing Matt's number.

He answers after the first ring. "There you are. I sent those texts hours ago."

I can feel my blood pressure rising, but I close my eyes and focus on my breathing just like Chess had suggested. "I'm on vacation, Matt," I say evenly. "I called as soon as I could."

"Fine," he replies, and I picture him there at his desk at work, his white polo shirt bright against his tanned skin, the nervous way he's probably rubbing his free hand over the top of his head.

Always a tell with Matt.

"I called because your lawyer hasn't gotten a response from you on the dissolution filing," he says, and I frown.

"What?"

Matt's sigh may come from thousands of miles away over a cell phone, but I swear I can feel it. "We talked about this. I think we should go for the dissolution of marriage now since the divorce is . . . obviously going to take awhile."

He doesn't come right out and say that it's my fault, but of course that's what he means. Because if only I'd agree to give him those royalties, this could all be over, and wouldn't that be nice?

A dissolution of marriage is a sort of in-between. It will mean we're no longer legally married, but that we still haven't finished hashing out the financial stuff of the actual divorce. My lawyer told me it's pretty common when one of the parties is ready to move on with someone else.

But then Matt already jumped the gun on that, didn't he?

"I haven't checked my email," I tell him now. "And I've been working so—"

"Right, I've heard," he says.

Outside, the sun is setting, and I can hear the gentle twittering of birds, the sound of wind in the trees.

Inside, I'm very still.

"What does that mean?" I ask, but what I really mean is *Who told you that?*

Two people know. Rose and Chess. That's it. Maybe he emailed Rose and asked her. Maybe his lawyer did. That's the only thing that makes sense to me right now, the only thing I'll *let* make sense to me now.

"You know, Em," Matt says, and I picture him sitting forward, his eyes darting around the office as he lowers his voice. "If you're working on a new book just to fuck me over—"

I bark out a laugh. "Right! Because everything in my life is about you, I forgot!"

"I'm serious," he continues, a little louder now. "If you write something else just to get out of paying me what I'm owed for the next Petal book, I'll sue you for part of that, too."

I feel my stomach drop. He's bluffing.

He has to be. No one would let him have part of a book I wrote *after* we split up. But the thought of it sticks in my gut, twists like a knife.

This project, which has started pulling me out of the hole I've been in for the past year . . . it's a thing Matt would make another anchor around my neck.

"Why are you doing this?" I ask him now, and I hate how pleading it sounds. "*You* left, remember? Why punish me?"

"This isn't about punishment. Jesus, you always do this. I took care of you. I supported you."

I can practically see him ticking off his fingers.

"I put in all this effort, Em. I wanted to save us. I wanted to save *you*. Look, if it were up to me, we'd still be living in the house we bought together, raising our child. *You're* the one who changed. Not me."

I feel the blood rush to my cheeks. "Matt, I got sick. I didn't change."

"You said you wanted a baby, but you never wanted to have sex, and then I found out you were still taking the pill. Even after you promised to stop, you never did."

"Because I was *sick*," I say again. "I didn't want to fuck with my hormones when I didn't know what was wrong with me."

"You lied to me," he insists. "Which means I spent seven years of my life with someone, thinking we wanted the same things when, clearly, we didn't. Seven years. So, excuse me if I want a little return on my investment."

I give a bitter laugh at that. "Serves me right for marrying an accountant, huh?"

"Am I wrong?" he presses, and I don't answer. He is and he isn't, and, honestly, maybe ostriches have the better idea because right now, I don't feel better.

I just feel tired.

"Look, I don't know what you heard," I tell him now, my fingers tight around the phone, "but your information clearly sucks because I'm working on Petal. And I'll email Robert about the dissolution. The sooner I'm not married to you, the better, honestly."

I don't let him reply to that, pressing End before he can say anything else.

The sun has fully set now, the villa dim as I make my way downstairs. True to her word, Chess is in the kitchen, and there's a frosted martini glass on the counter filled with a bright yellow liquid.

I reach for it, the stem bitingly cold.

"It's my own concoction," Chess says. "Limoncello, obviously, a little bit of that gorgeous floral gin Giulia brought the other day, some elderflower liquor . . ."

It could be antifreeze for all I care right now. I suck down almost the whole thing, putting the glass back on the counter with a raggedy sigh as Chess raises her eyebrows and reaches for the cocktail shaker.

"I take it the phone call didn't go great."

I accept a refill, leaning back against the counter, one arm wrapped around my waist like I'm trying to hold my insides together.

"He talks like I'm the one who fucked everything up," I say. "Like I tricked him or something by magically *not* having a baby. That's what started all this. Once he'd decided he wanted kids, it was like that was the only thing that mattered."

Chess is quiet for a moment, taking a sip from her bottle of mineral water before saying, "Did you want kids, Em? Really?"

"I did," I insist, but even as I say the words, I can hear how unconvincing they sound.

I drink more, the lemony taste bright on my tongue. We've never talked about this, not really. Chess knew we'd been talking about having a baby, but she'd never asked me outright if it's what I wanted. No one did.

Not even Matt.

"I mean, I didn't *not* want kids, I guess. It was just that it still felt kind of vague to me. Like something future me was going to figure out or suddenly wake up and know the answer to. Or that I wanted them for *him*, if that makes sense."

She nods. "That's very you, Em. You live to make other people happy. It's the one thing you have in common with Nanci."

Chess so rarely brings up her mother that I'm actually stunned out of my pity party a little bit.

"Did you just compare me to the person you wrote an entire book about? A book where the thesis is, 'this person is both terrible *and* useless'?"

Chess rolls her eyes, and picks up the dishcloth on the island next to her, flicking me with it. "I didn't mean it in a bad way! Well, okay, I kind of did because it's a trait you have to shake off, girl. Nanci never has. At least not where men are concerned. Making *me* happy? That was not exactly the highest of priorities, but some dude she met in the frozen foods aisle at Publix, well, *he* got whatever he wanted. And look where that's led. She's on her fourth husband, Em. Fourth."

Chess holds up four fingers. "And living in his shitty condo in Florida even though I bought her a house in Asheville last year. But nope, she sold it because it was Beau's dream to retire to Florida." She shakes her head. "And it's not even the pretty part of Florida. The beach is like a two-hour drive away, and Nanci hates everything about it, but, hey, if Beau's happy, she's happy!"

Stepping forward, she grabs my shoulders, giving me a light shake. "That could've been you! But it's not because you're free of all that now. You just have to get free in *here*."

Lifting one hand, she taps my forehead.

It would be nice if life were as easy as Chess seems to think it is. But then, I remind myself, she doesn't know how bad it all actually is. She doesn't know about the money Matt's asking for, or this new threat. I could tell her, but again, something stops me.

"Well, now that you've warned me I could turn into your mother, I am indeed a new woman," I tell her, and she grins, pressing a smacking kiss to the place she'd just poked.

"That's why they pay me the big bucks!" she singsongs, and I laugh, putting my now-empty glass back down.

I watch her back as she begins rifling through the cabinets for dinner supplies, and think again about Matt's call. He'd heard I was working, and suspected it was on something new.

Chess is humming to herself, something from *Aestas,* and I keep my voice casual as I ask, "You haven't talked to Matt recently, have you?"

She turns around, pulling a face. "Matt? Jesus Christ, no. Not since you split up. Why would I?"

She looks so baffled that I feel stupid for even asking. It was Rose, surely. Something to do with all this legal wrangling.

"I just wondered," I offer lamely. "You two were close, too."

She turns back around, pulling down a large serving dish. "Only because we both loved you. Once he was out of your life, he was out of mine."

She spins back around, squinting her eyes at me with exaggerated suspicion, her mouth twisted to one side. "Why? You haven't been talking to Nigel, have you?"

That actually makes me laugh. Nigel was Chess's last serious boyfriend, some rich tech bro who was obsessed with cryptocurrency and said "San Fran" instead of San Francisco and owned sunglasses that cost more than the down payment on my house. Still, Chess had been completely crazy about him, and their breakup had hit her harder than I'd expected.

Now, I joke along with her, saying, "Just every other Friday. We're talking about starting a book club. Maybe getting a time-share."

"You fucking traitor," she replies, and I laugh again. The drink has relaxed me, and I'm thinking about getting back to work on the book after dinner. I want to write a chapter about Mari's mom, about Lilith and the connection between Marianne Godwick's short story and Mari's book. It was clear her mother's death had had a huge effect on Mari, and given Lilith's influence on Victoria in *Lilith Rising*, it feels like there's something to say there. About the ways in which a legacy is both a gift and a curse. And given the villa's own legacy of both horror and beauty, I thought I could tie those two ideas together somehow, really dig into the idea of how artists are inspired and influenced.

Normally, that thought would fill me with a kind of giddy excitement, an itch in my fingers to get back to work.

Now, though, there's a weight in my stomach.

What if you write it, and it's all you wanted to be, and then Matt sues over the fucking thing?

He can't, I remind myself again. *Or he can, but he won't win.*

But would that matter? Wouldn't it just mean more lawyers, more bullshit, more—

That's when I feel it.

Not a sudden thing, more like a slow-motion wave approaching the shore.

It's been months, but I recognize the sensation immediately, and the terror makes me feel cold and hot all at once.

My head swims, the room tilts just the littlest bit, and I feel sweat beading on my forehead, my upper lip, the small of my back.

"Em?" Chess asks, but I'm already sprinting away, heading for the tiny bathroom in the hall.

I barely make it, retching into the toilet, my fingers clenched around the sides of the bowl.

It feels like forever, feels like my body is turning itself inside out, but finally, it ends.

I flush the toilet, but experience has taught me that sometimes there's a second wave, and so I don't risk trying to leave just yet.

I crouch there like an animal. My eyes are closed, but I still feel like I'm spinning, and I press my hand to the base of the toilet to steady myself.

Not again, I think, desperate, tears and sweat mingling on my cheeks. *Not again, please, please, please.*

It's been months since I've felt this way, and I let myself believe that everything was finally getting better, that *I* was getting better. Instead, it seems like whatever it is that's wrong inside me has just been coiled up, waiting to strike again.

"Em?"

I hear Chess enter the bathroom, the sink running, and then Chess is there, wet towels in hand.

Her face crumples in sympathy as she moves to kneel next to me.

"Oh, honey," she says, and then she presses the towels to my face. They're cool and damp against my heated skin, and I'm thankful for it, closing my eyes as more tears spill out.

"I thought I was better," I say, and I hate how weak my voice sounds.

"Maybe it was the shrimp you had at lunch," Chess suggests, helping me sit up. "Fish is always a risky business."

She's still got the towels pressed against my cheek, and she slides them to the back of my neck as she hands me a bottle of Perrier. I take a sip, grateful.

"Maybe," I say, hoping she's right, hoping more than I've ever hoped for anything.

I was better, I was better, I was better.

We crouch there in the bathroom, Chess's hand on my knee as I take slow, steady sips of the Perrier. "My doctors all thought it was psychosomatic," I say. "Stress or something."

Chess wraps her arms around me even though I have to be a sweaty, disgusting mess. "And talking to Matt stressed you out. I'm so sorry."

I close my eyes again, shaking my head against her shoulder. "It isn't your fault," I say, but I hope that it is. I hope that's all it is, my system going haywire because Chess insisted I call Matt back and then he pissed me off.

Because if it's not that, then what the fuck is wrong with me?

"I don't know why you're so insistent it's mine. Or that she's up the duff at all, frankly."

Noel is sitting on the floor in front of the fireplace in the main drawing room. The good weather has finally returned, and the day is sunny and warm, but Noel has, for some reason, insisted on making a fire. He jabs at it now with an ornate poker, scowling into the flames.

"It's yours," Mari tells Noel, her voice flat. "And she's two months late, Noel."

This is the third time they've had this conversation in two days, and Mari is getting very tired of it. It doesn't help that the room is boiling, and that Noel is in one of his moods, but Mari is determined to have this matter settled.

"And you're so sure of this, why?" he asks. "Because she told you so?" He scoffs. "Would think you of all people would know better than to believe *Janet* about anything."

Mari doesn't admit to him that when Lara had first told her, she'd had a moment of sickening free fall, her head spinning, her mind and heart a chant of *you promised, you promised, you both promised, never again.*

"I told him," Lara had said through her sobs, "I told him I was on the pill, but I wasn't. Or I was, but I forgot to keep taking it, you know how I am with that kind of thing, Mari."

There had been a wheedling note in her voice, her hand coming to rest on Mari's knee, and the camaraderie, the *love* she'd felt for Lara just moments before had dissolved. Right then, she had wanted nothing more than to grab that hand, push it off of her.

No, more than that.

She'd wanted to grab that hand and squeeze. Bend. Break.

And then Lara had looked up at the ceiling and wailed, "How can I have a baby with *Noel*?"

Relief rushed over Mari, dizzying and thick.

"We'll get through this," she had promised Lara, gently taking her hand. "We'll fix it."

What that actually meant, Mari hadn't known. Noel certainly wasn't going to marry Lara. He couldn't, seeing how he was already married. But he could support Lara in whatever she chose to do. Give her money if she wanted to keep it, give her money if she didn't.

Mari was sure he'd see reason, understand that he bore some of the responsibility. Yes, he was wild and rude and heedless, but he wasn't heartless.

Or so she'd thought.

Noel looks up at her now, but she gets the distinct sense that he's actually looking down at her, and for the first time, Mari truly understands that he's the son of an earl. Noel may play at being a bohemian, but his blood is deeply blue, and she suddenly feels very sorry for Lara.

"Be that as it may, I made it very clear to her how I felt about her and exactly how permanent I considered our situation. Which is to say that I considered it about as long-lasting as whatever hobby she decides to pick up next. Basket-weaving, perhaps." The words are languid, Noel's usual bullshit.

His eyes, though.

His eyes are hard.

"She's made her own bed, Mistress Mary," he finishes, "and I suggest she lie in it."

The nickname is usually affectionate, if a little ribbing, but now she hears it for the insult it is, and her hands clench at her sides, nails biting into her palms.

"You're such a bastard, Noel," she tells him, and he gives an elegant shrug.

"So my father occasionally claimed, but I think the only bastard you need to be worried about is the one your sister is going to have."

"So, you're not going to help her?"

Noel gives an extravagant eye roll. "Don't be ridiculous. If it's money she wants, she can have it. But you know as well as I do that she expects me to marry her and move to some country pile in Somerset where we'll raise this brat and probably two or three others. She'll name them things like, 'Archibald' and 'Primrose,' and I'll eventually die of terminal boredom."

He turns back to the fire, pulling his dressing gown tighter around him, and Mari shoves his shoulder as she turns away.

"You don't know Lara at all then," she says, and he makes a sort of grumbling noise in protest, but Mari doesn't hang around to indulge him further.

Money is all Lara really needs or wants from Noel, and money is what he'll give, so that's sorted, at least.

She goes in search of her stepsister, but Lara is nowhere to be found, and when Mari heads outside, she sees Pierce sitting by the pond.

The grass is soft underneath her bare feet as she makes her way toward him. He's wearing that pair of jeans he likes so much, with their faded patches and holes in the knees, and as he strums his guitar, Mari wonders if he's picturing the album cover already: the brooding rock star reclining in the Italian countryside, hair rumpled, chest bare, the leaves overhead casting atmospheric shadows.

He barely glances at her as she approaches, lost in his own thoughts, and Mari sighs, leaning against one of the trees, her arms folded over her chest. "Noel says he'll take care of Lara. Financially, that is, which to be fair, is all she wants. So that's a relief."

She and Pierce had spent last night whispering in the dark about Lara, about Noel, and what would happen next, so she'd assumed he'd be pleased that Mari had sorted it all out.

But he doesn't reply. He just keeps strumming that guitar, looking out over the water.

"Don't you have anything to say?" she asks him. When he finally looks at her, those blue eyes she's always loved so much are hazy. Mari can feel her book pulling her to her room, and wants more than anything to go back to it, back to Victoria and Somerton and the chaos she's about to unleash, but no. No, once again, Lara needs rescuing, so here she is, standing by the fucking pond with Pierce instead of at her desk, doing what her heart wants.

"I guess I wasn't all that worried about it," he says, shrugging those pale shoulders. "We're a family, and the baby is just gonna be a part of it."

He smiles lazily, and she realizes that the haziness in his eyes isn't inspiration or creation. He's just high, stupidly so, and Mari takes a deep breath. At moments like this, she tries to remember exactly how she felt that day when she walked into her father's house to see Pierce sitting there. How the same smile that now makes her want to scream used to make her feel like she'd swallowed pure sunlight.

But all she can think about are all the times she's seen that smile turned on Lara, or a maid at a hotel, or a waitress in a short black skirt, and she suddenly feels very, very tired.

"I'm not sure Lara wants to have the baby, Pierce," she says, and he shakes his head.

"I'll talk to her. She's just freaked out right now, but she'll see that this is what we need, the three of us."

He reaches out to encircle her wrist with one hand. The calluses on his fingers are rough against her skin, irritating, and she pulls her hand back in horror.

He's talking about Billy. Mari had a baby and lost it, but now, look! A new baby, coming along, just like magic.

This is, she knows, how Pierce thinks. Nothing in life is too hard or too ugly, everything can be worked out.

But only because the rest of them bear the hard and ugly bits for him.

Up at the house, an unfamiliar car is pulling up in the drive, and Mari glances over at it before turning her attention back to Pierce. "Lara has her own music, you know. Beautiful music."

"That's cool," is his only reply, and Mari moves closer.

"It is. And the point is, she deserves a chance to make it, Pierce. You can't . . . you can't talk her into having a baby just because you want your own little hippie commune."

But he's lost in the guitar now, the guitar and the drugs, and Mari turns away from him, her heart in her throat.

To her surprise, Noel is walking toward them from the house, his usually louche expression serious, his limp slightly more pronounced. He's holding a piece of paper in his hands, and as Mari gets closer, she realizes it's a telegram.

"What is it?" she asks, and Noel's eyes move past her to Pierce, and somehow, although later, she's never sure how, Mari knows in an instant.

It's Frances, Pierce's wife.

The details are blunt and to the point. Three days ago, she drowned herself in the lake behind Pierce's family home. His son, Teddy, is with Frances's family.

Mari watches Pierce read the telegram, and waits for some kind of reaction, for grief or regret to cross that lovely face.

She feels her own grief—and her guilt; god, the *guilt*—like the stones Frances placed in her pockets that summer morning. She never met Pierce's wife, never knew her as anything more than a name, but she had sometimes felt like a third presence in Mari's relationship, a ghost always haunting their steps.

And now she's gone.

Pierce crumples up the paper, shoves it in the back pocket of his jeans, and looks up at the sky, his chest moving up and down as he takes a deep breath.

"Pierce," Mari starts, moving toward him, and he lowers his head, meeting her eyes.

"She's free now," he says, and he actually smiles a little as he says it. "This world was rough for her, you know? She was . . . she was sweet and delicate, and it was just too much."

Mari stands there, unsure of what to say to that, unsure of why it suddenly seems very important that she remind Pierce that the roughest element of Frances's world was *him*.

"We'll go get Teddy," he goes on. "When we're done here. He can come live with us in London."

"In the flat? Pierce, it's too small now as it is with the three of us—"

"We'll make room," he says, and then he grabs her face between his hands, kissing her hard on the mouth.

"And we'll finally get married. Make an honest woman out of you."

He's openly grinning now, and Mari looks into this face she loves so much, and realizes that there's no grief there at all.

She knows she'll think about Frances Sheldon until the day she dies, but for Pierce, his wife's suicide is just another obstacle removed, another worry he no longer has to deal with.

Will it be that way with her one day, too?

"Mrs. Sheldon is dead, long live Mrs. Sheldon," Noel mutters as Pierce walks back up to the house, guitar slung across his back.

"Shut up, Noel," Mari snaps, but when she goes to follow Pierce, Noel catches her arm, bringing her up short.

"Mari," he says, his eyes surprisingly solemn. "I know you think I'm a despicable human, and most of the time, you're not wrong. But listen to me now. Cut yourself free from all of this."

"All of what?" she asks, and his mouth thins.

"You know bloody well what I mean. From Pierce and Lara and the whole mess. Use a knife, use a sword, use a pair of fucking kitchen shears if you must, but cut yourself free. Because if you don't, you'll drown just as surely as Frances has."

He lets her go then, limping off back toward the house, and Mari stands there on the lawn, wondering how, on such a sunny and warm day, she can feel so cold.

CHAPTER ELEVEN

The book is almost done.

Somehow, after a year of hardly writing anything at all, I've written an entire draft in just a handful of weeks.

As I sit at the little desk where I now know Mari wrote *Lilith Rising*, I close my laptop, taking a deep breath. Outside, it's another cloudy afternoon. Chess left earlier to go down to one of the shops in Orvieto, and the house feels very quiet.

I could probably push myself and finish the manuscript within the next couple of hours, but I'm not quite ready yet. I think I'm still waiting for Mari.

I've reread *Lilith Rising* all the way through again, certain that there must be another hint to discover, another clue in there about where the remainder of Mari's pages might be. Because I am certain now that there are more. That fight with Pierce and Johnnie, Mari's decision to stay at Villa Rosato—a decision which seals Pierce's fate and hers—can't be the note she decided to end on. She wrote about that night, I'm sure of it.

But what has me so convinced? A writerly intuition? Or something more?

I don't believe in ghosts, but it's not hard to feel Mari's presence in this house, and there are times when I wonder if it's her nudging me on.

There's more. Find it.

Or maybe I've just spent too long going down all these rabbit holes, reading and rereading the same book, filling my head with murder and secrets, and now I've completely lost the plot.

Sighing, I drop my head into my hands.

I haven't had another bout of sickness in a few days, and my brain has felt very clear as I've worked. But it's always there, this threat that my body might betray me, attacking me like some kind of boogeyman, rendering me helpless.

That fear is what makes me think I should just go ahead and finish the manuscript while I can, get it done and off to Rose before I somehow lose myself again.

Speaking of Rose, I remember that I've been meaning to email her to ask about Matt and his lawyers. I've been putting it off, first because I didn't feel well, and then because it had seemed silly. What was I supposed to say, "Hey, did you tell my soon-to-be-ex's lawyers I was working on a new book?"

And I know I'm also putting it off because if I email Rose, it'll mean there's this part of me—albeit a little one—that didn't really believe Chess when she said she hadn't told Matt.

That she hadn't talked to him at all.

But I know it's going to bother me until I get it over with, so I quickly pull up my email and shoot a missive off to Rose.

I keep it brief, breezy even, just checking in, legal stuff with the divorce, she understands, just checking what she told Matt's lawyers about the new book.

I hit Send before I let myself overthink it, and then close my laptop harder than I need to.

On my desk, my phone beeps, and I glance down to see a text from Chess.

It's a picture of a massive fish on ice, its glassy eyes staring out at the camera.

What if I brought this home for dinner?

Guilt sneaks into my chest, an ugly, oily feeling.

I don't trust my best friend. That's the truth of it, and I don't know if it's the house getting to me, if it's Mari, if it's just me, but there it is.

I type back, *I'm actually on this very strict no sea monster diet, so pass.*

Then the search continues.

Chess is determined to cook a big fancy dinner for some reason, wanting to buy all the ingredients herself rather than depending on Giulia. Personally, I think she's using it as a way to avoid working. She hasn't said anything, but I haven't really seen her at her laptop all that often. Luckily, she seems to have believed my lie about working on the next Petal Bloom mystery, and the questions about Mari and the book have trickled off.

But that's actually another reason to get this done quickly. Once it's in Rose's hands, I'll feel better—safer.

I know it sounds paranoid, I know Chess is not actually out to steal this book from me, but I can't shake the memory of her eyes glinting in the candlelight.

This really seems like one we should work on together.

Like she doesn't already have enough. Like the book she's

currently *not* writing won't sell tons of copies, even if it sucks.

She can't have this, I think, surprised at how ferocious the thought is.

I've probably been spending too much time in Mari's head, reading about how fiercely competitive she and Lara were, constantly locked in a struggle for the same man, for the same artistic recognition, for the same life in a lot of ways.

It's true that I haven't thought nearly as much about Lara as I have about Mari—choosing, I suppose, to be loyal to the woman I feel the most kinship with.

But now, as I sit here wondering where Mari's last pages might be hidden, it occurs to me that perhaps I haven't looked at Lara closely enough.

And with Chess out of the house for another hour at least, I could use this time to do a more thorough search of the place.

I start with the little bedroom Mari described as belonging to Lara. Chess has taken the bigger room, the one I think was probably Noel's, so this bedroom is empty and neat, though faintly musty since it's been closed up for our entire stay.

I search for loose floorboards, feel under the desk, under the mattress, but there's nothing. I make my way downstairs, back to the sitting room at the front of the house.

Chess was right about there being several copies of *Aestas* around, and I check each one, feeling in the sleeves even though I know that's stupid. All five of these albums have probably been taken in and out of their cases a hundred times over the years.

Mari would never have risked that. She hid that last section well on purpose.

I move into the main hallway, passing the dining room,

and notice that Chess's laptop is sitting on the dining-room table.

Open.

I stand there in the doorway, and for a second, I really do think about just walking away from it.

But there's a darker voice inside. *She read your shit without asking, why shouldn't you read hers?*

She probably has the screen locked. And even if she doesn't, I'm not going to go searching through her stuff. At least when she'd read mine, I'd just foolishly left it up.

I stop.

Had I? She said that I had, and I'd been too freaked out and pissed off to really think carefully about it, because I *did* sometimes walk away from my computer without closing the document.

But then I think about that little icon on my desktop with "THEVILLABOOK.doc." and how that might have acted like a siren song.

Chess's computer isn't locked, but she has her own icon calling to me. Not "SWIPERIGHT.doc" or anything that obvious, just "NewBookDraft2-July."

I sit down.

I click.

Have you ever asked yourself, "Am I grabbing all there is in life?"

I let out a slow breath.

It's her self-help book, no mention of Mari, the house, any of it.

God, I'm a psycho, creeping around on her laptop, thinking she was . . . well, I don't even know what I'd thought. But this is clearly a Chess Book.

I scroll past her usual stuff—*How often do you ask your-self if you're reaching your highest potential?*—and feel my shoulders unclench a little.

She hasn't stolen my book. She isn't telling my story.

I scroll further down. More New Age word salad.

Enlightened.

Powered Path.

Soul Cleanse.

I'm just about to scroll back up to the top when another word catches my eye.

Emma.

Not my name, obviously, but close enough that I pause.

And then I read.

It's not much, just a couple of paragraphs, but as my eyes move over them, nausea and rage surge up from the pit of my stomach.

Of course, there are times in life when we step off the Powered Path, and find we can't get ourselves back on. Settle in while I tell you a little story about a friend of mine. We'll call her Emma. Emma was always the Smart One at school. Perfect family—you all know what a mess mine was!—and she had gone on to an adult life that we'd say had allllllll the markers of success: A good career, a nice house, a loving husband. But what happened when Emma, who was so used to things going her way, lost two of those three things? She couldn't handle it. Complete life meltdown.

That's because Emma was never actually on the Powered Path. She'd just accepted an illusory version of it, and when that failed her, she was totally adrift. If Emma had had to work for any of the things she'd attained, she would have had the Titanium Core we talked about in chapter four, but she didn't. That's why you should never regret the hard work you do on yourselves! Otherwise, you can end up an Emma (repeat after me: Don't. Be. An Emma).

Despite my anger, a horrified laugh bursts out from me at that last line.

Holy fuck, this bitch is going to sell T-shirts that say "Don't Be an Emma."

This is what Chess thinks of me, then. As a woman who never worked for anything and who, when things fell apart, fell apart with them. That's all this vacation has been, probably, a chance to observe me in the wild, to get a few more anecdotes of Sad Sack Emily—sorry, *Emma*—for her fucking *book*.

I scroll down further, bizarrely, sickly hoping there's more. I want to read all of it, to suck down every bit of poison, an impulse I barely understand, but can't resist.

There's nothing, though. Just white space. Then I get to the bottom of the page.

When most people think of Villa Rosato—if they think of it at all—they think about the murder of Pierce Sheldon in 1974.

In a way, it hurts more, but at the same time, an almost dizzying wave of relief sweeps through me. I was *right*. I'm not crazy. Oh, she was smart, hiding it inside this document, but I knew it, I fucking *knew it*, and the satisfaction may be bitter, but it's still real.

I keep reading, my breathing loud in my ears. The first paragraph is just the basics, the story of the murder, who was there that summer, how they were all connected. It's fairly boring, really, a dry recounting, followed by a series of bullet points with dates. There's nothing coherent yet, nothing that actually feels like a book.

But I keep scrolling, and two paragraphs on the next page catch my eye.

The summer at Villa Rosato was supposed to relaunch Noel Gordon's music career while bringing Pierce Sheldon along for the ride. The women who came with them were only there to look at them adoringly, tell them how talented they were, and provide the sex part of the "sex drugs and rock 'n' roll" equation. The ever-powerful myth of the muse, right? But instead, it's those women, Mari Godwick and Lara Larchmont, who left us with two truly iconic pieces of art. Is that tragic irony or poetic justice?

Maybe Lara Larchmont herself had the answer. If you've ever had a broken heart, you've listened to Aestas, *I'm sure! But look closely at the lyrics of the final track, "Sunset." Boring title, killer song, and the last verse goes like this:*

Your light has faded/but you still think that it shines

Your once-silver tongue/tangles over worn-out lines

You think the sun is rising/as it sinks closer to the sea

Boy, don't you know? The brightest stars that lit your sky/ were the ones you couldn't see

How often are we bright stars in someone else's sky, but they couldn't find us with a fucking telescope, huh? And how do we not only find ourselves a new galaxy, but become supernovas?

It's a different approach than I've taken. It's definitely still a Chess Book, and I wonder if she just doesn't know any other way to write after all this time.

But . . .

I missed that line in *Aestas.* I've been so focused on Mari and *Lilith Rising* that I hadn't even thought to look more closely at Lara's writing. But Chess had found this, a lyric clearly referencing Noel or Pierce or—most likely—both of them. What other connections were there between the album and what happened that summer?

Beyond that, the bigger idea that Chess has identified— it's *good*. By zooming out to include Lara *and* Mari, Chess has hit on something I hadn't been thinking about, how the muses became creators. I want to keep reading, no longer to satisfy some dark urge, but because I'm interested in where she's going with this.

But the Word doc ends there.

Which just pisses me off even more.

I get up from the computer on shaky legs, turning away before I remember to scroll back to where she had been working in the document. I can be sneaky, too, I congratulate myself, even as I wander out of the dining room in a daze.

Chess thinks I'm a loser.

Chess is stealing my book idea.

But also . . . I really liked what I read.

I'm trembling as I walk upstairs, and when I pass one of the hallway mirrors, my face doesn't even look like mine. My skin is pale except for two bright spots of color on my cheeks, and my eyes are shining, my lips pressed together in a tight line.

If I raised one hand and covered myself in blood, I'd look just like Victoria on the cover of *Lilith Rising*, and the image stays with me, intense, visceral.

And then, suddenly, I know where to find the rest of Mari's pages.

After a brief reprieve, the rain has moved back in, but for once, Mari doesn't mind.

She's claimed this little spot of the bedroom to write, and write she does, sitting at the desk every day as downstairs, Pierce and Noel get into petty arguments about music that still isn't written, Johnnie broods and strums his guitar, and Lara merely drifts through it all.

But Mari is with Victoria and Somerton house and Father Colin, and she can sense the final web drawing tighter and tighter.

She's going to call it *Lilith Rising*, she's decided, already imagining how the title might look on a book jacket. A tribute to her mother, yes, but also a fitting title for a book about women, power, betrayal.

Survival.

The only thing left is the bloody and cathartic climax, Victoria laying waste to all those who've wronged her. Mari can see it like a movie in her head, but she feels herself putting it off, almost like she's not quite ready yet.

Rain patters against the window as she puts her pen down and stands, her hands pressed to her lower back. She's getting thinner again, forgetting lunch, sometimes skipping dinner altogether, and her stomach growls now, reminding her that it's been awhile since she's eaten.

Mari hopes she can grab a quick sandwich and then get back to her desk without having to see anyone, but when she reaches the foyer, she's startled to see Johnnie standing there.

He's hovering, almost like he was waiting for her, and Mari smiles at him, a little bemused.

"Hiya, Johnnie," she says, and he steps forward, jittery.

"I was hoping you might come down. I feel like I never see you anymore."

"I've been working," she tells him, gesturing vaguely upstairs, and he nods again, his movement a little too jerky.

This is the reason she's been avoiding Johnnie for the past week or so. Lately, it seems that he's always high, and Mari finds that both boring and annoying. She occasionally puts up with it from Pierce, but she won't from anyone else, Johnnie included, and now she hopes she can just scoot past him, get her lunch, and get back to work.

But he's blocking her path, his dark eyes pleading and liquid. "I've really missed you these past weeks," he says, and it's so plaintive that it touches her a little bit. She remembers that first day with him by the pond, when she'd thought how nice it was to have a boy with a crush on her.

"Johnnie," she says, touching his arm. She means it as a gesture of affectionate friendship, but Johnnie clearly takes it for an opening.

He surges forward, and then his mouth is on hers.

It's a clumsy kiss, more enthusiasm than technique, and Mari is so startled by it that, for the briefest moment, she allows it.

But the whole thing just feels awkward, like she's kissing

a little brother or something, and she pulls away, her hands coming to his rest on his cheeks.

"Johnnie," she says, her voice soft, and she expects him to give her that wry smile, that almost sheepish shrug. Worth a try, he'll say, and they'll laugh it off. Maybe he'll be a little embarrassed, but not actually regretful.

Mari can see it playing out all so clearly in her mind that she's confused when Johnnie's expression goes hard, his hands grabbing her wrists.

"Right," he says, his lip curling. "*Johnnie*."

There is an ugly kind of sneer in his voice, and Mari stares up at him as he pushes her away. "So, you'll have it off with Noel, and you'll end up marrying that prick Pierce even though he's fucked your sister and drove his wife to suicide, but I'm *just Johnnie*, right? What was it Noel said? Ah, right. *Bit of a spaniel*."

"That's not—" she starts, but he shakes his head.

"Nah, don't tell me that's not what it is. I can fucking well see it, can't I?"

He points viciously toward the front of the house where she assumes Pierce must be. "*He* treats you like shit, and you won't have the guts to actually leave him because if you do that, you gotta admit that it was all for nothing, right? That you fucked over your family *and* his innocent wife, all for some piece of shit who wasn't worth it."

The words come out in an angry torrent, every one of them stinging, and Mari looks at this man she thought she liked, this man she thought she understood, and realizes he might as well be a stranger.

And the worst part of it is, she knows he's right. Yes, he's hurt and he's being a massive wanker about all of it, but he isn't actually wrong.

She has thrown in her entire lot with Pierce. There's no coming back from it, the only way out is through. And, as much as she hates it—Christ, how she hates it sometimes—she does love him.

She always will.

There's a sound from the kitchen, and Mari looks over to see Elena watching them. She's pretending not to, her gaze immediately darting to the groceries she was unpacking, but her cheeks are red, and her hands are trembling.

Another story for the villagers, Mari guesses, about the decadent rock stars up on the hill.

"Johnnie," she says now, lifting her hands toward him. "Please don't be like this."

He rubs a hand angrily over his mouth, walking away from her, then coming right back, his eyes wild, and Mari backs up a step.

Johnnie has always seemed sweet to her, charming and boyish, and she doesn't know if it's the drugs that have done this to him, but it occurs to her, almost wonderingly, that she's actually afraid of him right now.

"I asked around about him. About your old man. Called some friends back home, and turns out one of them knew his wife."

It's the last thing she expected to hear, and she blinks. "Frances?"

He nods, and there's that angry gesture again, his hand across his lips. "Yeah. My mate Tom. He went to school with Franny's brother. Didn't know her all that well, but said she was sweet. She loved her family, and she could have had a happy life. Except one night, she and a couple of her mates snuck off to London to see some singer."

Mari's stomach sinks. She knows this story. Pierce told her his version of it, how Franny had, for the first time in her life, lied to her parents to go to a club in Soho. How Pierce had been playing that night. How he'd spotted her in the front row wearing too much makeup and a dress that didn't really fit since she'd had to borrow it from a friend and thought how pretty she'd looked.

How sad.

And even though she hadn't wanted to, Mari had imagined it so many times, wondering if after the show, he'd held her face the way he'd held Mari's.

How did I go so long without knowing you?

"Next thing you know, Franny isn't back at school. Family's frantic, calling everyone, but, sure enough, she'd run off with that prick. Married him in Scotland, and then he knocked her up. And what did he do the second he met someone else, huh? Took off, said that Franny was boring now, that he didn't want to be married anymore, that he wanted to be free. That he wanted *her* to be free, too. And now I guess she is, ain't she? All for some stupid cunt who never actually loved her, and she was just dumb enough to believe his shit."

Mari shakes her head, but before she can say anything else, Pierce is suddenly there, his hands clenched into fists at his sides.

"What did you say about Franny?"

Johnnie whirls around, and Pierce comes into the hallway, his face a mask of fury Mari has never seen before.

"You heard me!" Johnny yells back. "Think you're God's bloody gift because you can play a fuckin' guitar, but all you do is fuck shit up. You fucked up your wife's life, you're fucking up Mari's and Lara's, and you're fucking up *mine*. Telling

Noel I can't play guitar on the album because it'll be 'out of place.' Didn't think I heard you, did you? Probably forgot I was even fucking here. But what kind of pretentious bullshit is that, huh?"

Johnnie swipes at his nose with one hand, practically vibrating as he stares down Pierce.

"Yeah, well, maybe I didn't want some low-life dealer scum fucking up the vibe with his three shitty chords, ever think about that?" Pierce says, and Johnnie throws back his head, barking out a laugh.

"Rich coming from you, mate. At my door every day, asking if I've got more, but now I'm 'low-life dealer scum'? Well, you still owe this lowlife ten quid, you dickhead. Or hell, maybe I'll start giving it to you for free, hope you fucking top yourself. Say hi to the missus when you do, yeah?"

Pierce's face is white now, and then he's rushing at Johnnie, and Johnnie has his clenched fist raised, and Mari hears herself, shrill.

"Stop it! Both of you!"

Pierce grabs Johnnie's shirt just as Johnnie's fist connects with Pierce's jaw, making a sick, fleshy sound that makes Mari's stomach roll.

She can hear Elena in the kitchen, shrieking for Noel, and Lara comes down the stairs, still in her pajamas, her face pale.

"Mari, what—"

"Pierce, stop it!" Mari yells again, trying to grab his shoulder, but he spins around, hard, sending her tumbling to the floor. She hears Johnnie's roar and another one of those dull thwacks, and then Noel—she's never been so happy to see Noel Gordon—finally appears, dragging Johnnie away from Pierce with surprising strength.

"Get a fucking hold of yourselves, both of you!" he barks,

none of his usual lazy charm now, just the innate sense of authority that comes from your family owning huge swathes of England.

Johnnie skids on the stone floor in his sneakers, and Pierce is on his knees, panting, blood dripping from the corner of his mouth. Both of them are glaring at each other, but they don't make any moves in the other's direction, and after a moment Noel lets go of Johnnie's collar.

Pierce rises to his feet and makes for the stairs, swiping at the blood on his mouth. It leaves a crimson streak across his cheek, but he doesn't seem to care, taking the stairs two at a time. "Fucking bullshit, man," Mari hears him say. "Fucking *sick* of this place."

"Then leave!" Noel shouts up after him, and Mari's stomach clenches.

No. They can't leave now. Not when she's so near finishing the book. What if she leaves this house, and Victoria's voice goes silent again?

She can't let that happen, not now, not when she's this *close*.

When she goes into the bedroom, she sees Pierce already angrily pulling things out of the wardrobe, slinging them onto the bed.

His head shoots up when he sees her, his blue eyes bloodshot. "Who the fuck does that arsehole think he is, talking about Franny?" he asks, but he doesn't wait for an answer. "Like he knows. Like any of them know. I *loved* that girl, okay? You think I wanted her to die? I just wanted her"—he slings another shirt onto the bed—"not to live the boring life her fucking parents wanted for her. She should've been able to do that without me, and it's not my fault she couldn't."

Mari's mouth is dry, her hands shaking, and she approaches Pierce slowly, resting her hands on his back. He's burning up, his skin hot against her palms, and she thinks again of that long night, holding Billy against her.

"Calm down," she tells Pierce now, but he shakes his head, pointing at the chest of drawers.

"Get your things. We're not staying one more bloody night in this nuthouse."

Mari's eyes go to her notebook, still open on her desk. "Don't be silly," she tells Pierce, trying to keep her voice light. "We're supposed to be here another two weeks. We can't buy new tickets, we don't have the money."

"I don't give a fuck about that," Pierce replies, beginning to shove things into the suitcase, and Mari can't help the scathing laugh that bursts out of her.

"Of course, *you* don't, but you never do. *I'm* the one who has to worry about that kind of thing, right? Suppose you want me to call my father, beg him to help us out somehow."

Pierce goes still, then turns around, his chest heaving. "I've never liked you having to ask your father for money—"

"But not enough to actually make money yourself. And god forbid Pierce Sheldon ever lowered himself to grovel to his own family."

Pierce points at her, his hand shaking. "You just don't wanna leave because of *him*."

His hand moves, finger now jabbing at the floor, toward downstairs, and Mari picks up the nearest thing to hand, one of Pierce's jackets, flinging it at him.

"Oh, that's right, the only thing I could *possibly* care about is some other man and some other cock," she spits out. She has no idea if he means Johnnie or Noel or both, and, given that the idea she'd want to stay for either of them is absurd, she's too bloody angry to care. "What other reason could a girl have for not wanting to sprint out across Italy dead broke?

Never mind that I'm actually *happy* here. Never mind that I'm actually *working*, not that you've even fucking noticed. Or asked. Or *cared*."

Pierce just stands there, staring at her, his expression almost comically confused.

He looks like someone just hit him over the head, Mari thinks, and she sort of wishes she had.

"You're really not leaving," he says, and Mari folds her arms tight across her chest.

"I'm not. You can, but I won't."

Sitting heavily on the side of the bed, Pierce puts his head in his hands, sucking in a breath. When he finally looks back at her, there are tears in his eyes, but he's trying to smile.

"Then I'll stay, too," Pierce proclaims, and somewhere in the universe, a pair of scissors snaps, sealing his fate.

In the end, it was the testimony of Elena Bianchi that doomed John Dorchester. The teenager had been a maid at Villa Rosato for the entire summer and, it turned out, had witnessed far more of the various tensions and dramas that were unfolding between the inhabitants than they realized. On the stand for a total of three days altogether, Elena's testimony held the court—and the world—riveted. Thanks to her, it was revealed that not only had Noel Gordon impregnated Lara Larchmont, but that Lara had previously had a brief affair with the deceased, Pierce Sheldon. Elena also testified to drunken rages, petty arguments, and, most damning of all, a physical altercation between Johnnie and Pierce that had erupted after Elena saw Johnnie and Mari in a passionate embrace.

This, of course, led to the long-standing belief that everything that happened that summer was really all about sex. The rumors began at the trial, and really never stopped. Mari was having an affair with Johnnie; no, she was actually sleeping with Noel and Johnnie—or, even more scandalous, had Mari discovered that Pierce and Noel were sleeping together?

Perhaps, as Elena darkly implied before the opposing counsel could stop her, it was a more fluid situation, one involving bed swapping, partner swapping—a veritable orgy unfolding just outside the tranquil medieval hill town of Orvieto.

It was ironic that these five people, accustomed to being watched and scrutinized, seemed to have forgotten about the civilian in their midst, who was committing to memory all the private moments that eventually led to a brutal murder.

Elena enjoyed her brief moment of celebrity as well. She was able to parlay it into a brief modeling career and eventually married Giancarlo Ricci, the wealthy son of an Italian record executive before she sadly passed away in the mid-eighties.

It's a great irony, no doubt, that in being a part of something so horrible, Elena Bianchi's life was, indisputably, improved.

If she herself ever had any qualms about that, she never expressed them. If anything, she seemed to take the events of July 29, 1974, in her stride.

Interviewed a year after the trial, Elena was asked if she thought the courts got it right. Her answer was typically Italian: *Errano tutti pazzi.*

"They are all mad."

> —*The Rock Star, the Writer, and the Murdered Musician: The Strange Saga of Villa Rosato*, A. Burton, longformcrime.net

Mari doesn't know it's her last night at Villa Rosato on the July evening that she sits down at her desk to finish *Lilith Rising*. There's no warning, no sense of foreboding in the air.

That last day has actually been one of the nicer ones that she's spent at the villa. Noel has taken himself off to town, claiming he's going to throw himself down St. Patrick's Well. Given that he abandoned any pretense of disguise, Mari suspects he intends to put himself on display and be admired by the locals. Pierce spends most of the day writing in the drawing room downstairs. Lara is in her room, playing, and though Johnnie seems determined to get himself into the most altered state humanly possible, he's at least peaceful, for once. No more dark glares at Pierce, no further arguments.

It's a good day, all in all, and Mari will be glad for that, after.

It's past midnight when the storm begins, and Mari is still at her desk, a candle burning next to her. She hears voices in the hallway, but she ignores them at first, determined to see her story through until the bloody end.

Victoria stared up at the house, and knew. All this time, she had thought it was Colin drawing her to the darkness, but the darkness had always been there, inside her. It's why she loved the house, and the house loved her. It's why she was here now: to bring about her own ruin, but also her own salvation.

She stepped forward, the grass—

"I get a say in this!"

Pierce's shout rings out from somewhere downstairs, startling Mari, ripping her out of the world she's creating and thrusting her right back into the one she lives in.

If he and Johnnie have started up again . . .

But it's not Johnnie's voice that replies.

"Pierce, you're drunk," Mari hears her stepsister say, her voice weary, and Mari goes still, waiting.

"You aren't listening to me," Pierce goes on. "You don't understand that we could . . . we could all be happy, Lara. We *were* happy, right? Before we lost Billy."

The mention of her son's name has Mari rising from her desk, and when she walks halfway down the stairs, she sees Pierce and Lara are standing in the front hallway near the door. Lara was playing earlier, and her guitar is still loosely held by the neck in one hand, resting against her leg.

"Stop it," Lara says to Pierce, "and go to bed. We can talk about this in the morning."

Lara tries to move past him as a clap of thunder rattles the house, but Pierce grabs her shoulders, stopping her. The guitar falls to the floor with a surprisingly loud thwack, and Lara's eyes go to it, but she doesn't try to extricate herself from Pierce's grip.

"D'you know I talked to Frances's mum last night? She says she's keeping Teddy. She says . . . she says they'll go to the courts if they have to, and that my father—my own bloody *father*—will pay for it. Says that his grandson deserves a better life, a more 'stable' life, than the one I'll give him."

Mari hadn't known this. Pierce has been subdued today, but she'd had no idea it was because Frances's family had decided to take his son away from him.

But as she stands there watching Pierce sob, trying to coax Lara into keeping her unborn child, she can't blame them.

They should hold him tight and keep him safe, she thinks. *Safer than we kept Billy.*

If they hadn't been so poor, if Pierce had let her take him to a doctor . . .

"I'm sorry," Lara says, reaching out and stroking Pierce's hair. "I am. But you can't replace Teddy with my baby. You can't replace Billy with my baby."

Mari moves closer, feeling a need to intervene, and then Pierce says, "But it could be *my* baby, too, Lara. And that fucking well counts for something."

Time slows, and Mari sees Lara finally notice her over Pierce's shoulder. The wretched look on Lara's face says that it's true.

Or at least, it could be true—and isn't that just as bad?

Pierce follows Lara's gaze and jerks his head around to see Mari standing there.

His face crumples and he lifts a hand to her. "Baby, come here."

She thinks of that night, weeks ago: another storm, another offered hand, and how she'd thought that maybe she could live in Pierce's world, after all.

But now she wants no part of it, wants no part of any of it, and she just shakes her head, a trembling palm pressed against her mouth, holding in a scream.

"You promised," she finally manages to say, but it's directed at Lara, not Pierce. "You *promised*, never again."

"Mari," Lara says, and there are tears running down her face, lightning flashing in the hallway window, making Mari wince.

"This can be okay," Pierce is saying. "I can make this okay."

He steps forward, lurches really, and Mari sees it happen like it's in slow motion, his bare foot landing on the neck of Lara's guitar, his toes curling slightly as he stumbles, and then there's a horrible crack, wood snapping, splinters shockingly white against the dark wood. The strings give a protesting twang, but it's too late, the thing is mangled.

Mari looks at Lara in horror.

She's seen so many expressions cross her stepsister's face, but this one is new. It's not hurt, exactly. It's deeper than that. It's something animal, something primal, and all Mari can think about is Lara sitting in the parlor, Lara sitting by the pond, Lara on the edge of the tub, and how in every moment, that guitar has been a constant. Mari knows she hasn't always loved Lara, but goddammit, Lara loved that guitar, and she was doing something with it.

Making something with it, something of value. Something for herself.

And now, like so many other of Lara's dreams—and Mari's dreams, too—it's shattered under Pierce's foot.

But still, Mari thinks she might be able to forgive him. It's a stupid accident, after all, nothing Pierce meant to do. He's drunk and tired, and they're all upset, and Mari could absolve him the same way she's absolved him for everything else.

And then he laughs.

It's a shrill sound, high and grating, and Mari is moving before she knows it.

"Stop!" she hears herself yell as she runs down the stairs, her palms hitting him hard in the chest.

Harder than she'd meant to, but also not hard enough, not nearly hard enough for the rage in her heart in this moment.

He stumbles again, and his eyes meet hers, wide and confused as he falls back, and Mari will never forget the sound of his head hitting the stone floor, not as long as she lives.

It's bad, she sees that immediately. Pierce lies there, dazed, his hand going to the back of his head instinctively, but then that same hand jerks like some invisible force has caught it, and those beautiful blue eyes roll back, his body convulsing.

"Oh god, oh *god*," she hears Lara screaming, and Mari just wants it to stop, wants him to stop making those sounds, stop moving like that. . . .

There's a sculpture on a pedestal by the front door. It's heavy, solid stone, a naked and muscular man holding a harp, and Mari takes it in her hands now, feeling the weight of it, how almost impossibly heavy it seems.

But it's not impossible after all.

She brings it down.

On the floor, Lara moans, but Mari can't make herself stop.

She brings the statue down again and again, and she sees Frances, walking into that pond with stones in her pockets, and she sees her and Lara, locked forever in this sick triangle, and she sees Billy, trying to catch his breath and Pierce is saying, *He'll be all right, stop worrying,* but he wasn't all right, he would never be all right again, and nothing Pierce ever said came true.

Nothing he'd ever promised her had ever been real.

The statue cracks, but by then, Pierce isn't moving anymore, and Mari is breathing so hard it sounds like she's sobbing.

She is sobbing, she realizes, tears and blood mixing on her face.

Lara is still crouched on the floor, her face gray, her eyes wide, and when she looks up at Mari, there's something like awe in her face.

"What do we do now?" she asks, and Mari is so, so glad she said, "we."

They both remain there, and Mari thinks how quiet it is in the house. Noel is gone, of course, but Johnnie . . .

Where is Johnnie?

They find him passed out on the sofa, deep in a drugged stupor, and Mari understands how it has to happen now. Understands why Johnnie was here.

She's inevitable, Pierce had thought in his dream, and she was.

So was this.

Once Johnnie has been smeared with Pierce's blood, once she has smashed the statue into even more pieces and left them, bloody and broken at Johnnie's feet, she and Lara go up the stairs.

Mari's hand is still streaked with red, but Lara takes it anyway, the two of them silent as they make their way into the bathroom.

She turns on the tap in the bathtub, and Lara takes her dress, the black one with the red flowers on it, the one she'd bought the last time they were in Italy.

Pierce teased her that those flowers looked like splashes of blood, but he was wrong. She knows now because his blood is all over this dress, and it's dark and thick and nothing like those bright red poppies at all.

Mari showers, making sure there's not a single drop of blood left behind.

She's not worried, oddly. She has Lara, and Lara has her. Johnnie and Pierce had fought just a few days before. Johnnie is passed out, Johnnie is covered in blood, Johnnie has the broken statue beside him.

Mari is going to get away with this, she knows.

What she doesn't know, what she can't know then, is that even if you're never suspected, there's no such thing as getting away with it.

Not really.

But that night, she puts on clean clothes, and she goes back into her room, and shuts the door. The rain gets louder, but Mari can't hear it as inside Somerton House, Victoria wreaks her bloody revenge.

She finishes just as the sun rises. Outside her window, the first rays of the new day brighten the sky, chasing off the storm from the night before.

The End, Mari writes, and downstairs the front door opens, and after a moment, Noel begins to scream.

CHAPTER TWELVE

I don't come out of my room the next day. I tell Chess I'm not feeling well, and she seems willing to accept that.

But my body feels fine. It's my soul that is suddenly a little ragged. I don't know if it's from reading what Chess wrote about me, or from her lies, or if I'm still reeling from Mari's last chapter, but I don't feel capable of sitting across from Chess and pretending everything is normal.

So, I lay in bed instead, listening to *Aestas* on my phone and rereading Mari's confession over and over again.

It was stupid, not thinking about the album like I had the novel. Maybe I just felt more drawn to Mari because I'm a writer, too, or maybe, when I'd briefly googled Lara, there was something about her that felt a little off-putting.

Something in that bright smile of hers that made me think of Chess.

But that's not fair to Lara. Or to Mari. They came to the villa that summer as muses at best, hangers-on at worst, because that's how the men in their lives saw them. The only way they *could* see them.

And look at what they'd become.

So *Aestas*—and Lara—are just as important to this story, and that means I need to read, and listen. I'm hungry for further clues, any hint of the truth of that summer in Lara's lyrics.

It's harder with music, the language more metaphorical and flowery, the links not quite as clear, but I find—or think I find—a few.

There's the opening track, "Golden Chain," that's clearly about Pierce, Mari, and Lara's twisted relationship, and it seems obvious "Night Owl" is about Mari herself. Chess already identified that "Sunset" is about Noel or Pierce or both.

But I want more than that. In *Lilith Rising*, there's the horror, the blood, Victoria with Colin's literal heart in her hand, and now, it all makes so much sense to me. Mari couldn't tell the truth about what happened to Pierce, what she did, so she had Victoria do it for her.

Did Lara do the same in her songs? Or would she have? All I have is Mari's story, how Mari saw it. Stories change depending on who's telling them.

Look at how Chess saw me. I didn't recognize that version of me in her manuscript, but that didn't make it wrong in the end, did it? It was just Chess's side of the story. Didn't she look different through my eyes than she did to the rest of the world?

When the album ends, I start it over, then eventually hit the Repeat All button on my music app to keep *Aestas* playing on a constant loop.

I think there might be something in "Last at the Party," a line that goes, *I watch you drift out the door/the music so*

loud, but your eyes so sad/and do you ever miss me, too?/Do
the ghosts we knew come looking for you?

As I scratch that lyric down on a notepad, I flex the fingers of my free hand, my pulse jumpy. I want to tell someone about this, I realize. I want to compare notes, I want to share what I found in Mari's papers, explain how the story of the murder at Villa Rosato is so much bigger than anyone ever knew.

And the fucked-up thing is, I don't just want to tell *some-one.*

I want to tell a particular person.

I want to tell Chess.

Even after everything.

She's the only one who will get this, who will get why it's so significant. And she'll make these other connections, find different ways of looking at the story.

She'll take it, another part of my brain reminds me. *This is yours. With these papers, if you can get them verified, you don't just have a measly $10,000 payment for a cozy mystery, you get a chunk of a seven-figure advance. You pay your lawyer. You get even better, scarier lawyers, and you keep every dime of your money, forever.*

So I shove down that stupid, childish impulse, that desire to run to my best friend, to confide all my secrets. Instead, I keep listening to *Aestas*, keep making notes, and later, I sleep and I dream, but all my dreams are of bloodshed and screams, and Chess is there—she's always there, somehow.

I can't avoid her forever and, after hiding Mari's pages even better than I did before, I make my way downstairs the next morning.

I'll confront her, I've decided. Tell her what I found, what I read. She can't be mad given that she did the same damn thing to me, and her betrayal is now a lot fucking bigger than mine.

Chess is on the phone when I get downstairs, standing in the kitchen, and I'm just about to interrupt her when something makes me pull up short.

It's the way she's standing.

The late morning light is making a halo around her, and Chess could be sixteen again. She has one foot crossed in front of the other, her head tilted down as she talks into her cell phone, and her free hand is playing with the neckline of her shirt.

"Well, if you didn't miss me, I'd be worried," she says, and whatever the person on the other end says makes her laugh.

"Baby, you know this stuff takes time," she all but purrs, her voice rich with promise, and I back out of the kitchen before she's seen me.

Chess isn't dating anyone as far as I know, but it's not totally unthinkable that there might be a guy she just hadn't mentioned. Chess hasn't been serious about anyone in a long time, but there are always men around. This must just be one of them.

But she was almost whispering, keeping her voice low. Like she was hiding from me.

Why?

And it's more than that. It's completely crazy, but there's something about the furtive way she was talking that reminds me of those times I'd walk in on Matt, speaking in that low voice to whoever was on the other end of the line. An illicit intimacy that I wasn't part of.

It's not a comfortable comparison, but it lodges there in my brain and I can't stop touching it, like a sore tooth.

I'm settled by the pool when Chess finally comes out of

the house. I'm pretending to read *Lilith Rising* again even though, at this point, I practically have it memorized.

"There you are!" she says brightly. "I've missed you!"

I look at her smiling face and think, *You lying bitch.*

But I smile back. "Same. But I'm feeling better now, so I'm trying to soak up these last few days."

"Ugh, I know. Can you believe we only have a week left?"

"Fastest summer of my life."

"That's what happens when you spend it with your bestie," she says, and I grit my teeth and nod.

"Yup. So, who was on the phone?"

Chess had been turning to go back inside, but she pauses now, facing me. "What?"

"Earlier I came down, and you were on the phone."

Tell me it was some guy you're seeing. Tell me it was some guy who'd like to be seeing you. Just don't lie to me. If you lie to me, I'll have to ask myself why.

"Oh." She waves that off. "Just my mom. You know Nanci, doesn't want a thing from me until suddenly she wants *every-thing* from me. I guess Beau is late on condo payments, so it's Chess to the rescue again!"

I watch as she walks back inside, the pages of *Lilith Rising* squeezed tight in my hand.

WE'RE IN THE drawing room that night, the room I've started thinking of as *our* room, sitting on the sofas opposite each other. Music is playing again, *Aestas,* of course, but Chess is typing away on her laptop while I'm flipping through my phone. We've got wine on the table, but neither of us is really drinking it, and I keep stealing glances at her.

Rose's email came in this afternoon. Just a short couple

of lines, telling me she hasn't heard anything from Matt's lawyers, so no, of course she hadn't mentioned the new book idea to them.

I read it three times before deleting it.

It can't be Chess. It can't be Chess and Matt. That doesn't make any fucking sense. The guy she dated before Nigel had been a hedge-fund guy who drove a McLaren and owned a yacht. Matt got seasick on a cruise to Cabo San Lucas.

It's Mari's pages, getting in my head, that mess with her and Pierce and Lara. That's what's making me suspect Chess.

Or maybe I'm just looking for another reason to be angry at Chess. Something solid and valid, something that feels a little less petty than, *You were mean about me in your book!*

But this is the last thing I should want, because I'm not sure I could survive it. Matt's betrayal hurt, but Chess doing that to me . . .

That would be fatal.

It's stormy tonight, the first really proper storm we've had up here, and while we've got every lamp in the room on, we've also lit the candles again. It should feel cozy, tucked away in here while the rain falls outside, but it's anything but.

I sit up now, putting my phone down. "Can I ask you something?"

Chess closes her laptop, eyebrows raised. "Anything, Em."

"If you make 'Don't Be an Emma' shirts, do I get a cut?"

To Chess's credit, she doesn't pretend not to know what I'm talking about, or deflect it with some witty banter.

She just sighs and crosses her arms, her bangle bracelets clacking together under a cardigan that appears to be made of scarves.

"Was this an evening the score kind of thing? I read yours, so you read mine?"

"Kind of," I admit, and one corner of her mouth kicks up.

"For what it's worth, I wrote that the night after we had that fight. When you told me you didn't want to write with me. My feelings were hurt, and I was feeling cunty, so I wrote that. I was going to delete it."

"But do you think it?" I press, and Chess tips her head back, sucking a breath in through her nose.

"Sometimes?" she admits. "Yeah, Em, sometimes I do think you let yourself give up too easily. So what if Matt left? So what if you don't like writing about murder at the fucking cakewalk or whatever anymore? It shouldn't derail your whole life. Your sense of self."

"It's about a lot more—" I start, but then Chess shifts on the couch, putting her feet up on the coffee table, and the light catches that anklet I'd noticed the other night.

Then, the lights had been dim, and I'd just caught the barest glimpse of it. Now, the chandelier is on, the hem of Chess's pants is looser, and I can see the jewelry clearly.

But then again, I've seen it before.

A delicate gold chain, a tiny charm, a curling *M*, not unlike the *M* carved in the glass upstairs, but not *M* for Mari this time.

M for Matt.

Chess sees the moment I understand and stands up. "Emmy," she says, and now I know what people mean when they say they see red because it's like there's nothing in my vision but bright, bright crimson, and my heart is in my ears, my throat, my stomach.

I don't think.

I lunge at her.

CHAPTER THIRTEEN

Chess dodges me faster than I would've thought.

All that Pilates must pay off in unexpected ways.

But if she has agility on her side, I have blind rage on mine, and when she goes for the door, I catch her by all those floaty fucking layers, yanking hard, and she stumbles, crashing back into me.

"You're insane!" she shrieks, batting at me, and honestly, I do feel insane right now.

I think of Mari, bringing that statue down on Pierce's head, and I understand how she did it. How you can love someone, but be so angry at them that only their blood on your hands will quiet the screaming inside you.

We fall to the floor, my elbow cracking the coffee table, and I hear both our wineglasses topple over, red liquid spilling into the carpet, but Chess manages to pull away from me, shedding one or three of those layers in the process.

She reaches for her phone, but I get to it before she does,

throwing it as hard as I can against the wall, and then Chess whirls on me, her eyes wide.

We both sit there on the floor, panting, and then she lurches to her feet, her heel coming down hard on the hem of her palazzo pants. "If you will chill the fuck out for five seconds, I'll explain," she says, and I almost laugh because there *isn't* an explanation for this, but of course Chess would think there was. Of course, the great Chess Chandler can talk herself out of anything.

"When?" I bark, and she flutters her hands.

"Right now, if you'll sit down and—"

"No, when did it start?"

I'm already racing back through the last few years, trying to find the moment. There was that visit Chess made to us two years ago. There was the trip we took to see her in Charleston, then the week in Kiawah. But other than that, she and Matt hardly ever saw each other. How the *fuck* did this happen?

"There was no *start*, Em, Jesus. It wasn't an affair, it was a one-time thing. That week you two came to Kiawah. When I took him golfing."

After I'd gotten sick. Four months before Matt had walked out. Chess had just learned that Nigel was engaged and she was devastated. She called me, begging me to visit. She'd known about the baby stuff, but the rest of it—the doctors, the brain fog, the nights curled up on the floor of the bathroom—I'd kept a secret. The time never seemed right to tell her, and there was something about it that felt embarrassing.

Weak.

If I'd known what was wrong, if I'd had a clear diagnosis to share, it would've been easier. But "I can't think straight and I throw up for no real reason" felt too pathetic to say out loud—not to mention, impossible to explain—so I'd never mentioned it.

Instead, I'd agreed to come because she needed me, and then Matt had just assumed he was invited, too, and I hadn't been able to figure out how to tell him no.

It had been fine, though. Chess's house was big and airy, and I'd started feeling better the moment I arrived. Matt had seemed better, too—lighter, less stressed—and when he'd asked Chess to take him golfing, I hadn't thought twice about it. I'd spent that afternoon sitting by Chess's pool, working a little on the ninth Petal book, content and happy, thinking how nice it was that my best friend and my husband could easily spend time together without me.

"What, did you fuck him in the back of a golf cart, Chess? At least tell me there was some kind of 'ninth hole' joke. You know, to set the mood, keep everything classy."

"Don't be crude," she snaps back, and I almost laugh at that.

"Right, you're fucking your best friend's husband on the *golf course*, but I'm the crude one."

"It wasn't at the golf course, Jesus Christ, Em." Chess throws up her hands. "It was in my car, okay? In my car, by the beach. Are you happy now? Do you want any other details? We had too many cocktails at lunch, and then we were driving back to the house, I told him there was this really pretty spot closer to the water where I was thinking of building, I drove him there, and then . . . *it* . . . just happened."

I rise to my feet, hands shaking, a metallic taste in my mouth. "Why?" I ask, because what other question is there?

Chess bites her lower lip, looking away. "It was after I found out Nigel was getting married, you remember that," she says. "I was so crazy about him, Em. I actually thought that prick would be my husband, and then not only does he dump me, he finds someone else, like, five seconds later, and . . ." She blows out a long breath.

"I'm sorry, Em, but Matt was flirting with me, and I was sitting there thinking, 'See? Marriage is total bullshit. Even Emily's marriage is bullshit.' And I think . . . I think I just wanted to know if he would. If *I* would." She pauses. "And besides, you've always had everything."

That startles a horrified laugh out of me. "Chess, I'm pretty sure that by the time you were fucking my husband, you were also fucking *famous*. We were staying at your fancy beach house on an *island*, and you decided that the only thing you couldn't live without was an accountant from Asheville?"

"I didn't say it made sense!" Chess shouts in reply, throwing up her hands. "And I didn't mean it like that. I mean when we were kids. You had this gorgeous house, and parents who called you 'Pumpkin' even after you turned thirty. When college was over, you went running back to this perfect enclave where you never had to worry about anything while I busted my ass to wait tables where people ate two-hundred-dollar meals and left five-dollar tips. I had to live in a shitty apartment with *Stefanie* while you probably had Deborah still making your bed for you."

I gape at her, almost madder about this bullshit than I am about Matt. "I was miserable! I was a loser living with my parents, while *you* were reinventing yourself with new friends in a new city. Sorry, I didn't realize that came across as 'having everything.' Maybe I should've put sadder pictures on my Facebook or something. That's the one language you really speak, right?"

I'm so angry I'm practically spitting, and I point at her, adding, "And even if my mother was bringing me fucking filet mignon on a gold-plated tray, that's no excuse to have an affair with my husband."

"It wasn't an affair," she objects, holding up both hands. "I swear, Em. It was one time."

"Then why was he giving you jewelry? Why were you obviously on the phone with him *today, Jessica*?"

Her shoulders sag. "After Kiawah, he kept calling. You know, that's how I first found out you'd been sick. I had to fake surprise when you told me after he left you. And that hurt, Em. Knowing you were going through this big, scary thing and didn't want to tell me."

"If you think I'm going to apologize to you for anything right now, you are out of your goddamn mind."

She holds up her hands. "I know, okay? I'm just . . . I'm trying to make you understand. Matt tells me you've been sick, that the baby stuff is on hold, that he wasn't living the life he wanted." She laughs, but there's no humor in it. "He started reading my fucking *books*. Telling me he knew I 'got it' because this was the kind of thing I was always telling my readers, how to find their 'authentic life.'"

I absorb those words like a blow, but don't say anything, and Chess sighs.

"So that's when he started sending things, and I . . . I don't know. I couldn't *tell* you obviously, but I also couldn't let you stay with someone who'd fuck your best friend, either. I mean, I cover a lot of shit in my books, but even I had to admit that I was out of my depth. So, I kept talking to him, stringing him along, because I was afraid if I shut him down, he'd get angry and then he'd tell you what I'd done. And then you'd never speak to me again. I couldn't have lived with that, Em."

"Really? Because it sure sounds like you don't even *like* me, Chess."

She blinks, as surprised as I've ever seen her. "What? Emmy, I love you. You're my best friend. More than that. You're . . . you're my sister, basically. Of course, I don't always like you. Sometimes I hate you, but that's only because I love you. Don't you get that? Don't you feel that way, too?"

I don't answer, the words stuck in my throat, because if I say anything, I'm going to agree with her, and that is going to make me feel even crazier than I do right now.

Chess shakes her head, her bracelets jangling as she tucks her hair behind her ears. "I kept thinking you two would work it out. That it would just be this weird blip, and we could all forget it ever happened. Sometimes I told myself that it hadn't happened, that I'd just . . . dreamed it or something. Or that it was this weird intrusive thought, like, 'Wow, wouldn't it be fucked up if you'd slept with Matt?' That's what I wanted it to be, Emmy. I wanted that so much."

When she looks at me, her eyes are so sincere, so pleading, that I know she's telling the truth. And it kills me that I want to believe her so much.

That I want to forgive her.

"And then, a few weeks before he left you, he called me late at night. He was drunk, I think, or . . . or upset, or something. And he started talking about how he'd only slept with me because you wouldn't have kids with him. That if you'd only wanted to have babies when he did, he would've been faithful forever. That he'd actually thought about replacing your birth control pills with placebos or some shit, and I understood that as fucked up as sleeping with him had been, it had happened for a reason."

She reaches her hands out to me, but I don't take them.

"Em, I had to get that close to him to see what he really was. If I hadn't slept with him, he never would've told me all of that. He was bad for you, Em. All he ever wanted to do was to control you. And I couldn't tell you because of what I'd done, but I thought, I could at least try to make it up to you. And then, once I figured out what he was doing to you, I knew something had to give."

"What do you mean?"

She takes a deep breath then, and leans forward, placing her hands on her knees. "Em, he was killing you."

CHAPTER FOURTEEN

My eyes are watery, and my skin goes cold as I stare at her. "He was what?"

"You know I'm right," she says, coming to her feet. "You know how sick you were, how sick you suddenly got out of nowhere? Whose fault do you think that was?"

I'm shaking my head now, backing away. Matt is a lot of things, but a killer?

"Chess. There's no way Matt was poisoning me."

Chess stares at me, and there's that expression on her face again, that look that's half love, half pity.

And then she laughs. "Em, you've been writing those murder books for way too long. I didn't say he was *poisoning* you. I said he was *killing* you. When did you start getting sick? Honestly, think back. When was the first time you remember feeling that bad?"

My mouth is dry, my thoughts spinning, but I can pinpoint the date exactly. It was Valentine's Day, of all fucking things. Matt had made his big announcement to my parents the previous November, and he'd expected us to be pregnant by February. The thing was, I hadn't stopped taking my pills. I hadn't felt ready yet, had started working on that thriller idea, and figured I'd eventually get on board with the whole baby thing later, maybe by the summer.

But that night, while we were getting ready to go out to dinner, I'd been rummaging in a drawer in the bathroom and he'd seen the pills. Seen the date printed out on the prescription sticker that proved I'd just had them filled a week before.

We'd fought about it, really fought, the biggest argument we'd ever had. He said I'd lied to him, that he'd actually been expecting me to tell him I was pregnant at dinner that night, and here I was, knowing there was no chance.

And I'd argued that I was working, that I had never really told him that I was ready, he'd just assumed because *he* wanted it, I did, too.

That Valentine's Day ended with Matt sleeping in the guest room, and the next morning, I'd apologized. I was never really sure why, only that it seemed easier than fighting with him, and I'd agreed to stop taking the pills.

But later that afternoon, I'd been hit by the first dizzy spell, a wave of nausea climbing up my throat, and I hadn't felt like myself again until he'd moved out the next spring.

"The body always knows," Chess says now. "Chapter Six of *The Powered Path*. 'The world warns us about putting toxins in our body, and assumes toxic people can only hurt our souls. But there are people just as poisonous to us as any chemical.'"

"That's bullshit," I croak, but Chess shakes her head.

"How can you say that after what you went through? How many doctors looked at you and told you nothing was physically wrong? How many medicines did exactly fuck all for you? Your body *knew*. It was warning you."

She moves closer. "He was the wrong man for you, Emmy. And you were on the wrong path. Your body was trying to tell you."

I almost want to laugh as I slide back down onto the sofa. But could Chess be right? Was it all in my head after all, just like all those doctors said?

The ENT who told me it could be my inner ear tricking me.

My gyno saying that sometimes stress makes the body think it isn't safe to support a pregnancy.

The acupuncturist who told me I needed "healing sleep" in order to fully rest.

"That's why you got better once he left. Which is what *I* told him to do, by the way. Isn't that right? Isn't that when you started getting better?"

It is, and she knows it, so I don't bother responding.

"And that's why you got sick here when you talked to him," she goes on, crouching down next to me. "Think about it. You were fine for weeks; fifteen minutes after talking to him, you were on the bathroom floor."

It sounds like the same psychobabble bullshit that fills all of her books, but she's right. I can't deny how my body responded. It felt like it was shutting down all over again.

"You *told* me to talk to him," I remind her, and Chess smiles.

"Look, I knew I was right, but I still wanted just a little more proof. And come on, Em. Ostrich Moment? Surely you think I'm a little better than that."

"I knew I hadn't read that shit," I reply, and she actually laughs a little.

"Anyway, as soon as I saw you there on the floor, I realized you needed to know what happened between me and Matt. For us. But also, for the book."

"The book?"

"Honestly, as soon as I read the first pages, I got it. I understood all of this had happened to lead us right here. It's why Matt had to leave you, it's why we needed to come to Italy. It's what the universe wants for us, to finally write together. Like we should have been doing this whole time."

My world is slowly tilting on its axis, but Chess keeps going, pacing around the room. "I can't write these self-help books forever, Em. And even if I could, I wouldn't want to. Do you know how boring it is to come up with mantras? Do you know how fucking sick I am of lemon water? I don't even *like lemons*, Em. And there's no future in this. The only way this ends is with me streaming my vagina on Facebook Live, or being canceled for making one fucking misstep, and I want something better than that."

She stops in front of me. "You're a great writer, Em. Better than you know. Those cozies aren't setting the world on fire or anything, but that's just because you've been too scared to do anything but play it safe. You're *great*. Honestly. And I want you with me. I want us to write together."

"Then maybe you shouldn't have slept with my husband," I reply, my voice flat, but Chess is, as always, unfazed.

"Haven't you been listening? That was part of this journey, Em. It was an ugly part, and I'm so sorry I did it, but without it, who knows what might have happened? Maybe Matt would have actually fucked with your birth control. You might have gotten pregnant and felt a whole lot more trapped in a marriage that was slowly killing you. You might have gotten even sicker. In a way, that one stupid afternoon is the best thing that ever happened to you. To *us*."

"That's . . . actually fucking nuts, Chess," I say, but she only smiles at me, that beatific smile that has gotten so many women to download her app, even though it costs fifteen dollars a month and is just the same shit she puts on Instagram, slightly repurposed as "Your Daily Chess Move! ☺"

"I told you, stupid," she says, touching her finger to the tip of my nose. "It's fucking *love*," she says. "You're my best friend, Em. I did something that hurt you, but I promise, I'm going to make it up to you." She leans in close, pressing her forehead to mine. "And, admit it. Admit that you never would've started that book without me. Admit that Matt leaving you and you deciding to come here with me and writing something that actually *mattered* to you has made your life better."

I'm about to laugh at her, to tell her she's so horribly wrong, but . . .

She's not.

I *am* happier without Matt. I *have* loved writing this book about the villa more than I ever enjoyed the Petal Bloom books.

And, I realize, I like this story the best. The story where every mistake, every bad day, was leading me here.

Because the other story is that my husband, the man I thought I loved, was making me sick with his very presence. That he slept with my best friend. That the life I was so proud of was never actually real.

That the person closest to me in my life is lying and manipulating me.

I don't want that to be the story. I *can't* be that story. And after all I've been through, shouldn't I get to decide how my story ends?

So I reach down and thread my fingers with hers, squeezing tight.

Chess squeezes back.

We sit like that for a long time. Then she sighs, and I watch as she unfastens the anklet, tossing it to the floor.

"You wanted me to notice it," I say, looking at the piece of jewelry winking in the lamplight.

"I did," Chess confirms. "And I gave you that bullshit line about my mom on the phone. The last time I talked to my mom it was to threaten her with legal action, for fuck's sake."

"Why not just come out and tell me?" I ask, and when she looks at me, I roll my eyes. "If you say something about 'agency' or 'self-knowledge,' I'll tackle you again."

"Then I guess I'll be quiet," she replies, making a gesture like she's zipping her lips. She used to do that whenever I'd tell her a secret.

Chess and I, we have so many secrets.

"So, we'll write the book?" she asks after a beat, and I think about Mari's pages, hidden away.

The truth inside them.

Chess really does want to write this book with me, without even knowing just what a gold mine we're actually sitting on. That means something. Maybe it shouldn't, but it does.

And then I remember the secret I'm still keeping from her.

"Matt's after my money," I say, and her head snaps up.

"What?"

I nod. "He wants this massive cut of all things Petal Bloom, and he's threatening to try for anything I write after that, too. Specifically, this book."

"Fucking *dick*."

"To be fair, you're the one who told him about me writing it."

She sighs at that, tipping her head back. "Every time he called, he was always going on about how stalled out you were on your writing, how frustrating it was watching you throw your career away, given how much he'd sacrificed for it. But even though he'd talk like he was pissed off about it, he always sounded . . . I don't know. Gleeful, kind of? Like it was a schadenfreude thing. He always felt like you picked your career over him, so I think he wanted you to be miserable in it. And *I* wanted him to know that wasn't actually true."

Looking back at me, Chess ducks her head to look into my eyes. "I swear to god, Emmy, if I'd known he was doing this, I never would've said anything."

So Matt didn't just want my money, he wanted my joy, too. All of it squeezed out of me because he had written his own version of how our marriage was supposed to go, what his life was supposed to look like. He was supposed to be the successful, happily married father with the successful, dutiful wife. That was his story.

And there I'd gone, changing the plot on him.

Serves you *right for marrying a writer, huh?*

I reach out and squeeze Chess's hand. "When Matt doesn't get what he wants, he goes hard. I mean, if he's still calling you, he must think that he still has a shot with you. You're clearly *letting* him think he still has a shot with you."

Chess thinks about that, her brow wrinkled. "Well, you're right about him going hard. The one time I actually tried to blow him off, he said something about how interesting people might find it that the self-help queen slept with her BFF's husband."

"Not very Powered Path," I observe, and she grunts in agreement.

"I guess it seemed safer to keep taking his calls, to play up this idea that maybe we could be together at some point, but I needed time. That's what he thinks this trip is about, me finally telling you about the two of us. He thinks that once you know, I'll feel less guilty about it all and we can—"she makes air quotes—"'see where this thing goes.'"

I take that in, thinking about all of Matt's texts and calls. Not just about the legal stuff, then. Probably trying to get a sense of whether Chess had told me yet.

"So, Matt is trying to take my money *and* make sure I'm as unhappy as possible for committing the crime of not being the perfect wife. And he says he's in love with you, but will also go full scorched earth if you won't be with him?"

"That seems to sum it up, yes."

I sit back slightly, looking at her. Outside, the rain is still falling, thunder rattling the windows, and the lights flicker for a second, briefly leaving us in the candlelit gloom.

"So how is this going to work, exactly?" I ask Chess. "The two of us working on a book together, while he's still trying to claim a piece of what I've already written and he's determined to be Mr. Chess Chandler? What kind of happy ending exists there?"

She doesn't answer me, drawing her legs up and resting her chin on her knees, thinking.

There's another crack of thunder outside, and this time, when the lights go out, they stay out.

The candelabra on the mantel sends flickering shadows over Chess's face, its familiar lines shifting and blurring, hollows under her cheekbones dark.

"Maybe the advance for this book will be enough to pay

him off?" I suggest, and I'm only half joking. "I can settle with him over the Petal Bloom stuff with my share, and you can send him hush money with yours."

"And then what, he buys a fucking boat with money *we* made?" Chess says, her head snapping up. Her hands are resting on her upraised knees, fingers laced together so tightly her knuckles are white. "No fucking way."

"He gets seasick, so it would probably just be a really stupid car," I reply, and then I tilt my head back, looking up at the ceiling. Our shadows are up there, dark shapes sitting side by side, larger than life.

"I can't believe that asshole is actually going to win in the end," Chess murmurs, and her shadow lifts one hand, the movement elongated and slightly grotesque.

She's right. It doesn't seem fair that Matt should be able to take so much from both of us.

That *Matt* is the person to almost come between us for good.

That he will always be wedged in between us, our friendship—and now, even this book that we'll make together.

That we might never cut ourselves free.

The thought starts out so small.

It's just those words, really.

A seed that sprouts in dark, dark soil, a vine twisting into an idea, an idea that should horrify me, but doesn't.

"I need to show you something," I tell Chess.

Taking the candleholder near the door, I go up to my bedroom in the darkness, a pool of golden light just barely illuminating each step before me.

I fish under my mattress for Mari's pages, and when I bring them downstairs, I hand them to Chess without a word.

It only takes her a second to realize what I've given her, and her whole face glows as she reads.

We sit there in the drawing room, Chess reading, me watching her, until she gets to the end.

(Well, almost the end. There's actually still one more section that Mari wrote, but I've kept that for myself. I have to keep *some* part of this just for me.)

When Chess reaches the final page—Mari calmly writing the end of *Lilith Rising* as Noel screams downstairs—she looks up at me.

I wanted to see if she'd understand what needs to happen next, or if I'd have to tell her.

But she's my best friend.

She's always been able to read my mind.

ONE WEEK LATER

Chess hears the car pull up before I do.

We're at either end of the dining room table, each of us typing Mari's handwritten pages from 1974 into our computers, and I have my earbuds in, so Chess has to wave to get my attention.

"He's here," she says, and I smile, saving the document and standing up from the table.

You can see the drive from the window, and Chess and I both stand there now, looking at the little blue rental car, watching the man who gets out of the driver's seat.

He's still handsome, still achingly familiar in his uniquely Matt way, and for a moment, I remember what it felt like to be in love with him. Like Chess, Matt had a bright light, and when it was shining on you, it was beautiful.

So long as he was getting what he wanted.

He turns, sees us there in the window, and lifts one hand in a hesitant wave.

"What exactly did you tell him to make him come?" I ask, and Chess reaches down, taking my hand and squeezing it.

"That I figured out that we had to tell you together. That you'd be so devastated and upset, and I didn't want to deal with that on my own, and since he was equally responsible for how miserable you'd be, he had to actually see the consequences of our actions."

Gleeful, Chess had said. That's how he'd sounded when he talked to her about how unhappy I seemed. Because I deserved that, right?

Sometimes we don't really know we've won until we see the reflection of that win in the loser's eyes.

(From chapter two of *Things My Mama Never Taught Me.*)

Chess takes a breath now and looks at me, her eyes full of compassion. "He said he'd be on the next flight."

It hurts to hear.

But that's good.

That makes it easier.

TRAGEDY IN ITALY

Author and wellness guru Chess Chandler was struck by tragedy this week while vacationing outside of Orvieto, Italy. The frequent *Oprah* guest and self-help star had been renting a villa just outside the city with two guests when one of them, Matthew Sheridan of Asheville, North Carolina, drowned while swimming in a pond on the property. Both Chandler and Sheridan's wife, Emily, were away from the house at the time. Sheridan, thirty-five, was apparently a strong swimmer, but, early reports say, may have been drunk or otherwise incapacitated at the time.

Of course, the villa was also the scene of an infamous murder in 1974 when up-and-coming musician Pierce Sheldon was bludgeoned to death by Johnnie Dorchester, a drug dealer and wannabe writer also staying at the property.

Chandler and Sheridan are already understood to be back in the United States, with Chandler's lawyer issuing the following statement:

"Ms. Chandler is deeply distressed at this tragic accident, and requests privacy at this time. She and Mrs. Sheridan have no further comments."

"The house is just cursed," a local resident who wished to remain anonymous told us. "It's a bad place, and I don't know why anyone would rent it."

Others scoff at such superstitious ideas. "It's a house like any other," another local said. "The only thing this has in common with what happened all those years ago is that both times, people got stupid on vacation. It happens here. It happens everywhere."

—*People*, July 29, 2023

He's changed, but then haven't they all?

Mari stands outside the tiny restaurant he'd suggested, stamping her feet against the cold as she watches Noel walk toward her, hands in the pockets of a greatcoat, that same rolling gait she remembers so well.

But she can see even before he reaches her that he's different.

The changes are small in Noel, subtle. He was already completely himself when they first met, had probably been completely himself from the day he was born, and yet—he isn't the same man he was in Italy six years ago.

There's something more haggard about that beautiful face, as a lifetime of excesses has finally caught up with him, and he's thinner, his body seeming less solid than she remembered as she hugs him.

"So kind of you to make time for me in your busy schedule," Noel says, opening the door for her.

Heads turn when they enter, and they're all for Noel. Authors, even ones as successful as Mari, are not nearly as recognizable as rock stars.

Noel hasn't put out an album since 1973, but he still commands a room, and they're ushered to a large booth by a window. Outside, it's begun to snow, the streets slick and wet under the orange lights, but inside the restaurant, it's almost too warm, thick scents of garlic and roasting meat hanging in the air.

"When was the last time we saw each other?" she asks, and he leans back. He's still wearing his coat despite the heat, and she thinks again how pale he looks, how drawn.

But the smirk is classic Noel. "I think it was your book signing in London three years ago."

Mari snorts, picking up the menu. "You nearly caused a riot coming to that."

"That's precisely why I came," he tells her, and she laughs.

She's missed Noel, she realizes. More than she'd thought. Sometimes he feels like the last person standing from her past, like she became a completely new person after that summer in Italy with completely new friends, a completely new life.

Cut yourself free, he'd told her on that sunny day by the pond. And she had.

She just hadn't known how lonely that would turn out to be.

The waiter comes then, depositing a bucket on the table, a wine bottle inside, and Noel gestures to it. "I took the liberty of calling ahead to make sure they had this," he says, and when the waiter lifts the bottle, Mari sees the familiar word curling across the label.

Orvieto.

Mari doesn't say anything, doesn't rise to the obvious bait as the waiter fills their glasses, and when she lifts the wine to her lips, her hand doesn't even tremble.

She's proud of that.

"A toast."

Noel lifts his glass, still smiling that odd little smile.

"I'm not going to toast to myself, Noel," Mari replies, her

fingers wrapped around the stem of her own glass. "That's your bag, not mine."

His smile widens.

Curdles.

"To lost friends, then," he says. "Pierce and Johnnie, the poor sods."

Mari doesn't lift her glass to that, either.

Her pulse seems to slow, heart beating heavily in her chest. She's always wondered if Noel knew. If he suspected the truth of what unfolded that night. In the six years since, she's only seen him a handful of times, exchanged a few phone calls, maybe a dozen letters, but he's never so much as hinted at anything.

Until now.

"What are you doing?" she asks him quietly, realizing that he is quite drunk, that the bottle of wine on the table is not Noel's first drink of the evening.

He drains his glass, setting it back on the table hard enough that she winces, and then he takes the bottle of wine out of its bucket, water dripping onto the dark red tablecloth.

"Not sure, to tell the truth." Noel fills his glass. "Feeling maudlin tonight, I suppose."

The bottle sloshes back into the ice, and Noel studies her across the table. "I sometimes think I died that summer, too, you know. Nothing has been the same since."

"That *is* maudlin," Mari says, hoping they can change the subject, but understanding now that this is why Noel wanted to meet her tonight.

"Of course, you and Lara, you've both ascended to heretofore unknown heights, so I'm sure neither of you see it the same way."

Mari doesn't bother pointing out that Noel's long slide had

started before that summer, that what happened to Pierce and to Johnnie has nothing to do with where he's ended up.

"Do you ever talk to her?" Noel asks. "Lara? I tried once, you know. Went backstage at her concert in Paris. She had security throw me out."

Laughing at the memory, he slaps one hand on the table. "They didn't want to, but I let them because, Jesus Christ, if she had the balls to do it, I deserved it, didn't I?"

Pierce and Johnnie's names no longer have the power to hurt Mari, but Lara's . . .

"You know, I sometimes wish she'd had the kid," Noel goes on. "I would've liked to have been a father, I think. And lord knows your sister was a handful, but she was pretty. Talented, too, turned out. Would've been a good mix of genes at the very least."

Mari wonders if Lara told Noel she terminated the pregnancy, or if he's just assuming she did, but the truth is that Lara miscarried two days after Pierce's death. A loss and a relief all at once, for both of them, Mari thinks.

Now she only shrugs and says, "Last I checked, you're not even forty, Noel. Fatherhood is still in the cards."

He shakes his head, lifting his glass. "No, doors are beginning to close, Mistress Mary. I feel them slamming shut on all sides of me. Family?" He slams a hand on the table, their cutlery and glasses rattling. "*Bam!* Closed. Marriage?" Another slap. "*Bam!*"

Arabella divorced him in the middle of Johnnie's trial, heaping scandal on top of scandal. Last Mari heard, she'd permanently decamped to her family's country estate and gotten very interested in buying Thoroughbred horses.

"Friends? *Bam!* Rotten lot, all of them, though present company excluded, naturally. Music?" Noel continues, and brings his hand up to once again slam it down, but Mari reaches over, stopping him.

"That door will never close to you, Noel," she tells him, and she means it. "You mustn't let it."

His hand goes limp in hers, and Mari has the strangest feeling he might begin to weep.

"You're still seeing the best in us," he says, pulling his hand free. "In spite of it all."

Mari is grateful when their food comes because it derails this mawkish stroll down memory lane. Soon, Noel is regaling her with tales of how he found this restaurant, of other little holes-in-the-wall he's discovered all over the world, and by the time the meal ends, Mari feels on much more solid ground.

The air outside is frigid after the warmth of the restaurant. Mari wishes she'd brought a heavier coat because even though the snow has stopped, the night has turned bitterly cold, the kind that slips underneath collars, making her eyes water.

Seeing her shiver, Noel unwinds the paisley scarf he's wearing.

"Here." He wraps it around her neck, but holds on to the ends, tugging her close and looking down into her face.

"Mistress Mary, quite contrary," he murmurs, still smiling that odd little smile at her, and finally, Mari understands that it isn't mocking or knowing at all.

It's sad.

She doesn't know it then, but this is the last time she'll see Noel. In a month, he'll leave for Nepal, seeking inspiration, but also wanting to do something grander with his life. It's an impulse that will kill him, less than a hundred days from now, when the tiny plane he's flying in crashes into the side of a mountain. Mari will spend the rest of her life thinking about that moment, wondering if he knew what was coming, wondering how Noel Gordon could be snuffed out so quickly.

And there will be a little part of her that thinks, *Now it's just me and Lara.*

Now we're the only ones who know.

She'll hate how much that thought warms her.

Noel leans down then and kisses her, his lips cold but gentle against hers.

When he pulls back, there are tears in his eyes, and it might just be the frigid air, but Mari doesn't think that it is.

"I wish I'd never said it," he tells her now, and she knows he's thinking of the same moment she was earlier.

That day in the sun by the pond.

Cut yourself free.

"I don't," she replies, and he gives a huff of laughter, letting the ends of the scarf drop.

"No, you wouldn't, would you?"

Then he turns and leaves. Noel Gordon, once the most famous rock star in the world, now just another man on the cold, damp streets of a December night in New York.

Mari starts walking in the other direction, intending to hail a cab at the corner, but she spots a phone booth, and before she knows it, she's ducking inside, fumbling with gloved hands to pull out the necessary change.

She'd gotten the number months ago, not long after she'd heard that Lara had moved to California. She kept it jotted down on a scrap of paper in her purse, but she'd looked at it so many times, she now knows it by heart.

Punching in the numbers, Mari tells herself that Lara won't even be home, that this is a wasted call and a stupid whim that she'll feel silly about in the morning.

So, when she hears Lara's familiar, "Hello?" Mari is so surprised, she almost hangs up.

She stops herself, though, and stammers, "L-Lara? It's me, it's—"

"Mari. I know."

The last time Mari saw Lara, she was onstage at the Scala in London, the stage lights making a halo around her. She'd played all of *Aestas* from beginning to end, and Mari had listened in the dark, her hands clenched against her chest, her eyes full of tears.

She hadn't tried to go backstage, hadn't even wanted Lara to see her in the audience.

"I don't know why I'm calling," she says now. "I just . . . I suppose I missed you."

There's silence over the line for so long that Mari thinks maybe Lara hung up, but then she hears a sigh, and Lara says, "I don't think that's it. I've been waiting for you to call, actually. I knew you would one day."

Mari stands there in the phone booth, her breath fogging the glass, the city lights distorted.

"I'm proud of you," Mari tells her. "I've listened to the album more times than I can count. It's breathtaking, Lara." She laughs then, self-conscious. "Not that you need me to tell you that, given how it's sold."

"I bought three copies of *Lilith Rising*," Lara replies. "At first, I couldn't finish it because it was all . . . it was too close. But it's wonderful, Mari. Truly."

Mari feels her throat go tight, her eyes stinging. "Thank you."

There's another pause, and Mari rushes in to fill it. "I'm in New York right now for some promotional things and meetings with my publisher." She laughs, drawing a line in the condensation on the glass. "They're being very polite, but I'm sure they're all really thinking, 'Is this bloody woman ever going to turn in her second book?'"

She will, one day, she's sure, but it's hard to imagine anything following the success of *Lilith Rising*. Readers are bound to be disappointed, but it's more than that holding her back. It's that ever since that awful, stormy night when she finished *Lilith Rising*, whatever voice was inside of her seems to have gone silent.

"You'll get there," Lara replies. "The follow-up to *Aestas* was the hardest album I've ever written, but it was finished, eventually."

Mari has listened to it, *Golden Light, Silver Moon*, and she'd liked it, but it didn't have the magic of *Aestas*, something she suspects Lara already knows.

"Maybe," Mari offers, hesitant. "Since I'm in the States, and *you're* in the States—"

"No."

It's soft, but also completely unyielding, and Mari stands there in that phone booth, watching as across the street, a laughing couple walks hand in hand, their collars turned up against the cold.

"Mari, what happened that night . . . I've never forgiven myself for it. I never will. But the thing is . . . I think you have. I think you think it was all worth it."

Anger spikes her blood, her fingers curling around the receiver. "Aren't we both in a better place now? Would we have any of what we have if you'd had the baby, if Pierce had kept dragging us around, if—"

"We could've just left, Mari," Lara says, her voice tired, like they've been having this argument for hours instead of minutes. "That night, I believed the same thing. That it was the only way. But I realized a few years ago that we weren't trapped. That's just what you told yourself to make it seem like you didn't have a choice. But you did, Mari. *I* did. We can't take it back, but I can't sit across a table from you, or on a sofa with you, and pretend like what we did wasn't terrible, just to make you feel better. And that's what you want from me."

Mari doesn't reply, and outside, it begins to snow again, the flakes thicker now, falling faster.

"I'll miss you forever, Mari," Lara says. "But I'm not giving you absolution. We don't deserve it."

There's a click, and then Lara is gone, leaving Mari alone in the cold phone booth, snowflakes sticking to the glass.

She stands there for a long while with the receiver still clutched in one hand before, finally, she places it gently in the cradle.

The door of the phone booth screeches as she pushes it open, and a blast of cold air hits her as she steps out onto the snowy street and begins to walk to the corner.

Alone.

You are cordially invited to a reception at the

NEW YORK PUBLIC LIBRARY

to celebrate the authors of

The Villa,

Chess Chandler and Emily McCrae.

An instant #1 *New York Times* best seller, *The Villa* has sold over two million copies, and been translated into more than two dozen languages. An adaptation is currently in the works at HBO, led by Emmy-winning director Elisabeth Hart.

Called "an immediate classic that marries true crime, literary mystery, and memoir" (*Los Angeles Times*), and a "searing but deeply personal look at art, sisterhood, and the crucible of loss" (NPR), *The Villa* has remained on the *New York Times* list for more than sixty weeks, forty-three of those at the #1 spot.

The authors will be giving a short talk detailing the creation of the book, followed by cocktails and small plates.

ATTIRE: BUSINESS CASUAL

CHAPTER FIFTEEN

It's raining as I make my way into the café where Chess and I are supposed to meet for lunch. I had a phone interview that ran long, and by the time it was over I realized I was supposed to be at the restaurant ten minutes earlier.

But I'm here now, and Chess is already seated, a bottle of white wine sweating in a bucket of ice, a basket of bread untouched on the table.

"Sorry!" I call, making my way to her. People turn and look as I go by, and I don't know if that's because they actually recognize me, or if it's just my newly reddened hair. My stylist swore it worked on me, and from the look on Chess's face, I can tell she was right.

"Em!" she says, standing up and plastering on a smile to replace the grimace I just caught.

"Chess," I say warmly, wrapping my arms around her. She smells the same, that Jo Malone perfume she likes so much, but she's traded in all her beige and white for black today, a sleeveless turtleneck sweater setting off her tanned, toned arms.

"Love the hair," she tells me as soon as I sit down, and I tuck it behind my ears, shrugging.

"I wanted something new before all the TV promo stuff starts."

Her smile goes a little rigid, but she nods. "That's smart."

The Villa will be out next month on HBO, a ten-part mini-series with an award-winning cast, all shot on location in Orvieto. Chess and I got to visit the set last fall. A picture of us posing with canvas chairs, our names emblazoned on the backs, is currently my most liked photo on Instagram—634,932 likes, to be exact—and my Twitter replies are full of exclamation points any time I so much as hint at the show.

But I know it's not the show Chess wants to talk about today.

The Villa has been out for over two years and is still dominating the *New York Times* list. We don't even have plans for a paperback yet since the hardcover is doing so well, but already, there's that question.

What's next?

No one has asked about another Petal Bloom book, of course. Petal and Dex will forever be frozen in amber at the end of *A Deadly Dig*, and I'm happy to leave them there.

The follow-up to *The Villa*, though . . . that's another story. Not a day goes by that I'm not inundated with questions about it. On social media, on my website, in interviews, on phone calls with my new agent, Jonathan.

And now it's the question I see in Chess's eyes, a knowledge confirmed when she fluffs out her napkin and says, "So I was thinking it's time to start planning the next one. That way, we can have a big splashy announcement about the new book just as the show is really heating up. Buzz upon buzz, you know?"

She grins, putting her elbows on the table, her fingers folded as she waits for my answer, and I take a little satisfaction in making her wait. I unfold my own napkin, I take a sip of water. I contemplate the light fixtures for a moment, and then I finally say, "Are you sure we should even try?"

Her hands drop to the table. "What?"

"I don't know," I tell her, fidgeting with my napkin. "It's just . . . yes, *The Villa* was a big hit, and honestly, I'm so grateful for it, but maybe it should just be a one-off. What are we going to do, cowrite for the rest of our lives? I mean, it's not like mysteries are really your thing, you know?"

Her smile goes brittle. "Well, it's not like nonfiction was yours, but here we are." She gives a little laugh at that, waving one hand in the air. "We both brought our respective strengths to *The Villa*. That's what readers responded to."

What they responded to was Chess's name, my writing, and the story we could tell them, but I don't say that.

"We did," I agree instead, "but lightning isn't going to strike twice, let's be real. And what are we supposed to do, stay at another famous murder house, hope another terrible thing happens that we can write about?"

Chess leans forward, her eyes bright. "Okay, you say that like it's crazy, but what if we *did* do something kind of like that? Not with the tragedy aspect, but finding other places where famous murders happened, writing about them, what they meant, why people are still interested . . ."

What she means is that she'll find a spot, and I'll end up doing all the work. That's how it was on *The Villa*. Seventy percent of that book is the book I started, me, alone, by myself in Orvieto. Why should I have to share with Chess again?

"That might make us seem a little one-trick pony," I tell her now, opening my menu. Two years ago, the prices would've made my eyes water, but now, I can order two of everything and hardly blink.

At times like this, I feel such a weird mix of emotions. There's guilt, sometimes. I'd be a monster if it didn't raise its head occasionally. But mostly there's satisfaction.

Cut yourself free, Noel had told Mari, and she had.

So had I.

But, as I look across the table now, I wonder how free I actually am.

"Well, maybe it's something to think about," she says with a shrug that is clearly meant to be read as lighthearted, but actually looks like she's having some kind of muscle spasm. "I mean, we're a package deal these days, right?"

What can I say to that?

I'm not so stupid that I don't get that a huge part of the appeal of *The Villa* was me and Chess, best friends since childhood, experiencing this tragedy together. And what we did in Orvieto . . .

That binds you together a lot more than any pinky promise or friendship bracelet ever could.

It was the only way, I tell myself for what must be the millionth time. It's practically a mantra by now. *Matt was the problem, Matt was what drove you apart, and look at all you've done now that he's gone. Just like Mari. Just like Lara.*

But on the heels of that, as always, is the other thought.

If Matt was the problem, why don't you want to write with Chess again?

The waiter stops at the table, his black vest crisp against his white shirt. "Compliments of the ladies by the window," he says, holding out a very nice bottle of Chardonnay, and Chess and I both glance over to see a gaggle of women watching us expectantly. They're around our ages, their clothes chic, their hair expensively highlighted, and when Chess and I both wave in acknowledgment and thanks, they dissolve into excited laughs and chatter.

The bottle opened, our glasses poured, Chess and I look at each other.

She raises her glass, dewy with condensation, the Chardonnay inside a sickly yellow. "A toast," she says. "To *The Villa*."

"To *The Villa*," I echo, raising my own glass. "And friendship."

Chess smiles at that, and for a second, I'm ten years old again, and she's leaning over my desk, smelling like strawberry-scented markers.

I'm glad I'm next to you.

Then her smile curdles. "To secrets," she adds. "And partnership."

And that's when I know this doesn't end. Any chance I ever had of freeing myself from any of this drowned in that lake with Matt.

I chose Chess.

And I chose her forever.

I clink my glass against hers, and it sounds like a door slamming shut.

"To us."

No one understands why she wants to come back.

Mari isn't even actually sure that she understands it herself. It's just that when she sat in that doctor's office on Ebury Street and heard those words—*inoperable, too far gone, I'm afraid, dreadfully sorry, three months if you're lucky, less if you're not*—her only thought had been of returning to Villa Rosato, and spending one last summer there.

She won't get a full summer, she knows. There are no more full seasons left for her. But a week, a week in the sunshine of Italy—that she can have, and so that she takes.

It's not called Villa Rosato anymore, though. It's been renamed Villa Aestas, thanks to Lara and her remarkable album, and when Mari hears the travel agent say that over the phone, she has to cover the mouthpiece with one hand while she lets out a sob.

Lara has been gone for more than a decade by then, and of all the things Mari hates about losing her sister so soon, this is the one that hurts the most. How fitting that Lara, the one person it seemed no one wanted there that summer, should be the one to claim the villa in the end.

How she would've loved it.

Lara feels so present to her in that house. For the first two days, Mari wanders the hallways and half expects to see her sister around every corner, giggling or sulking, her dark eyes brighter than stars.

Noel is there, too. He slouches on the sofas in her memory, he sings from a rowboat out on the pond, he winks at her from his favorite spot by the fireplace, and there are times she swears she can still smell his cologne, like he's just left the room.

If Johnnie is still there, she won't let herself think of him.

But Pierce . . .

Pierce haunts every one of her steps.

He was not a good man. She can understand that now, at thirty-eight, in a way she didn't at nineteen. He wanted to be good, but he didn't know how, and he took his selfishness and immaturity and tried to make them into virtues, not flaws.

But he was young. He was *so* bloody young. They all were, and they'd made terrible choices, and they'd mucked it all up like young people do, but they had been trying to be something better.

Something bigger.

It's the memory of Pierce that sends her back to that little desk under the window, that has her pen moving yet again. The real story of that summer, all the ugly bits, but the beautiful parts, too. That night with Pierce and Noel, the first time she heard *Aestas*.

Mari even lets Johnnie have his goodness, because he did have some, after all. It was there inside him that day by the pond, when he told Mari her hair was gorgeous and he smiled his crooked smile.

She writes and writes until she gets to the last night, the night that ended everything.

Mari has spent nearly twenty years not thinking about that night, but she lets herself remember it all now.

She was sitting at her desk, finishing *Lilith Rising*, the storm raging outside, and from somewhere downstairs, Pierce was calling her name.

She'd ignored it. The end of the book was too close; *she* was too close, and what could Pierce possibly want?

The heavy sounds, those meaty thwacks, her annoyance, her *If he and Johnnie are fighting again, I swear to god . . .*

And then finishing the book. Writing *The End*.

She had wanted to share that moment of accomplishment with Pierce, despite all of it, so she'd gone downstairs and walked straight into a nightmare.

Pierce, his beautiful brown hair soaked with blood, the back of his head a ruin.

Johnnie, standing over him with something gray and heavy in his hand, his face splattered with blood, with *Pierce's* blood, his eyes almost like an animal's, blank, uncomprehending.

Everything that followed was a blur. Screaming, running, yelling for Lara, for the police, for Noel, for anyone to help them, as Johnnie just let the heavy sculpture in his hands shatter against the stone floor, before collapsing heavily next to it, his upper body swaying.

In the end, she hadn't been able to tell the truth, the whole truth, so help her God. She had left out seeing Johnnie there, the weapon in his hands, because, almost absurdly, she'd wanted to at least give him some kind of chance. Wanted him to have to explain why he'd done it, how it had all happened.

That was the part that still tortured her the most. Had Pierce been calling for her because Johnnie had already hit him? Had he just sensed that this fight would be different from the last? What had started it, and how had it progressed to Pierce lying dead in that hallway? If she hadn't been so focused on finishing her book—the book that had changed her life—would Pierce still be alive?

She'd never know. Johnnie never told, and within six months of his sentencing, he'd hanged himself in his cell.

Mari stares at the blank page in front of her.

She starts to write.

She doesn't tell the story how it happened. She tells another story, maybe a darker one, one in which she's the one wielding the statue, she's the one crushing Pierce's skull. That's better, isn't it? Grander, more important, less. . . . pointless.

Mari writes and writes, feeling the way she did that night as she finished *Lilith Rising*, a way she's never felt again. There have been other books, of course. Four in total, none as good as *Lilith Rising*, none she'd wanted to share with the world, but this story pours out of her.

When it's done—when this other Mari in another life has put pieces of the bloody statue in a sleeping Johnnie's hands and sworn this other Lara to secrecy—Mari expects to stop. Instead, she keeps going.

When Noel died in that plane crash in 1980, Mari hadn't seen him in three years, and that had just been a quick hello at one of her book signings. Now, she gives them this final meeting in a dark restaurant on a snowy night in New York.

Tears stream down her face as she conjures him up, remembering the way he moved, the way he talked, the way he might have been in those last few months before he died.

They kiss goodbye in the story, just like they never got to do in real life.

And Lara, flighty, mercurial Lara, she makes the moral heart of it all. The one who won't accept what happened so easily, who, in the end, has the noblest core of any of them.

As for Mari herself . . . well, she sends her off alone into the cold, because there are times when it feels like that's precisely what's happened to her. She has a life she loves, a life she very much doesn't want to lose, and one much happier than what she implies for this Other Mari. She and Lara had stayed close, had visited each other's houses nearly every chance they got, until Lara decided to have a little too much fun one night and climbed into her Jacuzzi bath when her blood was full of champagne and Quaaludes.

But there are times when Mari feels like she's spent her entire life fending for herself, so it seems like a fitting end to this, her own version of her story.

When she's done, she reads it back over and, for the first time since 1974, she feels something like peace.

She didn't kill Pierce. Johnnie Dorchester did, in some kind of drug-fueled rage—a sad and stupid ending for both men, and one she's never quite been able to reconcile.

But if she hadn't insisted on staying, if she'd let Pierce leave when he wanted to, if she'd gone to him when he called for her . . .

And she can't escape the thought that has haunted her as surely as her memories: If Pierce had lived, would there be a *Lilith Rising*? Would there be an *Aestas*?

Weren't those works—wasn't her life, and Lara's, too—born from Pierce's blood?

So, it feels better, letting herself wield the weapon.

Cleaner.

Truer.

But now, she sits in the fading sunlight and wonders what on earth to do with these pages.

It's an exorcism of sorts, the lancing of a wound. Nothing she'd ever want to publish, but also not something she wants to tuck away in her flat back in Edinburgh.

They belong here, she finally decides. Hidden away, but here nonetheless, an alternate version of the story the house already holds. The house that changed the course of her life, all of their lives, forever.

But she won't hide all of the pages together.

Together, they tell a complete story, most of it real, some of it not, but nothing about that summer has ever seemed so neat to her.

So whole.

It's always been a series of fragments, beautiful and horrible, shifting like the light on the water just beyond the villa, hurting her eyes if she looks too close. It feels right, then, to break this story up into fragments. Read the first, and it's sad, but there are moments of light, of joy, even if the reader senses the clouds rolling in.

Read the second, and now, the story twists. Heroine is villain, villain is victim, and that colors everything that comes before in a new light.

And yet that first bit still stands on its own, another kind of story, another universe of might-have-beens.

That's good, Mari thinks. *That's how stories should work.*

The first chunk of it, she hides in an easy spot, under the window seat where the *M* Johnnie Dorchester carved in the glass still occasionally catches the light.

The second, the parts detailing her very real fight with Pierce and her very fictional murder of him, those she tucks away somewhere more secret.

Only someone who has read *Lilith Rising* very closely would even think to look there, and it makes her smile as she pushes the papers into their hidey-hole.

If these are ever found, it will be by a true fan, and what will they do with them?

Mari doesn't know or care. She'll be dead by then, after all. She's hidden them too well for them to be discovered before her inevitable and swiftly approaching end.

Maybe they'll believe they've found the real ending to her story. Maybe they'll think it's some deluded piece of fiction. Maybe they'll toss them in the fire, and be done with all of it.

It doesn't matter to Mari. She's done what she can, reclaimed the narrative for herself in a way that makes sense to her, and if it means the world one day believes she murdered Pierce, at least it ensures no one will ever separate them again.

The car comes for her early the next morning, and Mari's last look at Villa Rosato—Villa Aestas—is of the house shining in the morning light, a perfect jewel waiting for some other story to unfold in its walls.

Mari presses her fingers against the back window, imagining she can still feel the warm stone under her palm.

She'll be gone soon, but the villa will stand for much longer, she knows, and that means she's never really gone. Neither is Pierce, or Lara, or Noel, or even Johnnie. They still walk those halls, and soon so will she.

So will others who come after her.

Houses remember.

ACKNOWLEDGMENTS

Obviously the first thing I want to address in these acknowledgments is this: To all my friends, I assure you, not a *single one of you* is Chess. Pinkie promise. I am so lucky to be surrounded by such empowering, supportive friendships in real life, and I think having that is why I was able to take such a dark look into the Frenemy dynamic. I love y'all even though you've never paid for me to go to Italy for the summer, a real failing on all your parts, quite frankly.

I remain staggered by the lucky break that was landing Holly Root as my agent waaaay back in 2008, and am equally staggered at how well she has supported and encouraged me as my career has taken more twists than any of my novels. Emily may say that good agents aren't necessarily good people, but holly is the best of the best in both regards.

Sarah Cantin, dream editor, Virgo queen, I hope I get to send you a thousand more completely bonkers ideas that you help craft into the books they were always meant to be. It is such a privilege to get to work with someone who is as good at their job as you are.

Sallie Lotz, I'll miss your notes on my stuff, but am so thankful we got to work on this one together, and am so excited for you and your authors as you move toward editorial superstardom!

I'm also so appreciative to Drue VanDuker. You blew me away from the jump with how smart you are and how quickly and instinctively you "got" this book.

Thank you so much to the entire team at St. Martin's Press, and especially Sarah Bonamino, Marissa Sangiacomo, and Jessica Zimmerman. Thank you for all you do for me, and how patient you all are when I email you back in my head, as opposed to, you know, in an actual email.

Danielle Christopher, a huge part of why people pick up my books is, in my opinion, their gorgeous covers. Thank you so much for the thought, care, and artistry you put into each one.

Emilio, our tour guide in Orvieto in 2016, I am sorry that I did not listen as well as I should have when you were going over ecclesiastical art, but to be fair, there was a *lot* of it, and also it turns out my brain was busy plotting a murder book set there. I'm sure you understand. Special thanks for taking us to the well that plays such a big part in this story!

I always thank my husband in these acknowledgments, but he's actually earned it this time, since he's the whole reason we went to Italy in the first place. Thank you for signing up to teach a summer in Rome and for finding the best bus route so that I could go to Percy Shelley's grave and tell him some things in person.

Thank you, William, for being my favorite travel companion.

And last, thanks to Mary Shelley. I don't think I need to explain why.